About

Maggie Power was born
from Portsmouth Polyte
and History, she then le
College until 1993. Her first novel, *Goblin Fruit* was
published in 1987. She now lives in Middlesex and
writes full-time.

Lily

Maggie Power

A Touchstone Book
Published by Simon & Schuster
LONDON · NEW YORK · TORONTO · SYDNEY · TOKYO

First published in Great Britain by Simon & Schuster Ltd, 1994
A Paramount Communications Company

Simon & Schuster Ltd
West Garden Place
Kendal Street
London W2 2AQ

Simon & Schuster of Australia Pty Ltd
Sydney

A CIP catalogue record for this book is
available from the British Library

ISBN 0-671-85289-2

Typeset in Sabon by
Hewer Text Composition Services, Edinburgh
Printed and bound in Great Britain by
Harper*Collins* Manufacturing, Glasgow

Acknowledgements

My thanks to Chris Wilson for his unstinting support.

In Memory of My Father,
Chris Lonergan.

1

The rain fell skittishly like nuptial rice on the morning Jonathan Hopgate brought home a limp bride who would begin dying in the east wing at High Withens. Beads of bright water hung on the long dark hair of the bridegroom. Scuds of wet earth, swampy as desire, splashed his wedding clothes. The horse's hooves slithered under him.

'Jonathan, have a care for yourself,' his bride of a few hours called from the trailing carriage, as his horse stumbled on the slippery track that led up from the valley to the moors around High Withens.

A hot rain, flung from a too blue sky on to the land that was unstable and sodden, must have drowned her voice for he didn't answer, riding on ahead into the thicket of lilac trees that grew low, awry, bent by the stern winds that whipped the moorland.

Bridegroom and bride toiled on over a sticky earth, under the canopy of stunted trees that dripped sap and rain all over them, and then, as the path narrowed and the ground became hard and safer for the horses, the progression of the carriage was impeded by the ever thickening branches of lilac that scratched the fading Hopgate crest from the lumbering vehicle. Three times Jonathan dismounted to cut away the importunate tangle of branches and already withering white lilac that smelled all the sweeter as it neared decay. Three times the bridal carriage lurched on, following Jonathan on horseback, until at last they gained the summit and a stout wind shooed the rain back down the valley to where the land churned and sickened.

'At last, my destiny!' His arm swept a flourish before the deformed house which had been built by his ancestors and was now ruinous with neglect having been shut up for three decades. Thirty years in exile from his inheritance!

His bride called out again from the black carriage. 'Jonathan help me out, I want to see High Withens!'

And so he dismounted and fetched the poor crippled thing to whom he had pledged himself from her cocoon of shawls and mantles, and held her so that her curved spine was cushioned in his gentleness, and showed to her the estate that had been ruined by his errant grandfather and finally lost by the Hopgate who had spawned him. His father had gone to damnation in the belief that the Hopgate line faced a greater curse: descent into penury and oblivion.

Two upright coffins beyond a stagnant tarn that was swampy with waterlilies.

Lily looked again, and she saw High Withens with its east and west wings lowering at her.

Her little shudder of awe thrilled him, her new money

2

turned to rust by old blood, Hopgate blood. He almost desired her; the fusty brown hair escaping from her bonnet chafed his neck and stirred him like wickedly probing fingers. Now she saw what he was worth, she saw the history and the land and the breeding in him – the breeding that after centuries had come to such a sorry pass of dissolution.

'Jonathan, I love you,' she said. She kissed him with her wet mouth and then the desire turned cold in him and he pulled her away because he tasted only her sickness.

He put her back in the carriage, remounted and rode on ahead, swiftly now, to take possession of his birthright, to make himself known to the servants and the gallery of ancestors; to be indisputably Jonathan Hopgate Esquire, the master of High Withens.

High Withens was damp with neglect. Rotting fabrics clung to the leaded windows. A cold house. As cold as disillusion. He carried his bride like a bundle of twigs to set down at the fireside. A rapt smile on her face kissed away the shadows of the angel of death, a smile to cheer the heart of any loving husband. He unwrapped the moth-brown shawls and rubbed her starved hands with vigour.

'How your strength revives me,' she sighed, and slept at once, drowning in a sleep from which she couldn't be roused even when the maid brought in a sop of milk and white wheaten bread for her supper.

The girl will not see Christmas out after all, he consoled himself. In sleep you could imagine her beautiful, those narrowed eyes of a beaten cur hidden in dreams, the dull hair raven with shadows – rough to the touch, it was true, but abundant, and in the dark you would not mark the frowstiness. The full mouth that repulsed him would narrow with pain or the seizures of nightmare; he only had to touch her and the fever would leap, the fever of sickness or the dull heat of her passion – he could not be sure which, and only the first did not dismay him.

The fire was set with spiced logs and the aroma of the mulled wine a servant brought him dispelled the gloom of the long uninhabited house. His wife slept, curled in the bow of the ottoman. Her crooked back, he realised, imitated the serpentine curve of the couch: deformed, a broken, erased beauty like his house. No, not beautiful, she had never had what men call 'looks' to speak of, and yet ... her scent of Hungary water, the spotless muslins and impeccable silks; her style, that flouted the indignities of the sick room; a plucky girl and, when she loved you, a bold one.

He carried her up to the room that was made ready for them, a room the sun never entered. The walls had been hastily hung with figured blue silk, but already the damp was turning the deep blue as green as corruption.

He laid her on the great bed that was draped with hangings embroidered by the long dead wives of High Withens. The bed had been warmed, the linen scented, and the antique drapes hoarded the warmth like a miser from the chill of the bedchamber.

He had ordered a fire to be lit in the room but the grate leaked smoke in sinuous wreathes like mourning crape that almost asphyxiated them. So he snatched the wedding bouquet from its vase, scattering the lilies his bride was named for, and

poured the water from the vase on to the smoking fire.

'I can quench the fire and put it out, but can I douse
your passion, my sick girl? Can I ever snuff the flame
that makes you hot for me?' he asked the pitiful sleeper.
She was lost in the great bed like a child beneath an
ogre's blanket. When he lay down beside her he put a
distance between them so that he would not crush her
bones that were fragile as egg shells.

He dreamed that once more he was returning to High
Withens, through mire and bog, along the valley that
led to his inheritance. The rain fell heavily as though
heaven had opened its sluice gates, rain that stank
like old slops, churning the valley into a treacherous
quagmire.

He dismounted and again heard his bride calling out
to him. He tried to shut out the sound of her thin voice,
which had the town and new money bred in it, so he
sang a sad song, a ballad, over and over, repeating the
words like a rosary . . .

> 'Last night I lay sleeping,
> When my dead love came in . . .'

Dead love . . . dead love . . . The slough began to
swallow him. Jonathan sang valiantly and soldiered
onwards, his feet sinking more surely than his swooning
heart, as he fled his bride and struggled vainly through
a land that ingested him, from the valley to High
Withens. Sinking into earth with a drowsy blood heat
pulsing in it, the mire clinging like a lover whose
passion is unrequited. Dead love . . . my only lover
. . . the earth sucking him into dreamless oblivion.

When he woke the sheets were wet and fetid. He looked at his bride and saw that fever rode her into delirium. He peeled the sheets away from him.

'Would that I could so easily divest myself of a sick wife,' he lamented. He dressed, then sent one servant up to the sick woman and despatched another for the physician who attended her.

One night of love and her passion will immolate her; she'll be dead by the autumn, he promised himself, and the impious hope cheered him.

Lily stared at him with dazed eyes. Her fever had cooled but the delirium of love still seized her.

'How strange it is – just being here alone with you.' She looked around at the shadowy room where they breakfasted. 'Our palace of enchantment,' she said. Her eager mouth pressed on his hand as it reached for the coffee pot. 'The miracle of doing such blessedly simple things as sitting here, eating and drinking with you. The very ordinariness of it beguiles me.'

He said nothing, smoothly disengaging his hand from hers, pouring the steaming coffee into his cup.

'Is this real? Will you pinch me?' She laughed, trading her hand with its new ring, bold as brass, for her plump ankle, which curved itself about his booted calf.

'This is all that is real from now on,' he said slowly, ruminatively, as if thinking aloud. 'There is no other reality, now that I am in my own world,' and his eyes were dazed, enchanted too as they drank in the heavily carved furniture, listing walls, as he swallowed the damp, fermenting air of history with his strong hot coffee.

He fell silent but Lily's joy, which for the moment dispelled suffering, was loquacious. His bride, with her large eager mouth telling him yes that was the best of it, that it had been in her power to restore High Withens to him . . .

Her power. She spoke of her power to rescue him from years of poverty and obscurity! No – she had conceded that! Power was no longer in her possession. He was master here now. He'd had too many long years of being powerless.

'You know so little about me,' he couldn't help himself from saying with resentment. And how could she know all there was to know after such brief courtship?

'I didn't mean . . .' Lily faltered. Her damnable loose tongue – now she had offended him. 'It's just that . . .' She licked her lips like a small child. 'Love loves to give, you know. And you've given me so much; you've given me life.' Her breasts rose and fell. How he despised her tawdry, mercantile sentiments.

And she was surely mistaken about her prospects of life. Love couldn't conquer death, and she was deluded about his love in any case. When she looked into his eyes, didn't she see coldness, indifference? But it wouldn't be the act of a gentleman to disabuse her. Let her die in her fool's paradise!

Let her die, let her die, the house echoed his thoughts triumphantly. Too soon to crow about life, surely!

He looked out of the window at the wide sweep of land that fell away from the house, stretching far beyond the horizon, and his sapphire blue eyes glittered with a desire that Lily mistook, believing it to be for herself enitrely.

Our world, she thought – ours, the world of love. A charmed life will be ours and death will have no dominion. Jonathan is as enchanted as I but thinks it not manly to demonstrate affection easily. He has the ways even if he has scarcely led the life of a gentleman.

But love that could conquer death could surely erase etiquette also! 'Tell me about your past,' she said, catching hold of his hand again, determined to make him open his heart to her. 'I want to know everything.'

'It's pointless going over and over these old tales. The past is dead. I've no wish to disinter it.'

'I don't want to stir up pain, dearest. I know how dwelling on childhood losses can be a torment.' She glanced at him coquettishly. 'I simply want to provoke myself into a passion by having you recount your . . . amorous exploits.' She coloured slightly. 'Have I had any rivals?'

He regarded her distastefully. 'Rivals?'

'Well, you're not such a great age. But you can give me almost fifteen years, you know. I want to know how you've wasted them,' she teased. How much livelier she felt this morning!

Wasted.

'Any life that is deflected from its true path is wasted,' he said, pouring himself another cup of coffee.

Little fool! Did she imagine she was the first? Was she expecting him to tell how he never tasted the delights of love until she succoured him? A true gentleman was discreet in these matters.

She needn't have worried. He'd never seen an eligible woman who'd matched his exquisite standards. Seamstresses, thwarted governesses, laundry maids, dollymops: these were the only kind of woman that had laid themselves out for him. He had tasted their wares and moved on.

One or two more fraught liaisons had occurred, it was ture. Girls in Lily's position had sometimes tempted him, but it was more than it was worth to forfeit his reputation and livelihood for a moment's fancy that could never come to anything. He had always calculated. And somehow, plaguing him, making sure he never took a wrong step, there was an insistent sense of destiny . . .

'There must have been someone,' Lily said.

There's always someone, he thought wearily. But never the right one.

'Oh, in my errant youth there were some dalliances,' he confessed.

'But someone special?' There was a quizzical twist to her mouth. 'In recent years?'

'In recent years I've been too concerned with scratching a living to pursue petticoats. But if you're trying to find out if I've been in love before, the answer is, finally, irrevocably, no!'

Love! Why he could only love an equal!

There had been a governess once, like him down on her luck, someone who had fallen below her station in life but retained a certain grace.

But of course filthy lucre, or lack of it, had made the thing impossible . . . Christina, her name was. He called her Christabel because it had a more poetic ring to it. A small faery of a woman, with astonishing golden hair that rippled to her ankles when she let it fall, loose as her morals.

That was the time he lived in London, in Blackfriars,

in a large but damp and bare set of rooms he shared with an opium-smoking artist.

'I'm only doing this because I love you,' she had said, 'you must know that . . . only because of love.' Love will excuse anything. Christabel had lost her position because of him. A maid saw them enter the Cremorne Gardens – pleasure gardens – and that was that. After this of course his beloved was destitute, and she expected him to marry her because now and forever she would be without a character.

Well, he hadn't married her. It simply wasn't possible to marry on the little a drawing master could earn. But he let her move into the dreamy, wet rooms, where the artist shocked her by painting naked women. Then, when the little governess was obliged to sit too – posing without any clothes on because she didn't have a mite to eat and barely a stitch left to wear in any case – she found she couldn't afford the last shreds of morality.

But her body had been sweet before it embalmed itself with opium. He had appreciated her delicacy, her shyness at first; she was a gentle thing after the bold caresses of dollymops. How young he was. He remembered drowning in her shower of golden hair, the colours so rich, so sunny, that they drove the grey fog out of the riverside rooms.

But poverty spoilt her.

'I've told you, I simply can't afford to marry you,' he had said. Now she was weeping more, and smoking the opium the artist passed off on her instead of money. She went on pleading and weeping, and when he made love to her it was like loving a sore thing – a disconsolate wound that his loving aggravated.

And soon the artist was passing her round with his opium pipe, in any case.

Before long she was no better than a dollymop. Jonathan moved out and moved on, and though there were other women, when he could afford the time and money for them, he always remembered Christabel's refinements, her faery princess golden hair, a little regretfully.

'Poor Jonathan,' Lily said sweetly. 'Not even love to comfort you in that grim succession of rooms and lodging houses where you resided. Were they very grim? The memory of High Withens must have goaded you, dilapidated as it is!'

'Yes, it goaded me. And it drove me. But the rooms didn't signify. It was the loss of my identity that mattered. I knew, I always knew . . .' he laughed ruefully, 'that my real self was here. I've not just come back to a house, I've returned to myself, Lily.'

And to me, she thought joyfully, watching the passion spark into Jonathan's eyes at his final words. You have returned to love in coming to me, my sweetest, truest husband.

Lily glowed. Her whole life shaken out like a bale of cloth, unfurling, endlessly unfurling before her.

Bridegroom and bride in a world of enchantment. When she looked into his eyes she saw they were dazed as her own. Such bliss! Husband and wife finished their breakfast, both trembling with heartfelt desires, both lost in their worlds of enchantment.

At first the space, the dimensions of High Withens, astonished him. The sheer physical delight of awakening in a room where the walls didn't press close as a coffin.

Initially his triumph was such that it threw a cloak over his distaste for the bargain he had made to acquire his inheritance. But when Lily said, 'I can smell the damp. I don't think these streaming walls will do my health any good. Perhaps we should go on a brief wedding tour, and I'll get papa to have proper renovations carried out,' he was furious.

'I hardly think your health is up to travelling. The mere journey here from your father's house fatigued you.' As he flushed she paled. 'Look at the state of you. Why, you can hardly stand up. Do you think I'm villain enough to risk your life dragging you around the country with me?' he said more calmly. It wouldn't do to be too brutal with the woman; after all, he reasoned with himself, she was to be pitied, at death's door without a doubt. And it was thanks to her, he had to admit . . . without her he'd still be nobody. And just look at her . . . so soon to be a bride of death. Not for long would she trouble him. 'Just think how I'd feel if your health broke down completely, miles away in a strange place. Put yourself in my position.'

'I hadn't thought. It was stupid of me,' she apologised. 'Of course I couldn't burden you with the responsibility of travelling with an invalid.' To cover her confusion she picked up her fan and began to flutter it like a moth over her ghastly complexion.

'If the house is too damp for you it shall be fixed. You must appeal to your father for more money. He can hardly refuse you. But the request must come from you,' he said proudly.

For himself, the little ruinations time had wrought on High Withens were like amorous lines etched by experience on the face of a courtesan, an intriguing history of seductions that enticed him.

Days passed in rapt exploration of the most secret inner chambers and labyrinthine passages, distilling his breath on the streaming windows, penetrating every curtained recess, prying open cupboards, forcing doors ajar, until he had inventoried every item of neglect and abandonment.

Until one day Lily jested, straining her face into a smile that forced out the pain distorting her features, 'Why, you're stroking those dusty curtains as if they were a woman's hair, Jonathan. You're like a man possessed.' Then she laughed her harsh laugh, because when she looked into his blue eyes she still saw herself reflected there, a young bride, and not High Withens.

2

It was Sabbath, and while Lily Hopgate lay on her
couch, Jonathan, dressed in his black frock coat and
old French linen, prepared to go to church where the
Hopgate pew was beeswaxed, the hassocks made over,
and the pew doors rehung for him.

'You're going out?' She seemed surprised, wounded.
Her honeymoon so soon ended?

'It's expected,' he said. His mouth tightened. He
hoped that in the brief time that was left to her she
wasn't going to prove a nag of a woman.

'Expected? What's expected?'

'I'm going to church,' he said.

'But I thought you didn't care much for religion.
Didn't you say that art was a surer path to divinity
than prayer ever could be?' She lay down the novel
she was skimming and looked quizzically at him.

What a simpleton the woman was. She knew nothing
about his place in society. A gentleman's duties.

'Belief or non-belief don't signify, you know. I've got to assume my position in local society,' he said.

'Why?' she asked him.

Why, the querulous tone seemed to suggest, isn't my society enough for you? And why, he asked himself, did women always assume they were enough; how could any one woman fill that gaping void in a man?

'I don't expect you to understand.'

'What do you mean by that?' she rejoined.

'You're not used to country ways. The estate is the lifeblood of the house. Things are done differently here. There are ties, affinities. There's the land as well as the house, and the land means families linked by work and duties. These families have always looked to the master of High Withens as the head of their community.'

She looked bored when he spoke of these affinities. There was only one affinity as far as she was concerned. A town girl, a daughter of trade, she believed in true love, romance – not the tiresome bonds of landed society.

'We don't have any need for them. Sell the estate,' she said carelessly. 'Why should we bother ourselves with responsibilities? Papa has enough money for all our needs. You don't need to work land now, Jonathan.'

'Sell the estate!' He was appalled. 'I'd as soon sell my soul.' As soon cut out his heart. He shrugged off her hand, which reached up to caress him, as though it were an importunate insect.

Till death us do part, he thought, watching her rebuffed hand, the one that wore the wedding ring her father had paid for, fall heavily to her lap.

An ornate gold ring. She was his wife, but in truth he was only wedded to his inheritance.

* * *

The congregation pretended to contemplate the good Lord as they stared at the new master of High Withens. The gossips were thrilled because he had the wickedly handsome looks of his ancestors.

'A dissolute eye,' said the impoverished Miss Hemp, who ran the Ladies' Repository.

'Hair black as a raven's wing,' sighed the five ebony-haired daughters of the incumbent clergyman.

'The stamp of a gentleman,' barked Brigadier Ashley.

'The devil's glint in his eye,' said Mrs Tow, who was too young to be widowed safely.

'I'll lock up my daughters,' decided Jabez Wicke, who saw all the lecherous former masters of High Withens pant for his girls in eternity.

'A pity he's a wife so lately taken,' complained poor Mrs Creedy, with eight blooming daughters and no sons to take care of.

'But she's not long for this world if all I hear tell is true of her,' Mrs Creedy's sister speculated.

And Jonathan, prepared to acknowledge all and not notice one of them, like a true aristo, forgot his brief triumph at becoming master of High Withens when he set eyes on the curate's daughter.

Her shawl, like a fragment of dun mist, fell dreamily from her shoulders.

'A quattrocento madonna,' Jonathan muttered under the guise of praying. She was pale as Italian marble, with a languorous tumble of pallid hair that silvery-yellow lights danced in. Who is she? Jonathan wondered, as a different kind of Marian iconography proposed itself and, for a delicious moment, he pictured the woman as the Magdalen, drying his tear-soaked, naked feet with her long hair and then, ah then, stroking between the crevices of his toes precious salves and unguents.

The choir sang psalm number fifty-one and Jonathan, though no Oxford man, for the moment regretted the absence of sensuous ritual, the litany of ascending tiers of candles that burn prayers through a fug of incense. He recalled the papist churches in Italy where five years before he had accompanied a young art student on a sketching holiday. In every church they had visited, rapt, painted statues of Christ, the Virgin, and a hierarchy of angels and saints, were assaulted by the devout; women in prickly black garments kissed Christ's nailed feet more passionately than their lovers. The saints had bejewelled robes, but like Christ their feet were bare and vulnerable. All over Italy penitents taunted the cold saints with human desire, biting off the plaster toes, sucking the warm flesh tints from naked feet. All over Italy saints were ravished by believers.

Agnes met Jonathan gaze-for-gaze as the Reverend Beech thundered how the mighty were fallen in the pulpit above them.

'Fallen . . . fallen . . .' echoed the sermon, and the words flew up the spire of the church and out of the sump of the valley, borne on a righteous wind to the crumbling parapets of High Withens.

A bright church, filled with the rational light of Protestant England – none of the dolorous mysteries of Roman ritual here to entice his gaze from the clear-eyed English woman with her sparkling complexion. Not an English rose, though; rather a slender tulip, with that long neck, like a lady looking out of a tower in a medieval painting.

The service concluded, Jonathan walked down the

nave, heedless that all eyes were fixed on him. At the church door the Reverend Beech waited to greet him with an inventory of need: the pews were carious with worm, the minister told Jonathan, the pulpit required restoration, the ecclesiastical vestments, that had lain too long in the damp, had mould in them and the roof, like church roofs everywhere, let the rain in.

Jonathan exercised the patrician smile that had grown rusty from all the years he was obliged to practise deference. 'Naturally, I would wish to take a lively interest in all local matters,' he assured the clergyman, who was stout on the profits of half a dozen livings. 'Perhaps yourself and Mrs Beech would take dinner at High Withens, say a fortnight on Saturday? I'm afraid the formal procedures of presenting cards and making calls are beyond my wife at present. She is a sick woman.'

But when Beech made enthusiastic acceptances Jonathan scarcely heard him. His eyes raked the throng of the departing congregation, though he sensed her presence before he saw her again, an exquisitely beautiful creature with a pale tumble of hair! She stood at the wicket gate at the end of the churchyard, still and composed as one of the stone angels ascending from the sepulchres. A tall man in clerical black was beside her.

'Your curate?' Jonathan asked Beech.

'Mr Septimus Slane and his daughter Agnes.'

'Extend the invitation to include them also – and any other curates or churchmen you think may wish to dine,' instructed Jonathan. 'And Mrs Slane?'

'Mr Slane is a widower.'

Jonathan nodded and went down through the church-yard towards her. At the wicket gate the curate was doing the honours for those poorer members of the congregation whom Beech believed to be beneath him.

Not stone. Not stone, after all. A guardian angel, a composition of ether, he thought as he saw her standing next to her father. Close to, she had a translucent, patrician beauty, as dewily moist and bright as the sunlit morning. A canopy of ivy over the wicket gate cast a delicious green shade, so that if he closed his eyes he could imagine he was in a bower of love with her.

'Mr Slane!' Jonathan greeted him with a voice so urbane no one would have guessed at the sudden tumult of desire in him.

Formal introductions; the polite invitation; chivalric terms: obliged, honoured, gracious – words drawn on like white kid gloves. He stood close to her, felt her languid breath, was entranced by the clean, long-limbed gentility that proclaimed itself in her every gesture; the lineaments of a lady. She expressed herself anxious to meet his wife whom she had heard was an invalid, and her voice was as cultured as his wife's was harsh and vulgar. Miss Slane's speech was all decorum but he felt her watching him, saw the fatal spell, which his good looks exercised over any girl or woman who met him, begin to work in the blush that suffused her long neck, darkening the complexion.

'Please call on us without any formality,' he said at once. 'No formality,' he repeated as he stripped the dowdy dress away in his mind's eye, staring at her frankly, unashamedly, with a little more than admiration. 'My wife's laid up with a diseased spine and has been too long without the company of her own sex, has neither mother nor sister to look in on her.'

Agnes smiled charitably. 'I will come.' Gladly she

promised him. 'Our situation is alike, then: motherless only daughters.'

When Jonathan stepped through the wicket gate he felt as though he had entered a world that was born again. Everywhere trees were festooned with tassels in variegated tints: emerald, jade and Lincoln green. He rode through an over-arching colonnade of trees. The branches of trees entwined like fraught lovers, but the sun pierced the cathedral dimness and stung him with an agony of excitement.

'Agnes Slane . . . Agnes Slane . . .' beat the horse's hooves in a rhythm of urgency. On he rode, riding into delirium. As he came out of the valley his steed slackened its pace as though loth to leave the warm swampy earth for the hard pinnacle of moorland.

In the Sabbath light he could see how friable were the walls of High Withens, how the thick stems of wisteria dragged the masonry awry, and the green rot and black fungus seeped up from the foundations. A pile of tin needed to be spent on the place to re-point the walls and secure the roof, that leaked even more than the church did. He envisioned thick carpets and curtains that weren't faded silk with a pall of dust on them.

He should have held out for a larger bride price. But what was the real cost of a woman with a cankered spine in his bed? Her father had plenty of tin with which to buy his girl's happiness but there should have been more, more filthy lucre to assuage the misery of having death in his bed at nights.

He remembered the day that she had thrown herself at him, hands fevered, tearing at his hair with an access of passion. With Lily he'd been lulled into safety; he hadn't expected a girl waiting for death to want a lover.

He had at once disliked her father's house, with its cache of fashionable paintings that the merchant had snapped up at the Royal Academy. It was a white stucco villa where the carpets were all crimson and velvet plush, a faeryland of crystal lights and ruby lustres, the wall hangings as sheeny as silk; a house that dust never entered. Fine panels of Honiton lace festooned the windows, not the inexpensive machine lace from which George Flood had made his fortune, and the furniture which had been ordered after the Great Exhibition was opulent, heavy stuff. No antiques, with their contamination of worm or the tawdry ravages of time, passed the threshold.

'I like a picture to tell a story. You always know where you are with a plain tale,' Flood had explained to Jonathan as he showed the drawing master his paintings of scenes from Shakespeare and the old faery tales, or the affecting contemporary sequences of degradation. Jonathan cast a swift, scornful eye over a tryptych entitled *Daughter of Intemperance*.

'What do you think of my collection, Hopgate?' Lily's father had asked in a voice that was accustomed to throw itself across the clatter of machinery.

Jonathan half closed his eyes, the better to veil the Hopgate haughtiness. 'Oh I'm a Renaissance man,' he said.

Lily had had far more aptitude than the rest of Jonathan's pupils – a not insignificant talent, in fact, although her taste ran to the morbid, because of her disease he supposed. She saw death in everything. The flowers she drew in full bloom were always spoilt by the one petal that had begun to wither, already shrivelling, and her preference was for faery princesses in the catatonic state of lovelessness before the prince arrived. He showed her prints of Botticelli, Filippo Lippi and Giotto, because her taste had been formed by her father's stuff and her appetite fed with sentimental portraits of lovers' trysts, broken vows and sobbing, abandoned women in exquisite evening dress — dresses as fine and modish as those she herself wore. Wore uselessly. Cumbersome crinolines, scarcely practical for a recumbent invalid, swelled over the couch where she generally sketched during her drawing lessons with Jonathan. So much of her time was spent on artifice, on self adornment. There were too many jewels, too many frills and ribbons, and she applied too much pomade — too much of everything, he thought wearily. And why should he complain, he who had always had so little, he who had been denied so much?

What he considered most was whether the work would last, or whether she would die fairly soon so that he would be obliged to seek another position. And wondering even now, *would* she die? Soon? How soon?

Sometimes, if it was one of her good days, she would be standing at her easel in the conservatory when he arrived at the house for her drawing lesson. He was always on time. Punctilious. He remembered the conservatory, the heat and the almost suffocating bouquets of hot-house flowers. When it was not too hot, canary birds perched in a little Arabesque cage of some gilded metal, but their trilling always distracted him and he had to ask her to remove them.

Yes, he remembered the heat. He remembered the choking ferns and rampant flowers that took his breath away. So sultry an atmosphere that he had to take off his jacket while he instructed her, and was embarrassed when she said, 'Oh you've a tear in your shirt sleeve, Mr Hopgate. You must let our maid repair it for you.' Her damnably vulgar directness!

'Excuse me,' he had apologised at once, reassuming his jacket and never again removing it at that house, so that from then on he associated her presence with the cold heat of perspiration that made the clothes stick to his flesh like leeches.

He had inwardly diagnosed curvature of the spine when he was first introduced to her. Her head hung to one side so her ringlets drooped over her pale face. Her shoulders were stooped so she appeared shorter than she was, which was no great height in any case. He towered over her, and was obliged to half kneel on a hard chair when he assisted her with drawing.

For a year he had attended the house, regularly at first, offering one lesson a week, and then the appointments were increased to thrice weekly as a passion for watercolours gripped her with an energy belied by her condition, which he had by now learnt was mortal.

Three times a week he tutored her, and because she was an eager pupil he continued to bring her prints of the old Italian masters, endless madonnas and countless annunciations, depicting hosts of angel Gabriels with flaring wings.

The girl had startled Jonathan when, after he had spent time perusing the painterly techniques of half a dozen annunciations with her, she said, 'But look at all these angels. Are they boys, young, hot-blooded Italian boys?' She was half murmuring to herself. 'And yet they have a girlishness, too — such prettily curled hair and flowing robes.' She had glanced up at Jonathan and smiled wickedly. 'Don't you think that's maybe why the Virgin looks so astonished? It's not the dreadful news the angel's bringing her; she's wondering: is this a boy or a girl thrusting its way into my bedchamber? Or perhaps a great bird about to ravish her.'

She had spread two of the prints on her lap to compare them. 'Just look,' she said, 'the energy in the taut wings and stirring draperies of this angel with such a Florentine face proclaims the hot-blooded male of the species, don't you think?' She laughed. 'But his skin is soft and whiter than the Virgin's. And now this one', she speculated, holding aloft one of the prints for Jonathan's scrutiny, 'is glacial as the Mary he's flown in on, and has . . .' Lily screwed up her mouth. '. . . I'd say a prettier, more delicate face. Is this Gabriel a boy or a girl angel, do you reckon?'

'I suppose all angels are of necessity ambiguous creatures, their being, strictly speaking, above the physical plane,' Jonathan had replied stiffly.

'You mean there are no men nor women angels either?' Lily asked, her face darkening. 'So they cannot love one another.'

Jonathan felt uncomfortable with the turn her conversation had taken.

'Then I wouldn't be one of them,' Lily went on with a sudden violence. 'I would never choose to be such an angel, dwelling in a passionless paradise.'

*   *   *

Passion, Jonathan thought distastefully, as his horse stumbled and slithered over some fallen branch half hidden by sodden earth ... passion prevailed over death in her.

The lessons had gone on, though now she was possessed with a desire to draw only angels. When he had reminded her – very gently and carefully, not wishing to upset this lucrative pupil – that she had declared the creatures passionless, and it was now time to extend her repertoire and progress to some other subject, she had challenged him. 'But I must find their secret. Such beauty must have a secret. Cold beauty, but it stirs a fire in me. How can something so cold ignite such a fever of admiration?' She went on, 'There is an ambiguity in all these quattrocento seraphims and archangels; they are a puzzle I must solve, whether male or female, passionate or ethereal – wherein does their true nature lie? Perhaps in copying them I may discover their truth. I cannot believe true beauty lacks passion.'

She worked avidly. Drew feverishly and made herself ill, so that her father was obliged to take her away for a brief rest cure although Jonathan was still paid for the cancelled lessons. But when she returned from her sojourn on the south coast her artistry somehow had lost its nerve, and her hand shook terribly when he coaxed her to sketch bowls of fruit and vases of flowers.

She sketched haphazardly, lying on the drawing room sofa. Her head was bent low, her voice thick with suppressed sobs, and Jonathan assumed a melancholia wrought by the certainty she must die had gripped her, and he prepared himself for the cessation of his employment in the merchant's house as she seemed to lose the heart for drawing.

'You grow too weary for such exertions,' he remembered saying resignedly when, after dropping her crayon, executing faulty lines and smudging a charcoal etching, Lily had at last dashed her portfolio to the floor in a rare fit of temper.

He remembered too how he had assisted her from the sofa and led her over to the conservatory, where the door was open on to a raised terrace, because he thought fresh air would soothe her. She leant on his arm, one hand fumbling with her chatelaine that was too tightly fastened. When they had reached the door leading to the terrace, a mesh purse attached to one of the chains suddenly snapped and fell from her waist, scattering sovereigns. He bent down to pick up the purse and the money and, when he stood up, an astonishing thing! Lily flew at him as if all the joys and sensations of the long life she should have had were to be tasted in that moment. Audaciously she had kissed him.

And what could he do? When a lady kissed him he, perforce, must embrace her. On the whole it was an unpleasant kiss, because he was conscious of her sickness and then her lips were too slack and she salivated grossly.

In stooping to pick up her purse it seemed the thing was decided.

He remembered his horror when she said, 'I must tell papa how it is between us.' He saw himself lose favour in half a dozen households: the philandering drawing master!

'Miss Flood, you're too . . . precipitous!'

'I have little time left to exercise patience,' she had said directly. 'Papa desires my happiness. Don't be afraid, Jonathan.' When she said his name she salivated as though she tasted the word in her mouth. She kissed him again, wetly. She wouldn't hear his pleas. 'I've lived too long in the fear of death to submit to the lesser fears,' she said.

The very next day he had received a message to call on Mr Flood, so he was obliged to cancel a drawing lesson that he was appointed to give, and had gone to the villa with the old arrogance masking trepidation.

'I'm not the sort to stand on ceremony, you understand,' her father had said. A short, stocky man. Blunt. Too blunt. Like father, like daughter, thought Jonathan. 'My girl wants you. You're a handsome fella, I'll admit. But there's no tin is there? Of course there isn't. A fine gentleman like you wouldn't be doing this sort of thing. I adore that girl, Hopgate. I'd cut out my heart for her. But she's a gonner, you know that, don't you? The consumption's after her like it galloped off with her mother before her. And what'll I have left? My heart's gone into her and my soul's in my work, man. Work is a great saver you know. It'll get you through anything.' The entrepreneurial wisdoms had gone on like a litany in the mouth of the merchant whose loud voice had cracks in it.

'No tin,' Flood repeated. 'Well that'd matter to some, but in the circumstances . . . D'you love my girl?'

'Yes,' Jonathan said civilly.

'I understand from the family who recommended your services that your people came over with the Normans. An old family . . . but bad blood in it, eh?'

'I come from a long line of gentlemen.'

'And there's an estate gone to rack and ruin, in the hands of bankers.' Flood spat out his cheroot. 'Marry my girl,' he said, his voice thick with emotion. 'Make her last months happy and, before God, I'll buy back your family estate for you. You can have the life of a gentleman if you give my girl a year of loving. Think of it! A year of loving for a lifetime's freedom from want. What do you say to that, Hopgate? Is it enough for you, man?'

'Yes,' Jonathan had said as he remembered how her wet mouth fastened on his. 'Yes, I'll marry her.'

3

'Marry her . . . marry her . . .' The horse's hooves beat out a rhythm of desperation. Riding, riding as he had ridden just weeks ago, the day he'd scarcely dared dream of . . .

He had ridden like a stricken lover, heart pounding, impatiently urging the horse onwards, then pulling, restraining the steed to fall back in pace with Flood's complacent mare. The agony of restraint, of civilly matching the slow, untroubled clip clop of his companion's mount when all the time his heart was fit to burst within him at the prospect that he would be his own man again and his lost identity would be restored to him.

The two men had ridden together to look over the house and estate that had so long ago fallen from the possession of the Hopgates; a house that haunted Jonathan. Returning like an ardent lover to the arms of a long lost mistress; going back to first love that leaves its mark forever.

He remembered Flood grumbling about the dampness of the countryside. 'How much further d'you
reckon, Hopgate?'

'Not far now,' Jonathan assured Lily's father.

'Can you remember much of the place, man?'

'I recall it as a series of disconnected pictures like a
dream that leads nowhere.' Jonathan's voice was cool,
distant.

Flood, slumped heavily over the mare's neck, was
unused to riding, and deeply regretted yielding to
Jonathan's arguments that they would make better
progress on horseback rather than travelling by carriage. 'It's a devilish tricky place to get to, anyway,'
he complained. 'I'm more of a town man meself. Don't
care for fields and cows much . . . Still, I suppose it's in
your blood an' all.' The older man looked at Jonathan
with some irritation. Hopgate was a cool customer, he
decided, pallid, straight-backed on the horse, his very
civility a form of arrogance.

Thinks himself too good for the likes of me – but not
above hankering after me money, though. He had to
admit he didn't much care for the fellow, but Lily, his
poor child, his one and only Lily, was half mad for the
drawing master. And was this the last thing he could do
for his dear heart, the final indulgence? Love conquers
all and all that flummery. Lily's love had swept aside
all objections. And could such love conquer death too,
he wondered.

'What of your family, Hopgate? D'you recall anything of them?'

Jonathan looked straight ahead so Flood couldn't see
the flush that mantled his complexion. 'I remember distant relatives, scattered cousins, uncles I lived

with, enough of them for more years than I care to remember.'

'But your own folk?' Flood persisted.

'Doubtless you know of the business with my father?' Jonathan retorted.

'I heard there was . . . a bad end.' Flood spoke cautiously.

'A bad end,' Jonathan repeated dully. 'That's almost a tradition with us Hopgates.' Seeing his prospective father-in-law's face darken, Jonathan went on quickly, 'My father lived in more dangerous, less effete times, sir. There were women . . . a certain, shall we say, recklessness, and a great deal of the sweet nectar of Bacchus, so — '

'He died by his own hand, they say,' Flood cut in.

'They say right, then. One minute my father was dead drunk, the next he was dead as a door nail. Blew his own brains out after swallowing a keg of brandy,' explained Jonathan. 'After the banks ruined him.'

They rode on for a while in an uneasy silence. Then Flood said, 'And you have no brothers or sisters living to share in the estate?'

A brief spatter of rain fell suddenly on the two men, and as they sought shelter under a solitary tree Jonathan said swiftly, 'After I was born my mother was delivered of a series of babies – all before their time, all dead, all female.' He bowed his head as he spoke, and trailing leaves fell over his face. They felt cool as a woman's hand in the morning air.

'How old were you when your father died?' Really, Flood was relentless.

'Eight.'

'What happened to you then? Your education?'

Jonathan's eyes narrowed. What did this tradesman know of a gentleman's education?

'I had a tutor, a retired clergyman who lived at the house, but when we lost High Withens I was sent to a grammar school in London. Every holiday I spent with a different family, sometimes kin, sometimes old friends, but none were willing to act the part of benevolent benefactor. I had to equip myself for the real world, and my first thought was to try my luck as an artist . . .'

'Then?'

'Well, Italy snuffed that particular illusion,' Jonathan said shortly. 'I saw there that I'd never have sufficient talent to be of the best.'

No, and second-best would never suit your infernal arrogance, Flood speculated. 'Working as a drawing master must barely earn you enough to keep body and soul together, man.'

Jonathan shrugged. 'I've supplemented my income with some portraiture — nothing serious of course, but then I never envisaged my profession would earn me enough to marry on.'

'No, marriage needs money,' Flood agreed readily. 'And so none of your own kin would do anything for you.'

Jonathan smiled briefly. 'Blood isn't just thicker than water, sir, it's also more venomous. My father had scandalised his family for years, and when he finally brought the house to rack and ruin they were only too pleased to see how the mighty were fallen, and mightily reluctant to do more than supply a roof and a crust for his offspring.'

The brief shower had spent itself and they continued

their journey in the sullen brownish light of the moor-land. The two men rode side by side as the path widened. Flood glanced across at the younger man, and for a brief moment a trick of the light and the sepia shade erased Jonathan's features. When he recalled the moment later, Flood shivered. It was as though he had looked over and seen an abyss, a chasm like the mouth of hell, where a man's face should have been.

They rode on silently, Jonathan with holy dread in his heart; a worm of doubt quickening the thicker arteries of the merchant.

When Flood first saw the dismal house, his spirits sank. Hand his only child over to this pile of malevo-lence! Common sense told him to deny her desires and ride back to town at once, but he knew there was no saying no to her, when that refusal would reach over into the everlasting nay of eternity. So, hopelessly, inevitably, he had dismounted. He dug his pouchy hands deep into his pockets and ceremoniously handed over the keys of the house to the last Hopgate, the keys of the house that, like a token of love, would forever bind his blood to the Hopgate inheritance. Keys to unlock the heart and its illimitable desires. Such heavy, rusty keys, and an impossible nail-studded door.

Jonathan accepted the keys silently.

'Lead the way, sir,' the merchant said, and then fol-lowed Jonathan into the penetralium of High Withens.

Breaching the battlements of the past . . . There was yet another door within the inner hall but this was stuck fast and they had no key. When Jonathan forced entry, thrusting his fist through the stained-glass panels, tiny shards of red glass, glittering like beads of blood, cut his hand badly, but he scarcely felt the pain although the sight of the wound shook the merchant.

'Go easy me boy. Here, let me.' Flood removed his stiff white cravat and wrapped it around Jonathan's bleeding fingers. Then he put his own hand through the aperture and opened the door smoothly.

The past, like a dream. Each room was skewed by a half-lit remembrance. He could remember a little, as he had told Flood . . . a room scented with Cologne, and the maid brushing his mother's endless hair . . . smooth it was, without a snarl.

He recalled watching the ritual through a half open door. The scene never varied until he spoiled it. Always the same ivory brush, bristling through the yards of golden brown hair. His mother wore some sort of white wrapper and pearly silken slippers. He watched her across the distance of the bedchamber as he regarded her across the length of the great dining table when he was allowed to eat downstairs. His father's promiscuity filled the house, but his mother was always a remote presence in her own set of rooms where she received her own set of female visitors. He spent his childhood simply looking at her, as he could now gaze on her portrait that still hung in the gallery. Look but don't touch, her loveliness told him, but he hadn't heeded it and she began to disappear when he broke through the magic pentacle that guarded her.

That devastating evening he couldn't bear the intimacy of the swooping brush in her yards of hair any longer and, though he was supposed to be long ago in bed, he tore across the room, heart aching for mama. Even now, when the rest of the night rotted to rags in his memory, he could recall her sibilant, indrawn breath as her cold arms repulsed him and she said, 'Take the thing out of my lap, woman, take it away from me at once. Do your hear me? Take it out.' And someone had dragged away a bewildered, yearning Jonathan.

How long after this it was that she withdrew entirely to that bourne from which there is no return, he wasn't sure. But when his father sneered, 'She's with the angels, your little sisters in Paradise,' he felt nothing. He thought no more about the matter. His mother, who was always almost there, had vanished completely.

Jonathan pushed open the door from what was once his mother's dressing room into a narrow passage, where the cobwebs hung like flags and a spiral of stairs descended to his old rooms.

'What part of the house is this?' Flood panted.

'Just here is the nursery and my old school-room.'

Flood followed Jonathan into a bare room with narrow windows. 'Bleak sort of an arrangement for a child,' he commented.

'Well, I remember it was always cold,' Jonathan told him. 'For some reason fires weren't permitted in the schoolroom.'

The nursery which led directly from the schoolroom still had a wooden chest and a bed in it, the very same bed where Jonathan, returning unexpectedly early from a walk with his tutor, had surprised his careless father with the nursery maid. Then the bed had had a little coronal. Translucent white muslin fell from it like a bridal veil. But the same diaphanous stuff that cascaded over young Jonathan's night-time slumber had been used on that unfortunate morning to strap and bind the splayed legs of the little nursery maid to the bed post.

Did the girl protest? Did she scream out on spying the young master? Was his father outraged, shamed; did he placate or beat the importunate Jonathan? And did his mother ever hear tell of the scandal? Jonathan simply couldn't remember.

A vivid lightning flash of memory brought him the girl's bare legs, stained with plum-coloured bruises, then all was a blank. There were other scenes though, that bled into one another from other occasions, or mayhap it was all one scene and his memory tricked him. A vision of rough woollen stockings floated before him, rucked around thick ankles. He heard a sound, not unlike Flood's stertorous breathing, whenever the image of a woman sweating heavily – her old skirts, the colour of dish cloths, turned back over her thighs, her hand labouring in his father's trousers – plagued him. And there were too many shadowy corners where his father emerged from a dim succession of sluttish petticoats.

His father had always smelled of the scullery maid, or the housemaids, the cook even, as well as an assortment of cheaply-scented town women. Only the fresher scent of the lady's maid never clung to him, because she had been fiercely loyal to his mother, he supposed, or perhaps she was of superior birth to the other servants and more likely a chaste woman.

Another scene: his father had been drinking claret. His voice was thick as raspberry cordial. 'Remember you're a Hopgate. I won't have you playing with stable boys.'

'I want a friend,' wailed the infant Jonathan.

'Pray hard and God will send down a little brother to play with you.'

'When?' demanded Jonathan.

'In a month or two, maybe.'

But the post between Heaven and High Withens must have gone astray, for no brother nor sister either was ever delivered to play with young Jonathan.

A cursory glance at some of the larger bedchambers was enough for Flood. The dust and the damp brought on his wheezing. The two men made their way down to the enormous kitchen. Jonathan remembered how this was always the warmest, busiest room, smelling of baked apples and bread and the steam from the next door laundry.

He must have been about seven, he reckoned, when, stealing jellies from the pantry, he overheard a kitchen maid boast to a scullery maid how the night before, in her tiny attic, the master had been so thirsty for her, his throat so parched with longing, that he drained the contents, every last liquorish dreg, of her chamberpot.

The kitchen, converted long ago from the brewery, was a large rectangle with rooms small as closets leading from it. The huge wooden tables were there still, as were the heavy skillets and pots that hung on walls larded with smoky sediment.

'Primitive, ain't it?' Flood said. 'Lily will want a new kitchener and all sorts of gadgets installed. I'll have to get men in quick to do painting and a bit of repair work. It'd cost a fortune to restore the whole place, though. We'll have to see how things go.'

Jonathan shrugged. 'It makes no difference to me. All that matters is I've come home. I expect Lily will want some comforts though.'

'The estate brings in little enough,' Flood went on, running a finger over the dust on a vast table. 'But perhaps in time, with a bit of planning, you could improve the revenues.'

'Naturally,' said Jonathan, 'I welcome the opportunity to take a full part in the running of the estate. My father never cared for his landed duties, but I, I'm a different man.'

'Good. That's settled then,' said Flood, sounding more resolute than he felt. It must be the damp, the infernal gloom of High Withens, that was bringing on a fit of the blue devils, he decided.

When they rode away Jonathan turned back to look at the house as he had turned so many years before ... taken quietly, someone's hand – he could never remember whose – leading him away from everything. He had possessed only the clothes he stood up in. The last thing he remembered seeing inside the house as he looked up before leaving was the long rows of ancestral portraits, staring down at him. They were there still. Again he could look on them. They kept faith. Mother gone, father wiped off the face of the earth, but there – safe, deathless, the proof of his lineage – his ancestors hung on the walls of High Withens.

4

Lily had chosen not to stay in bed, where the smell of the running sore clung to the sheets no matter how many times the maid changed her dressings. She was not to be found in the baronial hall nor in the library nor in any of the morning or drawing rooms. She'd had a wicker chair brought down to the old walled garden, where elm trees and oak and ivy-clad walls shut out the moor and barrenness, waiting in the garden for her husband to come home to her.

The grass was strewn with discarded papers as she drew, obsessively limned, endless portraits of Jonathan. For a man he was too beautiful. She tried to capture the blue depths in his Italianate hair, but the right tones eluded her. Then his brow, his haughty Hopgate brow that was pallid when a tempest of frowns swept across it, vexed her skills. He smiled rarely. 'My knight of the woeful countenance,' she had teased him. 'My knight who will conquer death for me.' She loved beauty more than life. A plain girl, but a fastidious one. Her care was all for rich things and bright colours, the finest silks, the plushest velvets. Every morning she drenched herself with delicate, thin scents, and at night always wore heavier French perfumes.

She drew fanatically, as though she could portray her very desire for him, or as if, like her finery, her art could atone for the deficiencies of beauty in her appearance. A plain girl, the looking glass said – and a sick one.

Her gauzy sleeves fluttered in the light breeze, and the white muslin veiled her grey skin with an illusion of translucence. In the sunlight, with her head bowed over her work, she might be any unblemished girl in summer muslin.

As she sketched, deliriously outlining his thin-lipped, sombre mouth, her heart flew out to him. She remembered the special day, the first day of love, the day they had kissed in the conservatory . . .

They had been together in the drawing room. She remembered how he had bent over her, urging her crayon to risk a bold tone here, a rich flush of colour underneath a rose petal where she'd scarcely noticed it. His breath was hung about with the scent of hot-house flowers; his black hair was luxuriant and had the depths of the deadly nightshade in it. She longed to touch his beautiful hair, press her lips to his sombre mouth. Her hand shook and the crayon missed its stroke. He chastised her.

'You must concentrate, Miss Flood.' His quiet voice had the authority of centuries in it.

'I cannot. I cannot.' Her voice was trembling like her hands; a salt tear slid down her cheek.

He was at once contrite. 'I forget. I work you too

hard. Poor child. I forget you're an invalid.' He took the
crayon away from her. His hands were warm and had
all the power of the world in them. She had attempted
to draw again but her hand would not work and to her
fury the paper and drawing implements defeated her,
and she flung them aside until through a sudden panic
she thought she had heard him hint that perhaps it was
all too wearying for her. He would leave her, her heart
told her as it leapt into her throat.

He raised her up from the sofa and, in a half faint,
her heart thumping, her very soul swooping, she knew
she had to stop him – she had to do something that
would bind him to her forever. She floated on his arm
through a bower of blooms. The floral perfumes were
stifling. At the door of the conservatory, where the
cooler air from the terrace met them, she tugged at
her chatelaine, dropping the purse of sovereigns that
hung from a chain.

He bent at once to pick it up, and when he slowly
lifted himself to meet her gaze the thing was decided.
She thought later that perhaps it was she who had
embraced him, but she could only remember the kiss
– the impossible, unbelievable kiss that had drowned
all the memories of sunlight and summers and the long
dark swoon of illness.

At fourteen she had been like any other girl. A little
bolder, perhaps, more headlong, pitching herself at
life, all impulse and spontaneity because she had no
mother to check her. She remembered her mother as a
large, ungainly presence issuing sharpness and warmth
in equal measure like the singing heat of the kitchen
stove, which dispelled the cold but showered you with

gritty cinders. When the warmth was withdrawn by death the coldness of absence was insufferable to Lily, so she had tried to wrap herself up in the comfort of things.

A brief blast of flaming love from Papa was always interrupted by the demands of the marketplace; she hardly ever saw her father and to assuage his guilt he encouraged her to replace him with trifles. So when morning cuddles could not be managed, because he was off before she had awoken, didn't that new looking glass with the gilt scrolls and winged cherubs reflect her kindly, as mama's eyes once had done?

Tippets and furs were soft as an angel's lap to repose in. A new fangled crinoline afforded the protection of a vigilant guardian: none could get near her when she wore the thing. Then there were the soothing salves and perfumes like caresses, pomades to beautify the hair and restrain its hectic kinks and corksrews, scented creams to stroke into her flesh, fragrances to anoint the body, lavender in pouches to secrete amidst lingerie.

To distract her there was an Ali Baba's cave of pastimes: shells for affixing to useless boxes; flowers for pressing flat as shadows until they were mere ghosts of themselves; ivory tablets and crayons for drawing; albums for sentimental inscriptions; a pianoforte; a magic lantern; a camera obscura she never mastered. There was a French speaking governess — a succession of them, in fact — they seldom lasted because she would not, could not, submit to their notions of decorum. 'A vulgar girl' was the universal judgement.

Lily, like her papa, took such obvious delight in material possessions. The house and its contents were always on show for visitors who visibly shrank as they made the grand tour of the latest acquisitions. If a man is what he owns, then Lily's father had swollen to a Colossus.

'D'you see this? Cost me half a year's income.' Flood always put a price to everything. Gold thread highlighted the heavy damask curtains he showed off to his guests. 'They match the two sofas, don't you see? I like things to match up. My Lily chose 'em.'

Meanwhile his Lily would be pirouetting in her new fangled crinoline, while her friends huddled in a flat group of unsupported petticoats.

Lily's fads were always honoured because it was a speedier business for Flood to buy things than actually spend time with his daughter, and though he hated to abandon the girl she would thank him later when she was set up for life with a substantial settlement. So if in the meantime it pleased her to cuddle dead cats – the live ones were kept for mousing, not petting – he would call on the services of a taxidermist. But when the inanimate creatures had arrived they were transfixed in glass cases, and she could only look at them.

'Doesn't it make you shiver, Lily Amadora?' asked Louisa, who at fifteen was a year older but unlike Lily hadn't grown breasts yet.

'Well at least they can't die on me,' Lily said, 'and the expression is most lifelike, you must agree, Louisa Elizabeth.' There was a craze just then for using second Christian names amongst their set.

Louisa Elizabeth looked unimpressed. She shuddered and her raven ringlets trembled. 'Isn't it just a little bit disgusting to preserve corpses? Unchristian, even!'

'Why, animals don't have souls, Louisa Elizabeth, so they can hardly be Christian in any case.'

Louisa Elizabeth wasn't up to theological arguments, but for nights afterwards her dreams were plagued by feline revenants, and the stuffed cats were regarded as a questionable luxury by the half a dozen girls who were Lily's friends.

The French gowns and undergarments, lavishly trimmed in the manner of a bride's trousseau, were another matter. No stinting of envy there!

Even if Beatrice Lorina's mother, who had lived in London and Paris, pronounced them fast, Beatrice Lorina would have given her crimped blonde tresses for them – almost.

The two girls, sitting on the little sofa in the boudoir adjoining Lily's bedroom, had gone into ecstasies over that first crinoline.

'See, you concertina the hoops, just so, then you may sit easily.' Lily demonstrated, the striped blue and white silk – silk for a day dress! – ballooning over the sofa.

Beatrice Lorina turned back the braided hem of the dress to inspect the marvellous construct of whalebone hoops and cambric. The circumference of Lily's dress was a wonder! And yet she swore it was weightless. When Lily told Beatrice Lorina the price of her ensemble, her friend gasped agreeably, her eyes narrowing with the anguish of desire for such a garment. To have been the first to wear a crinoline in their set! Her hips ached with the lust to swing capriciously, just as Lily's hips now swung as she arose and billowed across the room.

'Lets polka, Beatrice Lorina,' Lily ordered, wanting to show off how the crinoline bellied like a ship in sail when she danced.

Beatrice Lorina glanced in the mirror, the one with

the cherubs that showed her bright ripples of hair, her china blue eyes and innocent dimples. She stood up, slender in her lank petticoats, and held out her supple arms to partner Lily.

Lily la la'd some vaguely recognisable melody.

They danced. Or rather Beatrice Lorina danced and Lily spun and leapt but descended heavily, clumsily despite the ineffable grace of the hooped whale-bones. The mirror reflected them, displaying beautiful Beatrice, bella Beatrice in sad clothes like a nymph, an airy creation of ether and brilliance. Falling through the air Lily saw herself. Like mama's eyes with a cindery frown, the looking glass showed Lily for what she was: a clumsy clown of a girl with no poetry in her movement.

'Papa, I must have a dancing master,' she said. Although it was Sabbath, Papa was hurrying breakfast.

'What? Eh? Isn't Miss What's-her-name teaching you fancy steps . . . deportment?'

'Miss Kenny's a bore who thinks strapping a hard slate to my back's the be all and end all of elegance. She's too much of a puritan to waltz, and the polka is too energetic for her.'

Flood wiped a trickle of soft boiled egg from his mouth. 'Don't pay the silly woman for lolling about. Thought she had all the accomplishments, eh?'

'I feel foolish dancing with a woman in any case!' Lily wheedled. 'I need someone with a bit of life in him to partner me.'

Flood looked at her sharply. He tossed his half-eaten slice of toast down with mock exasperation. 'You squeeze every last penny out of me, minx, and now you expect me to fill the house with impudent young fellas.'

'Only one tutor, Papa. One is not so much, and of course he must be young. I can't polka with an old man.'

'Where you get these notions from the devil alone knows,' Flood grumbled. 'I wish your dear mama were here. She'd make a better job of taking care of you; the way you run circles around any governess I hire . . .' Flood was perplexed. Of course he wanted the best for Lily, but because they couldn't be bought over a counter he was at a loss when it came to the purchase of ladylike manners. Altogether a woman's job. What else did he pay that Kenny creature thirty-five pounds a year for!

Lily seized triumphantly on her papa's frown of confusion. 'It's expected, naturally, in the best society, that young ladies should be accustomed to dance gracefully and effortlessly before they're out of the school-room.'

'Well it's true your mama and I never had time or occasion for that sort of thing. But I know she'd a wanted better for her daughter.' His eyes, rheumy and crinkled, filled with a thick brine. 'Go on, then. One of these days I swear you'll squeeze blood out of me. Now, where do I go for one of these prancing fellas? Must I advertise?'

Something almost feminine, oriental about his features. He had looked at her shyly. A slip of a youth from Tuscany, his hair fell in a thick raven's wing over one brown eye. The other eye narrowed, squinting at her in the sharp spring sunlight in the conservatory. 'Buon giorno, Signorina Flewd.'

'Good morning, Giovanni.'

That first morning they hadn't danced properly. He had shown her how to glide, as if on castors, simply walking across the conservatory. He let her feel the swift rhythm of her own heartbeat. In twelve brief lessons he had taught her something more than grace, something she would remember and yearn for in the idle languor of illness – the pure joy of dancing.

At last Jonathan was returned from church. He came out of the house and over to where she sketched. She was dressed altogether inappropriately, he thought, in gauzy white muslin. A virgin's dress. Her hair, like the brown moorland, didn't shine in the sun. The light was harsher here. It was so high up there were no hollows, no glades to temper it.

He went up to her and kissed her peremptorily. Her grey hand caressed him. How curious she looked, already a cadaver – he shivered – with that odd, greyish-blue tinge to her flesh.

'Jonathan!' Her rough laugh with the rasping catch in it. 'It seemed an age, an epoch without you. And I wanted you close, so close dearest, I did the only thing that could conjure you up for me.' She laughed again, a harsh, discordant laugh in which her father's new money rattled. 'See, I've done a sketch of you.' She reached up out of her low chair, pressing her thin fingers upon his shoulders. She felt the almost negligent strength in him. A pang, half of love, half of sympathy in her breast when she saw how threadbare, almost frayed, were the seams of his coat. There hadn't been time to order a new wardrobe for him. She held up for his scrutiny a tablet of smooth ivory coloured in soft pastels.

The angel Gabriel looked at him with an excoriating gaze; a Gabriel with the haughty good looks of Lucifer and the rampant, flaring wings of seraphim. 'But my dear, an angel?'

'You are my angel. I'd say my guardian angel if I were a papist, Jonathan.' Again the coarse laugh that repulsed him.

'A somewhat fallen angel,' he said. He felt a sudden anger at this bold girl who found eternity in him.

'Now you must look with your professional eye and tell me what my faults are.' My beloved drawing master, she thought. Her beloved drawing master who was more beautiful than any angel limned in oils by some long dead Italian could be.

He looked at the angel, and at Lily's large portfolio marbled with colour, crammed with sketches and watercolours. No more of that. No more of that now I'm master of High Withens, he thought to himself. 'I'm your husband now, not your drawing master,' he said. But in his heart he knew that her father's money had merely paid for his services in another capacity.

'But I live when I draw for you,' she said.

He crumpled the angel. 'You'll do yourself no good, nor me either, if you try to recall past times. The past has gone forever and we'll have no more of it.' No more of Mister Hopgate, drawing master. A chimera, an abortive creature who never should have existed. 'I'm the master of High Withens now: you were a daughter of trade, now you're the wife of a gentleman, and there's an end of it!' He abruptly walked away from her, and the sun vanished behind one wayward cloud of vapour. She felt cold, as if she was back in the dark house again. As cold as it will be in my grave, she thought. Her heart was dull. She was too low bred. A plain girl. No fit wife for him. Her head drooped like a withered bloom. She continued drawing but with no heart in it. She sketched mechanically with swift, angular lines, a child's picture: a simple rectangle of a house with white shutters under an April sun. In the garden was a bower of love, and in the bower two lovers writhed passionately.

Tradesman's daughter. Old blood. Her beloved drawing master was gone forever. Oh, surely her soul was eaten up with a canker as irrevocably as her spine was.

They dined early, because of her illness, in the great hall beneath the gallery of ancestors. At the long table meant for a dynasty there was no hope of intimacy. He dined on a plump goose and spiced beef and drank two bottles of claret. She toyed with small messes of pulped vegetables and milk puddings. A sugary wine mixed with cordial was poured out for her.

A June night, but it was still too cold in the baronial hall, so a fire growled in the great hearth that she fancied was the mouth of hell gaping at them. Too many ancestors. Too much bad blood in the annals of this family.

He drank heavily. After the claret he poured port out of a chipped Georgian decanter. He drank with a swift, dissolute grace. The fire and the drink flushed him. Her heart quickened. For a man he was too beautiful. Forget Mr Hopgate, forget the fact that he was engaged by my father to instruct me in the elements of drawing, she told herself, remembering the promise to love, to honour and to obey him: my master, not my drawing master.

As he drank he assumed a Byronic insolence, slumped into the heavily carved chair. He dressed carelessly for dinner, without a jacket. His cravat was pulled away from his neck and his shirt was half unbuttoned. He sat with one booted leg tucked under him and the other stretched out under the table.

She wondered, does he love me or, as her heart grew cold, did my father buy him? All the while – and I love him so, love him far more even – a sudden chill passed over her. She shivered.

'You're cold. I'll have a servant bring more coals in,' he said. Perhaps the drink made him more amiable. He almost sounded solicitous.

'I think somebody has just walked on my grave,' she said.

'It's too cold in this house for you,' he said.

Lily looked out at the garden where the sun still lingered. 'Jonathan, it's this old house puts the blue devils in us. Let's go down to the gazebo and sit out the last of the warmth on the verandah.'

The drink had loosened him, the magic of good liquor that can make even a near corpse seem desirable. When he took her on his arm out of the shadowy room and into the sun-warmed garden, he joked because her hands were like ice. 'Cold hands mean a warm heart m'dear, but what can a cold house mean?' He laughed then, but his laugh sounded mirthless to Lily – a mocking laugh that went on too long.

The gazebo was built of stone with lattice carving like a diminutive Alhambra. Dust and dead leaves had accumulated in the circular chamber, but the cast iron bench on the verandah had recently been repainted. However, this love seat was too hard for his bride, so Jonathan had to cradle her in his lap like any lover. His body was so warm, so muscular, she was reassured – after all he had married her! A thrill of passion stifled the throb of the tumour. 'Forget . . . forget,' he had told her; so she forgot his harsh words and felt his body love her.

If he closed his eyes and felt the dress – only the gauzy stuff, not the friable bones beneath the soft material – if he sensed not her sickness but only the rare French perfumes in which she was drenched, he could fancy she was another.

So they both forgot and felt the warmth of the sun go down from the verandah. Next to the gazebo grew a cypress tree that flew up, straight and trim, to heaven. The hot sun of the day had warmed the cedarwood floor of the verandah. They curled close like lazy cats. Lily's weakness left her. She teased her husband's bared chest with moth kisses.

'I want to dance like when I was a girl,' she said, and unloosed her hair, and when he closed his eyes he didn't see that it was frizzed and broken. Her hair fell down like picked oakum. 'Dance, watch me dance,' she said. And she danced her own sick woman's dance. So love was an opiate, then!

Her brittle hair and butterfly bones . . . She weaved faltering, dazed steps along the verandah, waltzing unsteadily over to the cypress tree where she stood and looked at the generous rim of the sun in the west, far away from them.

'If I had the sun in my bones I might live,' she said wistfully, as the cypress tree threw a shadow over her.

Jonathan looked at his bride and remembered Agnes. He saw the other woman's mouth and eyes efface Lily's for a brief moment before the vision faded. Then there were black holes where Agnes' eyes had been, a terrible absence instead of her mouth.

He too rose and walked unsteadily. Passion and drink. He pushed the carefully ruched muslin from his bride's shoulder, put his mouth to her flesh and smelled only the essence of crushed roses.

Her masochism astonished him. She bore the brunt of the bare boards on her damaged spine. He was merciless, pushed guilt out of the gazebo and laid himself on top of her in a dead weight of drunkenness. For a sick woman she revelled in lovemaking. The little virginal ploys slipped away and she bit at him like a guttersnipe, a low woman. No breeding! Breed, breed, breed, his body taunted Lily, knowing only death and not life could be delivered from the mistress of High Withens.

5

———

'I should like to give a dinner or two for local society,' Jonathan said. There was a cool light in his eyes. His face flushed slightly as he went on: 'Some female company would do you good, my dear.'

'Having you alone to myself is the best thing for me,' Lily said at once. She handed him his tea, brewed strong and bitter to his taste.

He laughed shortly. 'You flatter me. I'm sure your feminine spirit must be weary after a couple of weeks' enforced intimacy with a taciturn male.'

Taciturn? She had fed too eagerly at first, drowned so recklessly in the sight, touch, the blissful intimacy of his presence she had scarcely missed mere words at all.

'Not enforced,' she objected. He said nothing, drinking his tea as she faltered. 'Oh, it has been confining for you. How selfish of me! I see that now, shut up as you've been because of my sickness.' Still he said nothing. She went on, a sliver of ice in her heart. 'Of course, you must mix in society.'

But she had wanted to seal the world of love around them, a charmed life, admitting no one.

Of course for a man it must be different. She had thought they would shut the world out, live in their own world of love, but he was reluctant to be alone with her it seemed. A man needed the world more than a woman, perhaps. Just short weeks of ardently loving him and his restraint made her love fiercer. He was afraid of passion, in case it devastated what was left of her health, she had told herself at first, and then a little later when his hard, dry mouth wrestled away from her fervid kiss, she thought, if it were only that he fears catching my illness.

He put his cup down. 'It's the way of things,' he explained. 'The tenants expect it.' His eyes narrowed. 'I have to assume my place amongst them. No matter if you don't feel up to it. Stay in bed. I can make your excuses,' he said indifferently.

'If it's your wish of course I'll receive your guests,' she said eagerly. Too eagerly. She would put her heart on his plate to carve if it pleased him. 'And I feel better, so much better.' Her face glowed – with passion or fever, he wondered.

When the tenants came, she was at ease in their company. The farmers drank heavily; their wives knew their place and openly admired Lily's elaborate costume, her pluck in overseeing all the finest details of service à la Russe. An exquisite meal and, though she ate little herself, merely sipping at her wine, her heart was warmed by Jonathan's easy conviviality with the hard-drinking men. And when they had gone very late he fell into bed with his boots on, then woke and loved her roughly and so briefly that in the morning he barely remembered a thing about it when she teased him.

'Like a quattrocento madonna, you were muttering, with skin cool as marble.' Though her back ached dreadfully she didn't mind it.

He flushed and said, 'If I said it, it was true.'

'Say it now,' she said.

But in the cold light of morning he would not be drawn. 'You look pale enough to be marble,' he offered. Like ice to touch.

When they entertained the clergy it was another matter!

Mrs Beech, at a loss without her five daughters who were sojourning in the Swiss Alps, had brought along Miss Hemp, a spinster of the parish. And Violetta Hemp brought an enormous cloth bag, hopeful of selling collectibles from her Ladies' Repository: doilies, shell boxes, mittens, ribbons, frivolous spoils – she depended on genteel charity.

'My dear, you're a saint to receive us with all your other trials,' Violetta said loudly, scattering shawls, hair trimmings, amusing Lily with her untidy style of dress. She was a stout, olive-skinned woman, a little deaf, with a disconcerting habit of shouting above the subdued murmur of polite company. 'There is fine air hereabouts that will set you up. You're better off away from that dirty little town.' She drew her chair alongside Lily's sofa.

Shortly after the arrival of the Beech's, two curates made their appearance in company with Miss Slane.

Lily's eyes glazed over the black-clad clerical gentlemen, and fluttered when Jonathan laid a proprietary hand on the arm of the curate's beautiful daughter. The woman's smile met her with something like pity in her glance, taking in at once the poor complexion, unruly hair and wretchedly curved spine.

When they went into dinner Jonathan accompanied Agnes and, as he bent over her, his dark hair shadowy against the woman's fair tresses, Lily thought with a pang that they looked like a portrait of perfect lovers so matched in their beauty.

Husband and wife sat at opposite ends of the table, Agnes seated at one side of Jonathan, Lily between Miss Hemp and the curate, Septimus Slane. Miss Hemp chatted throughout the meal, offering Lily large sweeps of meaningless gossip. Slane talked on theological matters with the third clerical gentleman, who was yet another curate from a neighbouring district. Mrs Beech entertained her husband. And Jonathan monopolised Agnes Slane.

Between the bursts of Violetta Hemp's chatter, the discourse between Lily's husband and the curate's daughter drifted through the air like candlesmoke.

'As Ruskin says . . . the individual freedom of . . .'

Miss Slane all ethereal in white, her neck and arms bare of ornament, murmuring, '. . . true . . . Tennyson's Palace of Art . . .' And was the creature even quoting poetry to Jonathan? '. . . A land where all things always seemed the same . . .'

And Jonathan was throwing back his head, his throat gleaming with the reflection of candleflame, saying with more animation than she had ever heard him speak, 'Ah now, lotus eating, Agnes . . .'

'Jabez Wicke's daughters are all unmarriageable because of their father's fussiness,' Miss Hemp cut in. 'Have they visited you yet, my dear?' The rest of Agnes Slane's affected recital was lost to Lily's ears. She turned dutifully to answer her guest.

After dinner the ladies sipped lemonades and Jonathan, an excitement in his step, a certain restlessness in his mien which Lily had never before noticed, was a solicitous host, offering views on church matters to the clergymen, nodding affably at Violetta Hemp and Ellen Beech, assisting his listless wife to her sofa before again monopolising Agnes Slane.

When she heard Agnes mention a certain Pre-Raphaelite artist, Lily called, 'My father's got three of his paintings; paid over a thousand guineas for them. He made the artist match the sitters' clothes to our drawing room carpet.'

Jonathan looked discomposed. 'My wife's father is a patron of the contemporary arts,' he said hurriedly. 'The Pre-Raphaelite Brotherhood are another thing, of course, but I'm sure you abhor the art of this crass, materialist age.' His head bent low over the woman, obscuring her face, so Lily never heard Miss Slane reply.

She was stern with herself. Anyone would be smitten by the woman's beauty, she admitted, even her artist's eye had to be a little in love with the dreamy quality of Agnes Slane's hair, her eyes, her slender figure. And the other company noted nothing untoward: how could they know that her husband's face was usually empty, blank with boredom, not mobile, alive as it was now? How could they ever know? None would ever watch him as she did.

None other could possibly imagine his hand rested too long in Miss Slane's lace-mittened palm as he bade her farewell; who else but a besotted bride would conjecture that the light in his eyes died as the servants snuffed the candles when their guests departed?

How she doted on him!

Alone in their bedchamber, her lace wrapper already discarded, the lawn nightgown artfully askew, she sat waiting for him.

He carried a lamp, the wick turned low, and when he opened the curtains the pallid reflection on his face threw his eyes into shadow.

'Still awake!' He put the lamp down heavily so the oil stirred and the flame leapt high. His voice was tight with exasperation. 'There's no need for you to miss sleep on my account.'

'I couldn't sleep. I dozed all afternoon. I was just about to come down again and see what kept you.'

'Nothing kept me. I wanted to finish my cigar and brandy.' He got into bed.

Lily moved across to him. He felt warm and his skin and hair were fragrant with Havana leaf. Her arms wound round his neck and she kissed his mouth. But as her body pressed against his he shuddered suddenly, violently, spat out her tongue and coughed until he almost retched.

'What is it?' she asked.

'One of your damn hairs. Can't you tie your hair back at night? You half choked me.'

'Is that all? I'm sorry. I'll plait it in future.' She laughed to make light of his coldness.

That must be all. That has got to be all, she prayed, as again she sprawled over him and laid her mouth on his tight lips though he lay still as an effigy.

At last they made love. But as passion quickened

him he turned his face aside at the moment her mouth
sought his kiss.

And then he moved across the bed far away from
her.

Lulling herself to sleep with the mournful thought:
he doesn't kiss me because he never loved me. In her
dreams Lily wept.

Love, sweet love. Oh love. And who better to appreciate the abandon of passion than one whose body was
imprisoned in sickness?

After the first kiss there were others. He did not turn
away then, his lips tightened with disgust. Papa was
never there, all governesses long gone, only a mildewed
aunt that papa had dug up from somewhere – not
a real aunt at all, only a third cousin or somesuch,
hardly a relation. And the woman was dotty and deaf
and could be bribed with a few glasses of brandy
and raspberry cordial. While this relic of assumed
respectability snored on the drawing room sofa, the
lovers stole away. To the garden, the conservatory or,
with the blinds pulled down, the gilt and plush dining
room – they sat side by side on a tête-à-tête set between
tall vases of lilies and fern. What she loved most was to
writhe her fingers through his hair or stroke the nape
of his neck that was white as a woman's.

He was the perfect gentleman. His lips were chaste
and cool and kissed her smoothly. The consummate
courtship ritual!

'May I write in your album, Miss Flood?' His
copperplate inscribed thrilling sentiments.

'What an exquisite verse. Is it one of your own?' she
asked him.

'I wish it might be. It's one of the *Sonnets From the Portuguese.*'

'Are the Portuguese a very romantic people?' Lily asked artlessly, adjusting a silken cushion to her aching back.

Jonathan was tactfully mirthless. 'I mean it's from a collection of sonnets written by Elizabeth Barrett Browning.'

Even Lily had heard of that lady's romantic fate. She read the verse aloud in her cracked voice.

I thought once how Theocritus had sung
Of the sweet years, the dear and wished-for years,
Who each one in a gracious hand appears
To bear a gift for mortals, old or young:
And, as I mused it in his antique tongue,
I saw, in gradual vision through my tears,
The sweet, sad years, the melancholy years,
Those of my own life, who by turns had flung
A shadow across me. Straightway I was 'ware,
So weeping, how a mystic Shape did move
Behind me, and drew me backward by the hair,
And a voice said in mastery while I strove,
Guess now who holds thee? – Death I said. But
   there
The silver answer rang: Not Death, but Love.

When she fell silent, she turned her face away from him for so long he half thought the verse had insulted her. He brushed a wiry ringlet back across her shoulder and turned her face towards him. Then he saw she wept. Her eyes, stung red with tears, regarded him desperately.

'Dearest . . .' His tone was plush and gilded as the dining room.

'Not death, but love,' she repeated through her sobs. 'My love, my love . . . it's as if this poem was written just for me. I know . . . I know now I can live because you love me.'

Oh life, oh love, her kiss said, and it seemed to him she struggled, fought in his arms, because never before had a woman kissed him with her life's breath.

Like tumbling into blackness. As if her indrawn breath absorbed and so defeated him. He felt lifeless. Carefully he withdrew his gasping mouth. Her head drooped, a dead weight on his breast and for a terrible moment he thought she had expired in his arms. Then she stirred.

'I will live because you love me.'

Oh life. Oh love, her breath rasped as a different kind of horror gripped him and he was entwined, her arms like bindweed, imprisoning him in outlandish passion, tasting her in his mouth, her greedy mouth fastening even now on his neck, gnawing at him . . . Pull away now or she'll suck you down into her deepest desires where you'll drown, reason told him. I'll love you as you've never been loved, her heartbeat threatened, as only those whom passion reprieves from death can love . . . and all the courtship trifles, the verse albums and nosegays and smooth promises, would count for nothing . . . devastated by the maelstrom of her desire.

For a moment High Withens lurched drunkenly over the precipice of destiny.

For a moment his tongue, coated with excuses, almost betrayed him into saying, 'Miss Flood, I never

61

can love you.' And then the choking sound of her too rapidly indrawn breath roused him. Her head had fallen back over his shoulder. Her eyelids were lowered, her face waxen. Why, her own passion had exhausted, sickened her! She was in a half faint. Vain hope to dream that it wasn't death but love that mastered her, not death but love ... a vain hope! He almost laughed. Why, only death, only death lay at the end of her passion, he exulted, and he fled to summon the aid of the aged relative – for brandy, for sal volatile, to revive her.

So then, her own frailty restrained her lovemaking. Her heart pounded when his dry lips brushed her mouth. When his hands took one of hers and clasped it to his heart, he felt the vein in her wrist flutter calamitously. He became careful not to rouse her. His speeches were cool but flattering. He praised her fastidious clothes, her artistic accomplishments, and was solicitous for her comfort, so for her health's sake it was best that they didn't sit too close. See how his strength could crush her! He gently stroked her fingers, turning round and round the amethyst, the ruby, the pearl rings of her girlhood, and playfully demanding that she must wear no other bauble when he had placed on her finger the slender gold wedding ring. He kissed each polished fingertip; her hands, softened with creams and potions, were limp and slippery. She had a strange fancy that if she didn't grip hard he'd slither away from her, so she was forever twining her fingers in his hair, binding him.

She wove little flowerets into manacles and bound his wrists.

'See what a fragile chain links our hearts,' she said.

'Your hands might so easily crush the petals. Your disregard might annihilate me.'

'My disregard?' His voice was low, cautious. He lowered his bound wrists to her lap. 'What is this disregard you speak of?'

She had seemed much weaker suddenly, and that day she had lain prone on the couch in a little morning room. All day she had been playing with wilting flowers, complaining of imaginary heat, lifting up her fan, snapping it shut, then restlessly dropping it to the floor.

He had never seen her so fretful. 'Have I slighted you in some way? Have I not been sufficiently attentive?' he demanded.

She flushed. With vexation or fever? She lowered her eyes and began to pick nervously at a wrecked nosegay of flowers. 'Your attentions are . . . assiduous,' she barely whispered.

'Then?'

Silence. Her fingers were growing sappy with the spoilt flowers.

'Have I done right in everything, or wrong in anything?' He forced a lighter tone to his voice. 'Really, we men may easily blunder in such matters; we require a lady's instruction when it comes to the gentler arts of romance.' Her continuing silence seemed mulish. She puzzled him. 'At least instruct me as to my misdemeanours.'

'Oh you've done nothing wrong,' she said at last. 'You've been the perfect gentleman.' She seemed to speak with difficulty, her complexion flaming.

'Clearly there's something, if you speak of disregard,' he said with asperity.

Her gaze fell on the chain of flowers. Her hand flew to her bare throat and in a flash he sensed how in his gentlemanly regard, his chaste distance, she saw herself disregarded.

'See, the link is strong but the blooms are crushed by my touch,' he said, slipping the floral chain over his wrists and holding the wilting but unbroken circlet up for her inspection.

'When the petals are crushed, the scent is strongest,' she said evenly.

Dutifully, he moved closer.

If her sickness required that she restrain her ardour, her love demanded he should trammel on the conventions. This sick girl wanted proof he loved her.

She lay still, very still, like a steady flame, her hands, throat and face were scorched, scorching.

His hands shook, unloosening her robe. He felt her desperately controlling her breath. He kissed her neck, her breasts, felt for the silkily stockinged limbs beneath layers of petticoat. She was limp and pliant, lying between him and some unknown danger. Feigning a passion he would never succumb to, never drown in, he demonstrated the love he should have felt for her in drawing back at almost the last moment like a perfect gentleman.

She held him still in her arms, not moving for what seemed like hours, feeling the heaviness of him crush her.

'Oh how I long for our wedding day,' she murmured. 'It will not be long now.'

To love freely at last.

Three days before the wedding, a perfect day, she had

the illusion of health again. She received him in the garden where a tea party was laid out for just the two of them. A good day, the sunshine and love had banished pain. She felt almost pretty with the desire that plumped out her flesh. Jonathan looked boyish with expectancy. In three days she would be his bride and be with him at High Withens.

When he spoke of the house it was of a different place than the ruin her father had deprecated.

'My spoilt beauty, she only wants loving,' he laughed, animatedly describing the gargoyles whose scowls had been erased by rainwater, and the battlements that were crumbling, and the acres of draughty halls where on moonlit nights in his childhood his own shadow had petrified him. A house filled with the magic of history and lineage, where water colours his grandmother and great grandmother had painted filled the bedrooms, portraits of Tudor ancestors lined the walls, china and plate handed down for generations were stacked in cupboards; where at any moment he might look up and his gaze might fall on the same sweeping prospect outside the windows that was viewed by his ancestors – and so he would be assured of his own place in the scheme of things.

'Can a house mean so much?' she questioned him. 'Mightn't we be happier in a more comfortable establishment?'

'Happier?' The thought puzzled him. He stared at the ignorant girl. 'It's been long years,' he said desolately, 'long years cast out from my inheritance, exiled from myself.' He hunched his shoulders and almost shivered like a lost orphan. 'I couldn't be any more comfortable in another house than I could be at ease in another's skin. You take us both, for better or worse,' he threatened suddenly. 'You must know that Lily, I *am* High Withens.'

6

———

'My dear girl, don't even attempt to get up,' Violetta said, plumping Lily's pillows and twitching the counterpane, all the while scattering provisions and dropping her shawl over the Jacobean bed wherein Lily was almost immured by the heavy drapes and covers. 'Where's that husband of yours? Isn't he dancing attendance on you? No, I daresay not. What man ever learned to tolerate the miseries of a sick room? They run like scalded cats when a woman ails. Believe me, I've attended many a sick room and I never yet came across a man, other than an apothecary or somesuch, in one.'

'Jonathan had some estate business,' Lily said loyally, allowing Miss Hemp to raise her to a half sitting position.

'Hmm,' Miss Hemp went on. 'You want to remind him he has wife business too.' She bent to pick up her shawl, her professional eye taking in the fal-lals and knick-knacks arranged on the old press, wondering if

Lily could be persuaded to purchase a few of those lace trifles Mrs Tow had made, from her Ladies' Repository. 'I made sure one of the maids was instructed to bring tea up as I came in. I hope you don't think me presumptuous. Is there anything else you need, Mrs Hopgate?'

Lily said, 'No. It isn't yet time for my tablets.'

'Are you eating? You're white as parchment, child. I've brought some homemade cordials and preserves for you . . .' Miss Hemp glanced around the gloomy room. 'You know, an invalid chair would be the thing. I'll see if anyone in the parish possesses such a contraption. Then your husband could wheel you out in the fresh air on days you're too poorly to walk. A young woman like you – you musn't be shut in like this,' she scolded.

'I don't want to be a drag on my husband,' Lily said.

'Mercy, child, you'd better lose that martyr attitude at once. You're speaking of a man, remember. A creature who needs to be fitted with chains and leg-irons if he's to slow his pace to the tempo of family life.' Miss Hemp laughed.

Lily laughed too. A hearty laugh. Shared laughter and merciless gossip billowed the inert air of the bedchamber.

When the servant brought tea and cakes for them, Lily found her appetite whetted by Violetta's store of local lore and scandal. Miss Hemp told the sick girl about the stir that Jonathan's marriage and return had caused in the local community.

'The talk hasn't died down yet,' she confessed. 'All the women are wild to have a look at you.' She drew her chair up close to Lily's bedside. 'I hope you won't be offended if I tell you, the Hopgates have a dreadful reputation in this part of the world; theirs is a long history of scandal, drink and ...' she lowered her voice' ... profligacy. Everyone's waiting to see if the new master lives up to the family reputation. But you, my dear, must see to it that he does not.' Miss Hemp smiled, grimly noting the younger woman's listlessness. 'Rouse yourself, get yourself well, and teach him who's truly master of High Withens.'

Violetta's direct talk exactly suited Lily, who wasn't at all offended by the older woman.

She mustn't let sickness make a martyr of her.

'Tell me more about the old scandals and the new ones too,' she begged, her eyes wide with pleasure.

Violetta's stories were ripe with the embellishments of repetition. Never were there such heinously ravished serving girls, piteously neglected mistresses dying in childbirth, such satanic rakes, besotted topers, as in the history of the Hopgates.

When she had rattled all the skeletons she knew were to be found in the Hopgate family closet, Violetta went on to thumbnail sketches of the local society, outlining the petty vanities of the Beech's; the crazy suspicions of Jabez Wicke, who beat his daughters if a man so much as met their gaze at church on Sabbath; the notorious drunkard of the neighbourhood, Farmer Belton, a fine cut of a man who, if only he'd give up the demon drink, shave every day, and pay more attention to his husbandry, would make some woman an eligible husband. Miss Hemp sighed the thirsty sigh of a woman who has endured the long drought of spinsterhood. Mentioning the impecunities of the industrious Mrs Tow brought her to the real purpose of her visit, however.

'You may remember I told you last time we met that some of us ladies, less fortunate than our sisters, widows or old maids like me', Miss Hemp laughed, but her eyes were narrow with fear and lost opportunity, 'have formed a business arrangement.' She went on to explain how ladies in a little local difficulty exercised their skills in producing fancy embroidery, quilts, honey, sweatmeats, preserves, arrangements of dried flowers and such like, which they deposited with Miss Hemp who made it her business to hector, coax and generally persuade the more fortunate, the more comfortably situated ladies of the parish to purchase the wares at bargain prices, combining enterprise with a little Christian charity, for it was Miss Hemp's business also to beg these beneficent benefactresses for donations – say odd pieces of fine china, a length of discarded silk – to add to her stock of fancies.

'In short, would you care to send down some more trifles to patronise my ladies?' Violetta begged, adroitly producing some ribbon and elegant lacework from her reticule. 'Or perhaps you'd cast an eye over these; the local peddlars will never bring you finer,' she boasted.

Lily's eyes caressed the skeletal web of lace that purported to be a handkerchief. 'Of course. I'll buy anything you've brought with you,' she offered with careless splendour.

'Of course, my wife can afford such largesse! Isn't her papa a veritable Midas!' Jonathan interrupted them suddenly, stumbling into the bedchamber, his boots caked with mud, his manner the worse for a luncheon spent at an inn in Farmer Belton's intoxicating company. 'Hasn't she told you, Miss Hemp, how her papa can buy anything, even a centuries old name?'

Insolently he swayed over to a small console table, opened a drawer and drew out Lily's mesh purse with its fistful of sovereigns, which he pressed into the reluctant palms of Miss Hemp.

'Oh this is far too much, sir,' she protested. 'Just a few shillings for a few trifles.'

But Lily was already dismissing her with a limp wave, saying, 'Please do take the money, Miss Hemp. I want the ladies to have it, but now I really must rest.' Treacherous in her abandonment of a new friend, simply because the husband she adored (although worse for wear, and although Miss Hemp might think he had cruelly embarrassed his wife) had returned. She wanted to expel this woman swiftly so it would be just the two of them in their own world of love again.

When Miss Hemp was banished, clutching her bounty, Jonathan threw himself down on the bed fully dressed and began to snore noisily. The local ale was stronger than he had imagined.

Lily didn't mind. She wasn't a woman to fuss about a man drinking. She rather liked him a little drunk; it made him less fastidious, less careful. She would allow him sleep and then she would press her body against his until he stirred in his stupor and made love to her like one who has eaten lotus flowers and forgotten everything.

She didn't mind the heavy boots soiling the bed, but she removed his jacket and drew the coverlet over him – his worn, dear jacket. She wrapped it round her shoulders, snuggling into his male warmth, thinking, I must have him measured up for new clothes; he's so careless about material possessions. She drew the jacket tightly around her, feeling the softness of the worn cloth, softness except for that stiffness in the inner pocket. She inserted her hand to remove the obstruction and drew out a wad of folded paper.

His sketches. She smoothed the sheets of paper and laid them out on the counterpane. High Withens, sketched in all the pride of possession. Jonathan had drawn the choked tarn before the great door; another picture showed the edifice with crumbling battlements; yet another depicted the east wing smothered by ivy; and a further delineated a tower. A tower. She looked again. The tower had a window that was open. A woman looked out, her hair long as Rapunzel's. A woman with a long neck – a beautiful woman. I know that face, Lily thought. Her thoughts were clear and cold as glass. She sat still, very still, for long moments, glaring at the sketch. A very beautiful woman, with a long neck; a cold beauty who lit such a fire in the gaze of the artist. I know who she is, Lily thought, I know the secret. The secret of angels, the secret of all cold beauty. The secret is the fire that is in the heart of those who yearn to possess the secret.

My Dear Lily,

    When I was a boy my pa told me, you can buy yourself any woman that takes your fancy, if she's over thirty. Before that they're all flibbertigibbets only wanting to be kissed half to death, romancing and ever afters. They go daft over the beast in a man until they're wore out with having young 'uns. As they say in these parts – a lass is nowt but a Lent lily until the first bloom has gone out of her. Pick yourself a flower of the field, my pa told me, not one of your altar blooms that toil

*not neither do they spin. Well I looked about
me. There was a stunner one time, a strapping
red-haired tormentor I lost guineas and sleep on.
But as you know I'm a toiler and moiler first.
There was business to take care of and I had my
pa's drapery shop in London to take on and half
an eye up North to where the real money was to
be had in the manufactories. A man must be at
liberty to pursue his best interests and a young
wife, I've noted, is more than a distraction, she's
as much a cross for an ambitious man to bear as
a guilty conscience. Your mother was almost past
child-bearing and could give me a decade when I
met her. Her first love died young and when she
got over it and didn't feel too squeamish about
walking out with other fellows she found she
had recovered from romantic notions. A good
provider was what she wanted. She'd had enough
by then of wearing her eyes out stitching fine
ladies' ball gowns for a pittance. She wasn't you
know what they call up here a comely lass, but she
was a sturdy 'un. A worker through and through
but canny enough to want to see the profit in it.
She didn't intend to be one of the undeserving
poor. No more did I. Poverty and shiftlessness
are bedfellows I say. And though she was ten
years older than me she was fit as a fiddle then
and ready for anything. I brought you up not
to lift a finger and I've no regrets about it and
as things have turned out it's no matter anyway
being as how you're so feeble. It's the truth you're
the spit of your mother in all but vitality. She had
you late of course and it's a fact that a late child is*

*always a sickly one. But you've been a good girl,
the apple of my eye, my rose without a thorn,
my little darling and what I want to say to you
Lily is – marriage is best seen as a contract in
which man and wife should be at liberty to pursue
their joint interest. It's no use you eating your
heart over some fancy you have for a husband
that's a hero out of a novel book. Your mother
was my right hand. At first, before you were
born, she worked hard helping me to build up
my lace manufactory. Right from the start when
we put the work out, before the factories came,
she'd rise at four in the morning and walk half
a dozen miles to collect from the outworkers.
And as my business prospered she did not sit
back. Her talents for accounts and snapping up
the best orders were second to none, superior to
mine in fact. A fine woman, Lily, and a good 'un.
We neither of us wasted time on the idle purchase
of romance. Nor did we spend time on love hot
quarrelling. Invest wisely, Lily, as your pa and ma
did, in rational discourse with your husband. Talk
to him about improving his estate, getting rid of
the shiftless tenants. Have your house made over
and if it's money you want (I thought it best not to
give your husband too much in case he's inherited
his father's propensities) for any trifles that would
gladden your heart, you've only to apply to me.
I wish I could spare time to visit you. But where
your interests are concerned you know well I'm
spendthrift. You write to me – I cannot humour
death and a husband – Lily you sadden me. Trust
in the Lord who gave your ma and pa strength*

to make a good living for you. No more talk of death then, any more than romance, both foolish palaver. Lily, don't make me ashamed of you. A grown girl of twenty-five writing like a fourteen year old! Does your husband beat you? Does he curse your name or ravish the housemaid? For goodness' sake child, don't make him despise you! Marriage is as much a business contract for a fine gentleman as it is for us toilers in Mammon. Humour your husband certainly if by that you mean keeping a sweet temper, a ready attention and a lively interest in all that concerns him. As for humouring DEATH! Lily I believe marriage could revive you. Don't give in! I know the pain gets bad, girl. I know and remember the spirited child you were at fourteen with your fashionable whims for deportment lessons and Italian dancing masters. I remember well your first sickness, the disfiguring skin eruptions. Then you got better but you never seemed my happy girl again. And now that tubercular spine! Fight it! Don't coddle yourself! I tell you a man can't abide a sick wife. She's no earthly use to him. No, Lily, don't talk of humouring death, humour your husband. He's a handsome fellow and many's the proud beauty would be glad to have him. No more nonsense of how he was bought for you. Develop a practical head on your shoulders, my girl. You're a lady and remember no one esteems the fact greater than

    Your loving pa.

P.S. If the symptoms do get worse you might ask Dr Briggs to fetch one of these specialist fellows from London. Are you eating eggs and cream as he told you?

Lily chafed the letter backwards and forwards across her lap. The afternoon sun shone down. She was alone in the gazebo. A new bride still, and already disillusioned. I cannot humour death and a husband, she had written. A man can't abide a sick wife, her father had said. He hates my sickness. He no longer kisses my mouth, she thought with anguish. I'm not a practical woman like Ma – she would tell her father if he were here now – nor a strong one. I need love; loving. So if I die before thirty it's as well for me. A plain girl and a sick one and a fool to expect a gentleman with the pride of Lucifer and the face of an archangel to be loving me.

'BUT I BELIEVED HE LOVED ME', she wrote in large letters in the dust on the floor of the gazebo.

The woman walked down through the sloping garden towards Lily, who sat on the dusty floor of the gazebo mourning her marriage.

Who was this woman and what did she want with her?

The woman that her husband already called Agnes instead of Miss Slane had paid calls on her twice already, as well as attending that dinner they gave for the clergy.

The woman found her in the gazebo amidst the dust and dead leaves, spoiling her dress. Her thin voice that was too well bred to express consternation said, 'Shall I restore you to your feet, Mrs Hopgate?'

And Lily, silently, sullenly, stumbled back to the house on the arm of her enemy.

When they were back in the dark, cool hall the

woman must have noticed her grimace of pain, her sudden pallor, for she said, 'Some sal volatile? Can I fetch any medicines for you?'

'No!' Lily said. 'Ring the bell, would you? A maid will bring my pills.'

'Do they help to dull the pain?' Miss Slane asked her.

'Not the pain, there's laudanum for that. Dr Briggs says they are a curative for my spine disease, but they don't work in all cases and there are side effects.'

'What are they, these side effects?'

Really Miss Slane was too curious. Lily didn't want to tell Agnes Slane how the pills turned her complexion grey as ditchwater.

Miss Slane tugged at the tasselled bell-pull by the great chimney piece, then sat down on an oaken settle next to the small table where Lily's portfolio was laid out. With her straight, narrow back she's more the lady of the manor than I, Lily thought with resentment. She envied Agnes Slane her smooth hair that had the sun in it, her long neck and the patrician body that had no need of style to achieve distinction. Lily eased herself painfully on to a low couch.

The curate's daughter had brought her some novels from the circulating library. 'I hope these books suit, Mrs Hopgate,' she said. 'I tried to select what I hoped you would find diverting, but I can hardly tell, I've so little time myself for reading stories. My father's a hard taskmaster.'

'I've time enough', Lily said, 'for pastimes.'

'I see drawing is among your accomplishments, Mrs Hopgate. May I look at these?' And without waiting for an answer Agnes Slane was turning over

Lily's sketches of Jonathan, her long, slender fingers caressing the smooth sheaves of paper: Jonathan as the archangel, Jonathan as King Arthur grasping Excalibur, Jonathan as Dante rapt before Beatrice, Jonathan as the hero of a Walter Scott novel, and Jonathan as the forlorn prince who loved Rapunzel and was repaid with blindness. When Miss Slane had finished studying the last sketch of the mutilated prince, eyes torn out on briars, wandering through the wilderness, she said, 'These drawings have a sure touch. You've been well taught, I think.'

'My wife was an attentive pupil. Her teacher merely focused the talent she so obviously possessed.' He stood in the shadow of the open door. Lily's heart skipped. Would he rage at her for displaying the sketches?

'I'm all admiration for your wife's talents, Mr Hopgate,' Agnes said swiftly.

'Do you sketch, Agnes?'

'No. I'm afraid I lack artistic accomplishments. As I was telling your wife, I have too many duties to occupy me.'

'The Lord's right hand,' Jonathan said with a smile in his voice.

Agnes blushed charmingly. 'Only the curate's. I think you blaspheme, Sir.'

Your beauty would make an angel blaspheme, Agnes, he thought. He said correctly, 'Mr Beech says he doesn't know what the parish would do without you, but if the parish can spare you for a day perhaps I could give you a little instruction in the elements of drawing?'

Lily interrupted as she saw another blush incarnadine Miss Slane's too flawless complexion. 'Jonathan, you surprise me. I thought you were half ashamed of your work. Would you believe, Miss Slane, my husband can't bear to be reminded he was employed by my father as drawing master? And Jonathan was the best tutor I ever had. I sometimes think it a pity he gave it up to marry me.'

Now Jonathan flushed. He walked over to the table where Miss Slane had spread out the sketches and threw a look of contempt at Lily. 'What I was once obliged to do, I may now choose freely; the disinclination lay in the obligation rather than in the occupation.' He went on, 'It's time my wife had some diversion. So I propose to accompany you both, ladies, on a sketching assignment. Name any day you please – I'm sure you must have one day free from parish work, Agnes – and I'm at your disposal.' He threw his gloves down on the sketches.

Lily felt as though he had slapped her. 'I feel faint,' she said in a cramped little voice. 'Where is the wretched girl? Miss Slane, would you ring for her again?'

'Stay where you are, Agnes,' Jonathan said, and he walked over to the chimney piece and rang for the servant. When the girl came and Lily was about to ask her to fetch the pills, Jonathan interrupted, 'My wife's dressings are soiled. Help her up to her room at once and change them, and then get her pills.'

Miss Slane was still, very still. Lily wanted to draw a line of pain across that flawless complexion; but she was obliged to go with the girl and limp across the great hall, away from her husband and the woman who sat on the Jacobean settee as if she was carved out of ivory.

7

She was sick in the night, spewing black vomit over him. He dreamed of swamps. Suffocation. Then he woke and tasted her sickness on his mouth.

'I'm fit to die, Jonathan,' she gasped. He got up and lit the lamp. She retched violently and when the spasm was over and she saw the disgust on his face she fell silent. He fetched her a clean nightgown and threw back the soiled bedclothes. The air in the room was noisome. Rest was gone from the night. She shook with the cold sweat that was on her.

'I'll get the girl for you,' he said.

'No, leave her. There's nothing she can do for me.'

'Shall I get your pills then?'

'No. They make me worse, I think.'

He went into the dressing room and got cloaks and mantles to lay over her in place of the bedcovers. Her hair was matted with the rotting matter and sweat.

'Oh God, I can bear no more of this death in my bed at

nights,' he anguished as he mechanically poured water into the basin for her and more water in a drinking glass. Her odour clung to him. He wanted to spit the acrid taste from his mouth. 'I'm going downstairs for brandy. Shall I bring some up for you?'

She looked at him vacantly. Her face was swollen, distorted. She didn't speak, only nodding her head.

He came back with the decanter and two large tumblers into which he poured cognac. At the first sip she heaved then she shut her eyes tight and gulped down nervous mouthfuls of the liquor. With the brandy burning the sourness from his mouth Jonathan felt calmer.

'You'd better get Briggs up to the house tomorrow. I've never seen sickness like this.' He began stripping the bed and bundled sheets and blankets into a black press.

'I'm sorry Jonathan,' she wept after a long silence.

'You look like death,' he said. But she was already in a purged sleep of exhaustion.

Jonathan went back into the dressing room and tried to rest. In the next room his wife slept heavily. A scent of decay drowned his senses like a perverse perfume. A bouquet of death filled the house.

In the dressing room hung all her finery: crino-line cages, laundered drawers and chemises, artificial nosegays, floral ornaments for the hair, a spray of ostrich feathers, the wedding dress – all the accoutrements of desire, only the woman was not desirable. He was too close to her sickness. It was as though her sickness claimed him. He got up and unhasped the window. A faint wild scent drifted up from the moorland, a sweet moist air, and he drank a languorous ease from the cool draught. Below him, beyond the wide acreage of his estate, Agnes slept the refreshing sleep of health. In the next room his wife slept heavily, fatally. He leaned out of the window and breathed the night air that made his head spin as though it was an intoxicant. Pure air, I must have pure air, he thought. And he envisaged opening every window, every door in High Withens, until the breath of sickness was extinguished at last.

The physician came at noon. At first Briggs thought it was the master of the house who was sick, so dull-eyed and feverish he seemed. After the doctor had been up to his wife Jonathan received him in the library where Briggs accepted a glass of his favourite port. The doctor seemed a commonplace fellow, Jonathan decided.

'You've been my wife's physician for some time now?' he queried.

'All her life, Sir. I delivered her.' Briggs was a large, stooping man without the deferential smile Jonathan was growing accustomed to.

'All her life! And will it be a short one?' he asked abruptly.

'I beg your pardon, Sir?'

'Has my wife long to live?'

Dr Briggs looked at the bridegroom curiously. 'Her case is a difficult one, Sir.'

'Difficult? How difficult?'

'Worse cases have survived. Less serious ones go out like a light when you least expect it.'

'You prevaricate, man. What are my wife's chances?'

'Chances, Sir?'

Was the man a fool? Could he only echo him?

Jonathan walked over to the mantelpiece and saw his own misery reflected in the mirrored overmantel. His black hair tumbled nearly down to his shoulders. Noon and still unshaven and in his shirt sleeves like a grieving husband.

'Your wife has a strong spirit.'

'I don't speak to you of her spirit. She vomited so violently last night. And her father fears the worst, I think.'

The worst. What is the worst, thought Jonathan. The French windows were open. A fitful breeze lifted the old curtains and blew little gusts of dust from them.

'For God's sake, tell me how sick my wife is.'

'With a decline', the doctor averted his gaze from Jonathan and looked at the younger man's handsome, haggard reflection, 'the illness may be protracted over a period of months or years, or it may suddenly reach a crisis without warning. I can give you no reliable prognosis in your wife's case. With diet, rest — '

'Residence in Italy?' Jonathan interrupted.

'That won't be necessary,' Briggs said at once. 'Her lungs are sound. There's no disease in them.'

'Her lungs don't squeak,' Jonathan said impiously, 'like all those dead poets'.'

'I wouldn't know about that, Sir, not being a literary man,' the doctor said heavily.

'Her father thinks it might be time for a second opinion,' Jonathan ventured. 'A London specialist.' Briggs went white. Now his professional spleen is up, Jonathan thought.

'I wouldn't advise that, but you may dismiss my opinion as a form of impertinence if you wish.'

'You don't advise a second opinion, and yet you don't sound over confident of your own, Dr Briggs.'

'Confidence is the handmaiden of quackery; that's my belief, Sir. I am confident that so-called London specialists would plague your wife no end with their experimentations. I'm one of the old school: rest, diet, traditional cures that are well tried and ... happiness.'

'And what happiness for me? If my wife dies, I mean.'

The doctor looked at his boots, flushed with anger or embarrassment. 'I will tell you this, Sir. Last night's sickness was the consequence of your wife's taking an increased dose of the pills I gave her. It was abuse of the treatment that sickened her, not the disease. I've warned her to be more cautious in future and I've given strict instructions to the maid, but you might watch your wife in case she develops any . . .' he ahemed delicately '. . . looseness of the bowels or occasional irritation of the nerves.'

'So you experiment, like the London doctors?'

'No, Sir. The pills are . . . an old remedy, to be used with caution, I think. Too large a dose can be dangerous. But have no fear, I have impressed on your wife that a small dose is in the long run more efficacious.' The physician looked up at the reflection of the master of High Withens. 'There is one matter I wish to speak to you about, Sir,' Briggs said quietly. He put down his unfinished glass of port.

When the doctor had left, her husband came up to the bedroom.

'Briggs says you must have quiet,' he told her. His

haggard face suddenly crimsoned. 'Why didn't you tell me your physician advised against marriage for you?'

'He didn't exactly,' Lily said dully. 'He said it would be having babies that would be the certain death of me.'

'Isn't that the same thing?' His bitter voice.

How he hates me, she thought. 'Oh Jonathan, how could I not love you?' she said passionately. 'Dr Briggs said I should be a wife in name only, and I promised him. But how could I not love you? How could I not love you? When I knew, when I know I'm soon to die in any case . . .' Her voice trailed off and to his horror he saw that she was turning back the bedclothes and beckoning him.

He backed away. Had he never noticed before how her lower lip jutted, that heaviness around the chin? A coarse woman. There was spittle in the corner of her mouth. Her hair stood out like a mad woman's.

'Jonathan, don't you love me at all? Don't you love me a little?' She crawled out of the sheets over the bed to him. Her poor twisted back. Lie with her. As soon lie with the devil.

Her odour of Hungary water and sickness. She put her frail arms around him, dragging him down, down on top of her. Her eyes narrowed, her lizard tongue darting at him. She kissed his body. She slavered on his mouth and he thought of Lamia and Geraldine and all the female monsters, the serpent women the poets wrote of. This is hell fire. This is sickness. Her body was hot, salamandrous, as it wreathed over him and, despite himself, his body responded to her embrace. Was it his very disgust that excited him? Perhaps the devil was in his flesh. She sweated bad humours. His flesh stuck to her flesh, her burning ardour. 'Married to death, married to a dying girl,' the house whispered, as he thrust, thrust, thrust his revulsion into a black lake of oblivion.

She remembered. She remembered the summer sun, the salt wind, and again she waded out from a beach on the south coast of England. But there was another summer, long ago . . . another summer when just such a sun shone down and the air was crisp with excitement. Another sun . . . another time before the time of the sun on the south coast of England.

She leaned on the stout, red-faced bathing woman who half carried her out of the striped hut down the steps into the fathomless sea. Her brown bathing robe floated up and around her. 'I'm a waterlily,' she laughed foolishly to herself.

The bathing woman passed the rope down over her shoulders and fastened it at her waist. She remembered the clammy touch of the seaweed, the taste of salt, the briny sea, the exhilaration of her first dip. Her feet just touched the seabed. Pebbles and crabs. She splashed warily. Iodine in the water will fix your spine; the ozone will restore you, Papa had promised her. A crisp sun shone down. Her hair floated like seaweed.

I wish I could draw the feel of the sea and the taste of the brine with the sun on it, she exulted. And in that instant she knew. The sun blazed suddenly hot and the cold water chilled her.

'I love him. I love him,' she cried to the gulls circling above her. 'I love my drawing master.'

The bathing woman had gone to another cabin and

didn't witness her madness. Oh then, how she'd wanted the days to fly. She wanted the sea-cure over. Over. Over. Over. On the train going home it was as if she flew back to him.

———

The carriage bowled along, reviving a half-dead breeze in the July sunshine. The two women sat like sisters in wide-brimmed straw hats. The two hat boxes had been identical, and when the tissue was laid aside there was the confection with a blue ribbon for Agnes (to match her eyes, Jonathan had said), and there was a green ribbon on his wife's hat. Lily put on the straw hat and looked at her reflection in the mirrored overmantel with her hazel eyes that had green flecks in them.

Agnes Slane wore the shady hat atop the deft coils of her pale hair. Was it proper of the master of High Withens to buy a chapeau for the curate's daughter, Lily wondered, and then the thought drifted away from her like a dandelion seed as she mounted the gig.

'Now ladies, you needn't fear for the sun spoiling your complexions.' Her husband smiled a too accommodating smile. How could any woman not be moved by him? He was dressed in white linen, wore a poet's shirt and a wide-awake hat. I will not be sad; I won't have him despise me; Papa's advice shall be my guide; I must be rational, Lily catechised herself. She smiled, a crooked smile, that was half hidden by her wide-brimmed hat.

Jonathan drove them at a brisk pace that had the two women clasping their hats and doing their best not to bounce up and down on their seats in rhythm with the gig wheels. Agnes, cool Agnes in her much repaired muslin. Lily dressed up to the nines. Rice powder dusted her bare arms and shoulders. Her dress was cut low, immodestly low for the daytime. She was full bosomed and, when the rice powder disguised the silvery moons of pigmentation that pocked her chest, her bosom was her best feature, her only beauty. Her dull hair was knotted under her hat. The broad brim cast an agreeable shade that softened her grey skin to olive. For the sketching expedition she flaunted a dress that was sumptuous as a ballgown. The turquoise silk was sprigged with clusters of wax flowers; lilies of the valley foamed on green satin leaves, and she had been half convinced that she looked beautiful until Agnes arrived. Agnes — slender and immaculate in simple white, ungarlanded, unencumbered with hoops or cages — lovely, lissome Agnes threw her in the shade.

The carriage sped down the brown moorland towards the valley that lay on the other side of the vale of Low Withens. They passed into a leafy glade where the track narrowed, and Jonathan was obliged to drive at an almost somnolent pace for once. Brambles tore at Lily's crinoline that frothed over the edge of the open carriage. Some lace trimming was snagged and she left one of the nosegays of artificial posies, which was caught up on thorns, after her. The glade was rampant. A moist undergrowth bathed them in a dank, greenish light. Agnes Slane's white dress looked spectral. Her insubstantial flesh . . . There was scarcely any substance to the creature, thought Jonathan as he glanced back at the woman. Like some enchanted spirit of the glade she's possessed herself of my heart. His wife looked overdressed, he thought, and the exposed bosom was a species of vulgarity. Her coarse flesh . . . A lady does not reveal herself in the daylight, he would have said if the enchantress hadn't been beside her.

The mare ambled through the clamorous glade. Febrile fronds of fern stroked them as they passed. Tall grasses fanned their procession, stirring a languorous heat from the humid undergrowth that teemed over the earth. Wild flowers and weeds and uncultivated bushes were crushed beneath the gig wheels that were vexed by thorns and twisted about with bindweeds; grass stains and sap smearing the yellow spokes of the equipage.

The mare struggled valiantly through the rank vegetation and at length the choking weeds thinned and the sinuous tendrils sprang back from them as the glade gave way to a wood or small forest of beech trees. Here the ground was peaty, the colour of cinnamon, and the great trees stood like venerable giants athwart a shadowy labyrinth of footpaths.

'Jonathan, don't lose us,' Lily panicked, reminded by the dark wood of the old tales of children who were variously abandoned, set upon by wolves and witches or mysteriously gobbled up by the ineffable evil that lurked in forests.

'Perhaps you should leave a trail of madeira cake after us,' Jonathan mocked her.

The wood smelt of spices, dead leaves and small

animals. An alien smell. The silence, a silence of wariness and anticipation, appalled Lily. 'An eerie world, a world the real world has forgotten,' she said.

'This is the real world, not your shops, your factories,' Jonathan muttered.

'And I have never felt so unreal,' Lily said. But Jonathan and Agnes, lost in the labyrinths of their own thoughts, scarcely heard her.

The gig rolled on pliantly over a spongy earth that was carpeted with fragments of bark and leaf mould. The dim light and the cool aura of the beech trees cast a spell over them. The path dipped and the tall trees gave way to an orchard of crab apples. A hot sun beamed furiously again, and the little gig gathered pace. Agnes drooped like a parched peony. An uninhabited valley spread before them like the garden of Eden.

'Such fruit!' Agnes exclaimed as they passed a bush overburdened with fat gooseberries.

'Would your father relish a gooseberry pie for his tea, Agnes?' Jonathan asked her cheerfully. He reined in the horse, jumped down from the gig and garnered the green berries until his straw hat was brimful with them.

'If the berries burst, your hat will be ruined,' Lily scolded him. But Agnes looked at Jonathan with her eyes like wild cornflowers, and it was obvious he would gladly have gathered all the fruit that grew in the wide valley for her. His blue-black hair tumbled, it seemed to his wife, boyishly. For a man he is too beautiful, she nearly wept. Her throat was almost as choked as her ribs that chafed beneath the constriction of whalebone.

Agnes said smoothly, 'There's enough fruit for half a dozen pies. Let me bake one for you, Mrs Hopgate.'

Jonathan mounted the driving seat and they toiled on again. The hot sun burned down, and Agnes was glad of the wide-brimmed hat of Italian plaited straw that Jonathan had given her.

The valley undulated deliciously, fragrant with flowers and fruit and strange berries that were so bright there must be poison in them, Agnes said. At last the gig was tethered in a resting place and the mare allowed to drink from a stream bordered by succulent pasture land.

Before the serious business of the day, the company picnicked. Jonathan lifted down the heavy basket and Agnes spread over the grass a cloth of white damask that had been laid away in the linen closet at High Withens since the last century.

Out of the basket came flasks of lemonade for the ladies; for Jonathan, two bottles of claret. There were sandwiches cut fine as communion wafers, cooked pheasants, two cold chickens, a portion of tongue, pies of spiced meat and apple, terrines of cold vegetables, celery in long sticks tied together like a bundle of lucifers, a pink blancmange in a mould for the dessert, as well as little jellies in earthenware pots. There were madeira and heavily spiced fruit cakes too, wrapped about with damp linen, and then there were silvery grapes and a tin of peeled nuts and currants to finish with.

'This is a feast, not a picnic,' marvelled Agnes, who over the years had become adept at contriving recipes for economical dishes comprising cheap cuts and leftovers.

Jonathan ate heartily. The ladies would not or could not do justice to the repast: Lily because her stays, which were laced too tight, made digestion impossible, and Agnes because she was unaccustomed to plenty and had the bird-like appetite of a lady in any case.

The hot sun was a trial to Agnes, but Lily revelled in the heat. She was always cold, it seemed: too cold for the passions that riot in her, Jonathan thought ruefully. They sat on a grassy slope. A cold stream frothed enticingly below them.

Taste me, I'm pure and sweet – you've never tasted such sweetness, the stream gurgled at Jonathan. Pure and sweet. The water was clean and refreshing after the heavy wine he'd been drinking. He cupped his hands in the stream and splashed the water over his face even as he drank from the brook. He looked up at the two women who were packing away the remains of the picnic. Above them the hill was mantled with bracken and a tangle of undergrowth. From the summit the view would be a fine subject for a landscape, he decided.

Jonathan fetched the ladies' sketching materials from the gig then he gave Lily and Agnes their instructions.

'Lily, you were always inept at contriving the flow of water, you know. Your assignment today is to draw that brook and try to capture the vitality, the life force in the water's current.'

Oh how glad she was to receive his instruction again. Lily heard the drawing master once more, like an old friend, her beloved.

'Agnes, as a novice', he went on, 'you shall tackle perspective. The view from the brow of the hill is your task this afternoon.'

'You are to separate us?' Lily quizzed, but Jonathan ignored her and was already leading Agnes up through the tangle of undergrowth.

Lily rearranged the cushions behind her aching back

so that she drew from a half-reclining position. The stream was bright as nickel below her.

They climbed upwards. The cool fronds caressed Agnes through her thin petticoats. Jonathan clambered above her. There was a natural ledge of slippery terraced earth where the hill grew suddenly steep. Her long skirts imperilled her. As she staggered and went to clasp the knotty root of a bush just above her, she found his hand instead, waiting for her. Her hand was steady in his. She looked at him gravely.

'We nearly lost you Agnes,' he said, and his voice shook with an emotion that surprised him. Hand in hand they climbed upwards to where the view Agnes was to sketch awaited them.

Never had she negotiated such treacherous ground. The earth was slippery as beeswax. The undergrowth slithered with urgent saps and the too bright, crushed berries that were poisonous. But his hand never failed her so that she was assured that howsoever her feet missed their aim and slid, stumbled, jabbed ineffectively at the footholds that denied her, he was there like a steady ballast that held her. She felt the strength in him, and his protection seemed an intimacy that was shared like a secret between them.

They arrived at the brow of the hill. Lily was hidden by the bracken below. He sat her close, very close to him and taught her to look at the horizon and then, as she studied the fecund landscape, his hand guided her in slow voluptuous movements over the blank paper. The sun beat down on them. He almost tasted her languor that had the perfumes of the valley in it. So close now, her cornflower eyes growing paler, paling to match the

azure of the horizon. Just one kiss – to steal one kiss
from that pale mouth and she's mine forever, his heart
instructed him. He kissed her chastely on the hand he
manipulated. Her eyes narrowed – her eyes that are
clearer than I have ever known a woman's eyes, he
thought. He bent over her and kissed her mouth. She
made no attempt to rebuff him. It was as though he
drank once again the crisp water his wife sketched far
below them. One kiss and we are pledged for eternity,
his eyes promised her. Her eyes were sad, a virgin's eyes
that told him, forever, forever, a love that she must deny
him. One kiss, then. One kiss must suffice him.

The water leapt in a minuet of elation, dancing over
the scoured stones. The cold, clear water that you
could look into and not see yourself looking back
again, the current in too much of a hurry to hold your
reflection, clear cold water that had no horrors in it.
He is too long with her, Lily anguished. She imagined
Agnes drowned in a juicy vat of the poisoned berries
that grew in this valley.

  She threw one, two, three poisoned berries into the
swollen beck that serpentined across her ivory paper.
The current raged and foamed in a crazed dance of
death in her drawing. But the cold water was clear
and innocent, as clear as Agnes Slane's eyes. Lily drew
a fat toad under a large stone winking one eye of
malevolence. Where is my husband, and what is he
doing with that beautiful woman whose eyes look at
me with too much compassion? Is the compassion for
me or for my husband? I must heed Papa, she told
herself. The stream ran clear and smooth over the
stones beyond her.

'I am his wife, the mistress of High Withens.' She chanted the words like a prayer as she tore to shreds and scattered over the meadow the unfinished vista of disenchantment.

For the first time in the day the heat was too much for her. Lily longed to loosen her stays but could not manage the laces herself so intricately were they threaded and so painful her back. It was impossible to unbind herself. She slipped off her satin slippers instead and peeled away her silk stockings. Then, barefoot, she limped down to the stream. The water was even colder than she had imagined. The icy flow stung her flesh; sweet water that still had the chill of the dark centre of the earth in it.

As she waded, holding her crinoline aloft like a sail, she saw Jonathan, hand in hand with Agnes, clamber down the hillside. She waded upstream. Let him follow her, finding her gone he might suppose she had vanished off the face of the earth. He might believe her drowned. He might repent, briefly lament his dalliance with Agnes. Her flesh burned and even the water couldn't cool her. The sun hat fell from her head and dangled by its ribbons. She looked dishevelled, a spectacle, a holy show; but Agnes will look composed, she thought, as lovely as a flower scarcely budded she supposed, when, as alas her husband didn't come in search of her, Lily turned and waded painfully back downstream.

9

It was quiet and dark in the library, a room where he could be alone. The old books didn't interest her – the old knowledge. A room on which she wouldn't be spending her father's money just at present. A place that was left undisturbed to its quarter century of decrepitude.

The library had been well stocked in the last century. There were few acquisitions from recent years. In his wife's opinion the thousands of dusty volumes of religious essays, disquisitions on natural science and moral philosophy, the original editions of Bacon, Hobbes and Locke, could be put to the fire if the brittle leather spines didn't polish up nicely. If she cared to look she might find something to amuse her, he imagined: sensational gothic tomes such as *The Monk* or *The Castle of Otranto*, or even a novel by Maria Edgeworth. But then she preferred her reading material pristine, the pages uncut. These old volumes held no charm for her; too much dust had been allowed to settle on the antique books and lodge as dirt. The pages were stained brown as tannin and had a verminous smell to them, the ancient wisdom mere scaffolding for the spiders. She'd sent a maid in to clean up, but the feather dusters raised the top layers of dust so that the library resembled the lint-choked atmosphere of suffocation in her father's lace manufactory. The long windows had been opened and the powdery dust expelled on to the brown swoop of moorland. But the years of contamination could not be cleansed from the brittle pages of the old books, and too many of the shabby leather covers had been gnawed away by rodents or had the gold lettering effaced by the depredations of time.

He hoped he'd be left in peace here, then. He smoked a Havana cigar and dropped the ash carelessly on the old desk top of scarred walnut and rosewood. Blue smoke streamed like a genie from a bottle top. He had a glass of rum, and the cured flavour of the tobacco leaf cooled the smoky heat of the liquor in his mouth. He tried to read but Pope's couplets seemed vapid today, the poet's wit a mere form of emotional fatigue. He felt weary and thought for the first time, what if she grows old alongside me? He dismissed the thought at once. He remembered her father's assurances: 'Marry my dying girl', the merchant had said. Her father had assured him she'd so little time to live the marriage would secure just a few month's happiness for her.

He poured himself another glass of the Jamaica rum and relit his cigar which had extinguished itself. A dying girl – in a year I'll be free of her. In a year I'll be at liberty, have purchased my freedom, done my part. She dies in the delusion she's a lady like her papa wanted.

Her money's bought back my inheritance; without it I'd never have stood a chance with Agnes, in any case. My fair and beautiful Agnes. A real lady on my arm, one you'd never be ashamed of. One kiss and his fate was sealed forever. He remembered ruefully the first kiss Lily had planted on him. Five minutes before she was just a girl – a sick one it was true, and a pampered one – but just another rich girl in search of ladylike accomplishments. He'd taught a dozen such and always made an impression on them. How could he not, with his Byronic good looks and that innate Hopgate haughtiness? All these girls, mad for romance, half crazy for a gentleman who'd demonstrate his superiority to them. How such little misses love to prostrate themselves, he thought, the idle daughters of the newly rich with no place in the community, no duties by which they might know themselves – only the impossible fantasy of romance.

The bottle of rum was half finished. A pall of cigar smoke hung in the library, although the long French windows were open. Outside, an unkempt lawn fell away from the house. Even trees and bushes planted close by couldn't soften a dour northern light that scoured the shadows from the library. The curtains that were pulled back were cobwebby and grey as shrouds, he thought, but he had not drunk enough yet to be maudlin. The rum made him think he was happier than he was, as he planned the honeymoon he would have in Italy when Agnes was his bride, when Agnes Slane was the mistress of High Withens.

She would be dressed simply, with impeccable taste; he always imagined her in a white dress with the ghostly glimmer of the cameo he would buy in Florence at her throat. He lived again the never to be forgotten moment when he kissed her. But she was a pure woman and further endearments were denied him; how he esteemed her for that.

A scraping of wood. A shuffle. His wife came in. She walked unsteadily. *So even here she fastens on me. Her eyes were red; a vampyre's eyes. Death feeding on my life,* he thought.

'You're drinking!' she said.

But my drunkard's eyes aren't as inflamed as yours, my dying bride.

She was got up in a blue riding habit.

'I thought your spine wasn't up to horse riding,' he said.

She went white, the dirty greenish white she always coloured when her sickness was mentioned. 'No, I can't ride,' she said. 'This habit is the latest thing from Paris.'

Equestrian style for his crippled bride!

'Jonathan, I hoped you might take me for a turn around the estate in the barouche.'

'Barouche be damned!' he hissed very quietly. 'Get the groom to drive you.'

'If I were Agnes Slane . . .' she said. He saw that she carried a riding crop, pointlessly. '. . . you wouldn't . . .' The catch in her voice! '. . . be long about dancing attendance on me.'

His crippled bride!

She tried to straighten her back and lift her skirts archly. She had a little velvet hat on. An ostrich feather dangled foolishly.

'A real lady', he said, 'would be defiled by such words as you seem to delight in.' *Your factory mouth,* he thought. Your wet mouth. Shut your factory mouth that spews pestilence.

She looked deformed in the blue riding habit. Her dress was an empty ritual, a sham. My sham lady wife, he thought and poured another glass of rum for himself.

'Get out,' he said. 'Harry the servants if you must, but leave me alone.'

She dropped the riding crop and backed away from him in a cruel parody of obeisance. Her servile, bent spine, her skittering, lame steps; shuffling blindly away from him, all the while weeping, weeping noisily – and what else could you expect of a factory girl, he thought as he drank down the glass of rum.

10

She drew the bed hangings around her and shut out the daylight. The room was cold, vast, comfortless. As cold as my grave will be, she thought. Her pillow was chill and stiff with starch, the great canopied bed like a mausoleum without him. The drawn bed curtains smelled of must and were so heavily lined they stifled such air as crept in to her.

'But I can't reconcile myself to the darkness,' she sobbed, 'not yet, not now that I want his love.' She put out her hand and tugged the drapes that fell by her pillow. A wan sliver of light, and she could breathe again and smell the moor from the open windows and the bowls of flowers that were in the room. She had insisted on hot-house blooms everywhere, although her husband said they stole his breath from him by stealth in the night.

The canopy over the bed seemed low, oppressively low to her, and she remembered a tale she'd read in a journal about a woman haunted by her dead lover. How was it the story went? Ah yes – the woman had made a happy marriage at last, but her dead love, a spirit bound to the earth by his jealousy, had asphyxiated the bride and groom as they embraced on the nuptial bed, pressing the canopy of their four-poster down on top-of them, extinguishing breath so that they were suffocated in their ecstasy.

A knock at the door and her heart knocked at her ribs as though death itself demanded entry. The maid brought in a papier mâché tray with a dish of ointment, a pot of pills and swathes of clean bandages.

'I wasn't expecting you, Reeves,' Lily said.

'No ma'am. The master rang to say you were taken bad and I should attend to you.'

'But not with my old malady. I need none of your pills. Take them away again!'

'But the master insisted – give your mistress her medicines and be quick about it, he said.'

The ointment, which was usually deep blue, today looked grey and oily. Like my skin, she thought. 'Where is my usual salve?'

'Oh, this is the same lineament ma'am, only a bit stronger, I think. Dr Briggs wasn't too happy with the ulcer last time he examined you so he had a stronger potion made up and the druggist brought it in.'

The girl had become adept at nursing her. She had warm, light hands that were careful not to chafe the sore. 'Dr Briggs said you might leave off your stays, don't you remember? It's maybe the whalebone rubbing you that encourages the runny stuff. He says to me, "if your mistress is unbound the sore'll dry nicely. Hard and dry as a button it should be," he said, "if there's to be a chance of healing."'

Like a broken heart, Lily thought as the maid bathed and anointed her back, then dressed her with the bandages. 'If only my heart was hard and dry as a button, I'd be healed of love,' she whispered into the cool pillow.

'What's that, ma'am?'

'The pills, Reeves. The master's right. It's time I had them.' Beautiful pills like enchanted sweets. Little blue pills to cure the canker in her.

'The master said better give you four.'

'Four? But I thought Briggs said two or three at the most if the sore weeps green pus. I don't want to be sick again.'

'I'm sure you're right, ma'am. Dr Briggs was very particular and told me, "I prescribe two pills at one time for your mistress. We don't want to poison her." Truth is, ma'am,' she said nervously, 'I think, if you don't mind my saying it, the master's a bit in his cups today.'

'A gentleman's privilege,' Lily said wanly. 'And it's unseemly in you to mention it. I'll take the four pills as the master wishes, Reeves.' She swallowed the pills quickly with raspberry cordial.

When the maid left her the silence was terrible, but then an ominous scratching as of mice grated on her nerves. Reeves had drawn back the curtains again. The sun was up and the room was agitated with a multitude of grey motes and pallid silvery particles of dust. An odour of damp, even in sunlight, impregnated the walls of High Withens. In this room there was still the old lofty furniture, nearly as decrepit as the house; the wood black with age and dimmed with neglect, like spurned love, she thought. I must get Papa to send over some of my things, she thought. She needed her familiar objects around her again: the mahogany dressing table with the muslin petticoats, the blue silk jewellery case, the china dogs and, of course, the japanned sewing table – all the light, feminine things that the house lacked to replace the gloomy venerable stuff: the black presses that lowered at her, the lugubrious chests of carved Tudor oak, all the antique furniture that oppressed her with the weight of the Hopgate past.

It's this old house that has put a curse on us she thought – these old things. Love needs a bright house, a conservatory of flowers, gilt mirrors and plush furnishings, crystal and velvet, not dull tarnished metals and faded textiles that have mildew in them. Even her bed was soaked with history; the great bed where Hopgates had been delivered into life for centuries. No more of the old. I want new things, she decided, and the decision invigorated her.

She remembered how her father had promised to indulge her whims. High Withens must be made over entirely: new paints and fabrics. Out with the old! We'll import new things. I won't have the Hopgate pride kill my spirit before the consumption shrives my flesh, she thought. If she didn't fight it, the Hopgate pride, Hopgate blood, Hopgate inheritance, would nail her down more inexorably than any coffin lid.

I must make plans, she thought. A new bedroom – a room alight with colour, a room to love in. Her thoughts raced like fever. New things. A new life. Love. Again.

But that infernal scratching! I must stop it. She got out of bed stiffly, picked up her satin slippers that had curved leather heels, and threw them at the wainscot. The scrabbling stopped. She felt oddly nervy and yet fired with intent. I am the mistress of High Withens after all, she thought. She put on a pale green wrapper over her nightgown, then donned the projectiles that were her house shoes. I've never faced this house alone, but I'll put my mark on every stone of it. I'll make an Italianate villa out of this gothic tomb.

She opened the bedroom door, but before she went out she lit a candle and held it aloft to illumine the dark territory that lay ahead of her. The candle flame convulsed and her flimsy robe lifted a little in the wild draught that swept down the gallery from a broken window. From the west wing where the sun sets to the east wing where it rises, she swept along, almost forgetting her afflicted spine in a mad surge of determination. I am the mistress of High Withens, she told herself, as if the mere words could transform her.

The candle flame steadied and lit the way for her along the narrow winding stairway that curved up from the gallery. Round and round; narrow stone walls pressed in on her. The steps were slippery and steep and there was no hand rail to hold on to. Her green train slithered like a snake behind her. Up and around and about the twisting turret of staircase, her determination borne on frail limbs, up into the forgotten regions of High Withens.

Here there was another gallery, but narrower and darker than the last. The ceiling was high, and a soft whirring sound could have been bats, she thought fearfully. She listened for scratching. Her eyes raked the dimness for spiders, vermin, old family skeletons or dispossessed ghosts – but all she saw was the emptiness.

A dozen rooms like cells led straight off the landing. A dozen doors like dungeon traps had stout nail heads hammered into them. She looked over the wrought iron balustrade that ran the length of the gallery; a short leap below was a barrack of a room or bleak corridor hung with old banners and armoury. Bare floorboards and stone walls, and a door that led to a watch tower, she supposed. At the end of the gallery was another staircase but with wider less hazardous stairs that were carpeted with threadbare royal blue plush. One by one she tried the dozen door handles; one by one the stout cells resisted her until the last lock, the twelfth, yielded and the door sprang back with such sudden force she was flung into the room as violently as a captive might be incarcerated by gaolers.

The morning sun scalded her. She was on a parapet of light. It was one room, not twelve cells, and the doors which had looked like dungeon traps were only mirror backs, stout but innocuous. A long room on the top of High Withens, flooded with light from twelve gothic-arched windows that glittered on twelve mirrors, framed with gilt. Except for the light and the looking glasses the room was empty. Bare boards. Stone walls. No lumber from the past. No detritus of history. My room, at last. Lily breathed fresh air again.

I will not be ill, she told herself. I will be beautiful and well again and he will love me in our glittering room that will have none of the past in it. She saw a roseate room: pink carpets and puce curtains, rose silk cushions and counterpane. All the light of the morning sun would be caught up in the warm, flushed glow of love again.

*   *   *

She was alone all night. He did not come to her. He slept in the library with the rug over him.

'The best sleep of my married life,' he said when she asked him how he had slept. She flushed and the tea she drank nearly choked her.

'I'm sorry,' she said dully. Sorry. Sorry. A sorrowing penitent. Love me and I'll be well again, her heart pleaded with him.

His hangover had perhaps made him grumpier than he'd intended. 'I suppose it's your malady that encourages sick fancies. Did you take the pills?'

'Yes. I had four yesterday.'

'And?'

'I thought perhaps two pills was the prescribed dose.'

'Briggs is a fool. You should get a London man. You've been on a low dose for God kows how long and much good it's done you!'

But with four pills my skin will look like mud in no time, she thought.

'I was obliged to spend half the night on the commode,' she said.

'All to the good – it'll purge the disease out of you.'

'And my nerves are a little frayed, I think.' She started suddenly. 'I wish one of the men would put down poison for the vermin.'

'You're probably listening out for the things. All these country houses have rats in 'em.'

Her eyes were swollen and her mouth fell open. She's getting to look like a half wit, he thought.

'You'll have to exert yourself if you want to be well again. If you really loved me, if you wanted to be a proper wife, you'd put up with the little unpleasant side effects of the treatment.'

'It was too many pills made me ill, made me sick all over you,' she said.

'That's as maybe, and that's why of course I don't think we should risk further intimacies until . . . When you're fit and well we can have a proper married life,' he said.

'You won't lie with me?'

He looked at her warily. 'I think it's unnecessary to go into these . . . distressing matters. It's distasteful to discuss such things.' He looked away from her.

And I'd take the whole pot of blue pills if you'd only love me. He can't lie with a sick woman, love a near corpse, she told herself. He does love me, only he wants me well again.

Her mouth filled with saliva. 'You're right,' she said. 'I must bear with the rigours of a more drastic treatment. But you can't go on sleeping in the library, and most of the rooms in this place are uninhabitable because of the damp.'

He was silent.

'I've found a room,' she went on, 'a warm, dry room on the top of the east wing. A room that has the morning sun in it. Papa would give me money to furnish it, I know he would. Let me have it decorated for a bedroom, Jonathan.'

'Very well,' he agreed smoothly. 'An excellent idea. Have it made over. The sooner the better. And when you're well I can . . . return to you,' he said.

When the girl next came to change her bandages Lily asked her to leave the little glazed pot of pills after her.

'Is that wise, ma'am? You might perhaps forget the right times to take them.'

'Don't be impertinent, Reeves. When these run out you might get some more from the druggist.'

'Wouldn't it be best for the doctor to order them?'

'No it would not. I intend to dispense with Briggs' services. He's done me no good at all. He's much too cautious and old-fashioned in his treatments. Now take the soiled linen away and send up Richards. I intend to look beautiful for dinner tonight.'

The pills went down easily with the glass of madeira. She swallowed three, then, after hesitating, four. She thought, four will tear my innards out of me. She stared into her little handglass. I look like grubby white laundry before it's dipped in blue bag, she thought. Her skin was slick with oil and leaden. Her eyes were inflamed and had shadows under them; her swollen mouth was engorged with desire. She was still looking into the handglass when the lady's maid came. The woman went into the dressing room and asked what things she should lay out for her.

'A quiet dress, one that doesn't make a noise,' Lily said. The maid was puzzled. She suggested the muslin, perhaps.

'Yes, the muslin.' Her mistress clapped her hands and the dainty handglass slipped, shattering.

'Bad blood! Bad blood!' Lily said. She looked bewildered. Now why did I say 'blood' when I meant 'luck', she wondered. She gazed vacantly at her shattered reflection. The woman hurried over to clear up the mess and fretted that the pretty trifle was beyond mending.

'Good!' Lily said. She clapped her hands again. 'Now

I can have a new reflection.' Mend me, mend me, little blue pills, and when I look in his eyes at last I'll see myself reflected there: a lovely girl, a charmer, the exquisite mistress of High Withens.

11

It was hotter than any summer he had known. Even High Withens, that had the chill of death in it, could not cool him. He slept fitfully. The drink didn't bring sleep no matter how much rum, brandy or claret he swilled down his throat, and the refreshment of untroubled dreams eluded him.

Wherever he went in his house it seemed as if her fever followed him – her thin colognes or suffocating scents overlaid with the musk of sickness. He felt her presence palpably, as though some parasite burrowed in his flesh. His clothes chafed him. He thought perhaps his blood was overheated so he took sulphur powders to purify himself, and the sulphur brought out the badness that was in him and a scarlet rash flared on his chest. For the first time in his life his white skin was marrred by blemishes. The corrosion of the hot sun, the poison of death, turned the blood thick and bad in him.

His head throbbed and hysteria lodged in his throat

so that he had difficulty swallowing; then his neck was stiff and sore as though a vampyre fastened on him.

He drank his tea very hot as if it might scald his mouth and strip the sediment of drink and misery from his gullet. Only her death was the price of his liberty – and why is the malodorous scent of her perfumed flesh the most terrible thing about her he wondered. It was as though her essence resided in the very atmosphere that stifled him.

He thought of Agnes and he knew how true it was that cleanliness was next to godliness. Her unperfumed skin was wholesome, soaped pink and white with only the breath of fresh air on it. A clean, long-limbed country woman. The very thought of her made him long for the outdoors.

He put on a worn, very fine cambric shirt with a turned-down collar that would not irritate his inflamed skin. With his scuffed boots over brown cord breeches he looked like any gentleman farmer hereabouts. He wore a low crowned country hat, tilted over his eyes that could not bear the light on them, and he picked up a blackthorn stick with which to go out walking.

Sulphur powders and healthy walks, that is what I prescribe for myself, he resolved. And Agnes, Agnes, Agnes, his heart told him. Before the sun was too fierce he planned to have covered half the circuit of his estate, visiting some of the tenant farmers. The land here was poor and there was scant grazing, but he had not raised the rents because he took a certain pride in maintaining the Hopgate tradition of indulgent management. A gentleman had duties as well as rights, he believed. He scorned the new mercantile ethos that would regard agricultural workers as mere wage earners. As they were in thrall to the master of High Withens so the master of the estate was bound to them by custom, by ties as inexorable as blood even.

A sultry morning, with a moist greenish light over it. Jonathan leaned heavily on the blackthorn. He felt dizzy as if the real world was far away from him. I must curb the drinking, he promised himself. The ground soared up to meet him. He pulled the brim of his hat further down over his eyes and breathed in the air of the countryside, walking shakily over the scrubby moorland down to the lower slopes where there were scattered farms and straggling herds of grazing animals. All around stood the hills that were older than the Hopgate lineage. My land, he thought. Mine. The inheritance of my children after me. And then, inevitably, he thought of Agnes again. Agnes, Agnes, his heart sang. Agnes, Agnes, the very pebbles called after him in a litany of enchantment. Turn back and you'll turn to stone like us, the stones reminded him as they always do in the old stories. Turn around to find the source of the enchantment and it's lost forever. And you too, you will be lost, his heart instructed him.

He walked on, strolling now as his feet drew confidence from the solid clean earth beneath him. He was almost on top of the first farm before he knew it. The land fell away and a black slate roof seemed to grow out of the hillside below him. Mosses and grass flourished on top of the farmhouse wherever the slates were broken or dislodged. At first glimpse it looked as though the hill was growing back over the old dwelling. The farm might have been a gateway to the secret heart of the moorland. And what world of enchantment awaited within, he thought fancifully.

He half ran down the steep descent of a path bordered by rampant grass that grew shoulder high, towards the low, sprawling house. A waterfall sprouted somewhere beyond the dwelling that was secluded from the valley below by a small copse of silver birch trees. The water splashed on lichened stones and smooth pebbles. A soothing sound, thought Jonathan. Thirst raged in him.

An aged labourer in a grimy smock was digging over the front garden which was a functional affair that disdained useless cottage flowers in favour of fodder for humans: potatoes grew there scratchily.

'Is the master of the house within?' Jonathan hailed the old rustic who was either deaf or foolish, a string bean of an octogenarian who wielded the shovel with an astonishing vigour. The fellow mumbled something in the local dialect, which Jonathan had long ago forgotten, and continued gardening. Jonathan walked up to the front door and rapped on the blistered wood with his blackthorn. The servant, a slight, kippery ten year old, opened the door to him.

'Tell your master Hopgate's without,' he said.

The girl bobbed and said excitedly, 'Farmer Belton's off to the races today sir.'

It was a low-lintelled house and the entrance was little more than the height of the child who stood in front of him. Behind lay the cramped dark, and the smell of a rough stew in a cauldron.

'Who is it, Annie?' a clear voice called. Then the darkness moved; a long stem, as of an arum lily, and Agnes bent over the child. She simply looked at him.

'Agnes, may I enter?' he said.

The child hurried away to the scullery, which was a

shed built on to the kitchen where the family generally resided.

Agnes led him into the parlour which was used mainly for the guests who scarcely called any longer. The eldest daughter of the house sat there with a Bible. She was a gingery sprite with sharp plain looks that had a quality of nervelessness.

'Esther, please be so good as to give the Bible lesson to your sisters now.'

'But we've not finished, Miss Slane,' the scholar objected.

'Yes, I rather think we have.'

'What portion of the text are you studying?' Jonathan asked the girl.

'The story of Jezebel and King Ahab,' said Esther, and she might as well have said Jonah and the whale or Noah and the ark, for the holy scriptures were all as one to her, the stories lost behind the strictures of morality. She disappeared to spread the word of the Lord to her sisters. Agnes went and fetched a tray which she loaded with tea and plain cake.

'I daren't leave the tea to Annie. It would have the scum of the stew on it.'

Jonathan sat down by the mantelpiece where a dusty bouquet of muslin flowers was arranged in the grate.

'I come here once a week to instruct the eldest girl,' Agnes explained. 'She in turn teaches her younger sisters, poor motherless mites.'

'It's a wonder Belton don't remarry. All these girls must be a hard thing on a man,' Jonathan said.

'No sane woman would have him. He's plagued by the demon of intemperance, and when he drinks the devil catches hold of him. He kicked his wife half to death, then what little health was left to her was extinguished in childbirth.'

'Perhaps she was a disappointment to him,' Jonathan said. 'A man must be disappointed to turn to drink, you know.'

'Disappointed? A woman isn't a birthday present to be regarded as either inferior goods or a gift providing infinite satisfaction to the recipient.'

'Are you a champion of women's rights, Miss Slane?'

'No. Only God's laws, Sir.'

'And should God's laws tie a man for life to a woman who is loathsome to him, whose very flesh makes him cry out in revulsion?'

'I do not think God's laws do that, Sir. It seems to me that is more likely to be the unhappy result of man's bargaining.' She flushed and to cover her agitation she arose and poured out another cup of tea for him. Then she cut portions of the cake which she set out on one of the willow plates that she got down from the dresser.

'You're right, Agnes. A man should marry for love and only love,' he said.

They drank their tea in silence. From the next room came the monotonous chant of young Miss Belton's Bible reading. Flies buzzed around the room, sated from feeding on farm animals. The sun was hot through the windows. Agnes stood up and swatted at the flies with her fan, then went over to the window and drew down the holland blinds so that there was an intimate dimness, an unbearably domestic quality to their drinking tea together in the shabby little parlour.

His skin began to itch again. She was growing nervous and poured yet more tea which she drank slowly to avoid the ineffable menace that lurked in coversation.

He finished his fourth cup of tea and put the cup down. 'You know I love you,' he said.

She was white, pale as a parian statue. 'You must not . . .' Words, conventions failed her.

He went up to her and took the little cracked china cup away. He held her close to him. 'Wait for me, Agnes,' he said as he breathed in the country air from her pale ringlets.

She succumbed to the male authority in him and yet she resisted the sin and the darkness with the word of the Lord that was bred in her.

'No God, no vow will keep you from me,' he threatened her.

When he kissed her he forgot he was a gentleman; the codes of courtesy and chivalry fell away like so much finery and he kissed her with the same angry desire, no doubt, that stirred Belton's boots when he assaulted his wife; the same passion thrusting from the same terrible absence within.

Yet despite her qualms it was he who pulled away first, violently, trembling, his legs suddenly too weak to support him. This infernal irritation to his flesh! The flies settled on him as if they scented his blood that was thick and unwholesome.

For the first time he noticed the blue Staffordshire jug full of wild flowers she had brought for the girls, placed on a low table by the window. He saw them as a painter might, not blooming but exploding in celebration of earth's vital powers. The radiant flowers soared out of the jug with a brief glory of life. Wild flowers with their scarcely perceptible scent that had the innocence of the world before man in them.

'I must go,' she said. 'I've distressed you.'

'The distress is at myself. It's my own fault that I love you. My own sin. I am responsible for my soul as you are for yours.'

No, I'm not responsible, he thought. It's not my fault that I love you. Not my fault my forefathers were profligate. But in a year I'll be free of her.

'I'm a victim of circumstance,' he said. His skin itched violently. The headache started up again. The flowers exulted in their own loveliness. 'Let me walk part of the way home with you, Agnes.' He expected her to refuse but she agreed readily as though by holding on to his company she could discover a way out of this malady of love that afflicted them.

Her pale blue dress shimmered with a threadbare translucence in the sunshine. Another of one of the eldest Miss Beech's gowns made over and passed on to her. She wore the wide-brimmed hat he had given her.

When they had walked a short distance from the farm and were by the waterfall he undid the ribbons, took off her hat and again kissed her hair that smelled of mountain streams and rainwater.

'You must not. You have a wife. You mustn't touch me.' And then she kissed him with her soft mouth that had the dryness of prayer in it.

His hand was on her bodice, on her slender body that was trussed in whalebone. He forced her on her back and she thought her spine would snap when he pressed her down on to the smooth hollow that was damp from the spray of the watefall. The earth felt slippery, treacherous under her.

'Love me. Love me,' he urged her, his intemperate fingers lightly grazing, like blades of grass, the fastness of her white stockinged limbs. He leaned heavily over her and as he worried at her petticoats she pulled her mouth from his, her narrow unsmiling lips forming an O of protest.

But she knew the moment of danger was only delayed, that virtue itself was dismayed, when she surprised herself and merely said like any doxy, 'But you have a wife! You have a wife so you can't have me too. You'll have to wait for me, Jonathan.'

But I won't have to wait. I won't have to wait for death to take my wife, sweet Agnes. No waiting, I promise you!

He kissed her again, the last kiss before parting; the seal of life on the death that was before them. They walked on a pace, then she turned and said, 'The gossips will have a field day if you don't leave me now.' And before he could touch her again she picked up her trailing blue skirts and ran down the hillside, holding aloft her straw hat with its long ribbons that waved farewell at him.

Now he felt the sun stinging the rash that spread over his chest. A high sun scorched the moorland. He leaned heavily on the blackthorn as he made his way back towards High Withens. He felt thirsty again and when he came to a small beck he knelt and cupped his hands in the water. The sulphur in his skin tasted brackish as he drank. He must have taken too much of the powder; his skin had broken out so angrily. Then the heat made his blood sluggish as ditchwater. His neck felt very swollen. His head ached abominably. I need a cure and the only cure is her death, he thought.

12

───────

'Hard and dry as a button,' the girl said. 'Your sore is hard and dry as a button.'

Her mistress stretched out on her exquisite bed with its rose satin drapes and gilt coronal. A new room and a new life. Pale pink muslin curtains fell in swags from the twelve gothic arched windows, netting the light so that its first harshness was veiled with a lambent glow. A soft roseate dawn filled the room and the twelve oak-backed looking glasses reflected an intimate boudoir light.

She always woke with the dawn now. Like a princess in a tower her first view on awakening was of the sky. The brown moor was far below, a world away from her.

Sugar almond pink ribbons were threaded through her lawn nightgown. In the room there was a capricious tumble of pale satin robes and dancing pumps, silk bodices, flounced underskirts, cambric caps, mantles worked with tambour lace, and even gauzy petticoats to the dressing table. All the myriad combinations of pink: deepest rose fading to barely flushed ivory in the most precious clouds of fabric that flared like the sunset or paled to the silvery blush of dawn.

Papa had been generous. The last gift of all, he supposed. The room cost him nearly as much as the husband did. But perhaps not the final gift, after all; mayhap endless dawns and sunrises were to be lived through in the roseate room on the top of High Withens.

The canker was hard and dry as a button. No suppuration. No pus. No softness. Ladling on the mercury ointment, dosing heavily with mercury pills had worked after all, and Briggs was a fool as Jonathan had advised her. But she looked as if she'd never been in the sun in her life, she thought – as grey as rainclouds on a thundery morning. Her eyes were crusty and sometimes she felt as if her stomach had dropped away from her, as if she was purged inside out and only her heart was left intact, only her heart remained to her.

When Reeves had gone the lady's maid helped her on with her gossamer bodice and the Spanish skirt that fell in limp tiers of the finest hand-made lace. She wore her hair unbound, weaving tiny wax rosebuds into the curls wherever her hair split and frizzed into corkscrews. The maid laboured on Lily's complexion. Rice was pressed over the grey skin until she looked like a stage Columbine with a theatrical whiteness. But her eyes betrayed her, eyes that glowed preternaturally red with the purple shadows of insomnia under them. She stared into twelve looking glasses. Twelve mirrors – twelve reflections.

In the first mirror, when she looked at her reflection,

she raised her fan to just beneath her eyes and regarded her bare feet and ankles, which were swollen. She remembered the steps, the carefree skip-the-night-away steps of the polka.

She leapt giddily and her petticoats fluttered down before her second reflection. She looked at the flounced skirts, the pale lace frothed in tiers as she twirled like an opera dancer.

In the third looking glass she admired her waist, grown slender and crushed by whalebone.

In the fourth mirror she curtsied and watched the eerie glow, like fireflies, of the silvery pigment on her breasts where the lesions had long ago faded.

The fifth glass foreshortened her.

The sixth glass showed the swell of her bodice over the breasts of a fourteen year old.

The seventh mirror – ah the seventh mirror – saw an elusive ghost, almost disembodied, vanishing into the farthest corner of the room as it prayed for courage to gaze into the eighth mirror which revealed the carnage the sickness worked on her flesh.

The eighth glass, like disillusioned love, showed her grey skin through the mask of rice powder.

Before the ninth sheet of glass she stood very close, breathing on the surface that darkened with her tainted breath.

The tenth pier glass reflected her eyes that were inflamed with drugs and loneliness.

The eleventh mirror showed her swollen mouth when she lowered her fan. It was a grey reflection and had an ugly woman in it.

The twelfth looking glass. She braced herself. She thought of Jonathan and told herself that she must be well and beautiful. She proceeded to the twelfth glass in her limp Spanish dress, her hair hung about with wax flowers, and stared. The glass was empty. The silvery surface glittered but she wasn't reflected there.

'Aren't you pleased with me?'

'Of course,' he said. 'Naturally I'm delighted to see you get well again.'

'You were right. You must be pleased you were so right after all and Briggs was wrong,' she said.

Three candelabra with ascending tiers of light stood on the sideboard. Her lace dress glowed. The wax flowers hung like stars. Her face was animated by the hot dance of candle flames. He sat in the shadows, on the heavily carved chair, fingering a glass of warm cognac.

'And this is the first time I've been downstairs in weeks.' She looked at him eagerly. Come to bed with me tonight, her heart pleaded with him. Tonight in the new room that has the heat of the sun in it. She left her place at the table and went up to him. She had lost weight with all the purging and she was light on his lap. As light as a confessed soul he thought. The canker had dried and the smell of rottenness was gone from her. She snipped grapes for him and opened his mouth with her cool little hands. She fed him the grapes and then she poured out some port that was redder and darker than the bad blood of the Hopgates.

Drink me. Drink me, her mouth prayed when it fastened on him as he swallowed the port. Her coarse hair scratched his neck. Her cool hands lay on his inflamed skin. Then she felt the pustules and the lesions on his chest and removed her hands quickly.

'That's an ugly rash you have. You're running a fever!'

'Nonsense! I don't share your woman's sense of melodrama about sickness. I was too long out in the sun, that's all,' he said. 'Only a heat rash disfigures me.' Too long in the sun but the night will hide us, the shadows mocked him.

Lily poured more port into his glass. 'Hard and dry as a button, my canker is,' she said.

Hard and dry as my heart, my girl.

He drank the port. He intended to get very drunk and already the fever elated him. In the dark one woman's like any other, the drink urged him. So when she kissed him he kissed her back – hot, meaningless, heartless kisses; the way a man can kiss with his body, the heart hard and dry in him.

She grappled with him like a pugilist for all her finery. One by one the whalebones snapped in her bodice and her lace flounces were torn to shreds. She sat on his lap, on the great carved chair where the masters of the house had sat for centuries beneath the collective gaze of the gallery of Hopgates. Her burgeoning health made her savage him. She dug her nails into the angry spots and drew blood. Her clothes were wrecked. There was no restraining her. They loved as if they had abandoned the tariffs of matrimony; a terrible freedom at too high a price, he thought, as her immodest gestures displayed that she had left the old codes behind her, abandoned feminine grace much as an entrepreneur leaves his manners at home to go and haggle in the market place. The old codes have gone, he thought drunkenly, as she began furiously to undress him.

He looked down at the stone floor where his dark

clothes were wrapped around her ruined costume. As if we have peeled ourselves away. It's not I who sits here naked on this ancestral chair with a factory girl splayed over me.

Thirst ravaged him. He was sick of desire. Desire isn't love, he thought. And when the act of love was over a terrible sobriety possessed him. She was too unattractive to delude him. He put on his clothes and saw that her nakedness was loathsome. Loveless loving had exhausted her. He covered his wife with the torn lace dress, carried her up to their old bedroom, and shut her away behind the bed hangings woven by the long dead brides of High Withens. He left her there to sleep alone and came downstairs again. For the rest of the night he sat up, bleary eyed and dry mouthed, for drinking only aggravated his thirst. He still felt the light pressure, the insistent contact of her damp skin on him. She had straddled him like a succubus. Blasphemer, blasphemer, he accused himself at first for so betraying Agnes. And then, as the dawn rose, he was flooded with relief as he realised that loving Lily was the foreplay to killing her.

She got out of bed and put the torn dress on again. Like a barefoot gypsy girl she tiptoed across to the window and pulled back the drapes. The moorland, lit with a low uncanny light, possessed the dark clarity of a silhouette. She felt the rain on her skin, hot rain that waited to fall from the livid clouds above High Withens, and she sensed the crumbling weight of the old house, listening, tensing itself against the assault from the elements.

Was it mercury that made her skin sensitive as a

spider's to the coming rain? She felt the plash of thundery drops before the rain fell. Her flesh soaked in the grey light.

Rain fell at last. Rain fell heavily over the parched moor, spilled with rapt urgency upon the porous walls of High Withens that drank in the moisture and darkened, glistening wetly. The odour of damp overlaid with the revived scent of wisteria and the smell of the rain itself that had the scent of the earth and the heavens in it. And the house was still, still as a cat waiting to pounce on a canary bird.

She sat at the end of the bed and waited. She heard him move across the stone flagged floor of the great hall, the only sound in the house she listened for. Barefoot, in her torn lace dress, she waited for him. She held herself straight with the miracle of a supple spine again – waiting. But only Reeves came. The girl, who had looked all over the house for her, brought lint and bandages and the slick mercury ointment. Lily sent her away. When the servant had gone she listened out for him once more, but all she heard was the army of vermin marching in disciplined ranks below the floorboards. The rain fell quietly now, the urgency purged from it. A soft rain veiled the moorland. She went to the bedroom door and listened. The house was quiet. She opened the door on to the hall which was dark, lit only with the scant gleam of daylight. The house seemed to be waiting to pounce, or maybe brooding because its prey was elusive. She walked down the corridor with her smooth, cool feet. A loose nail from the uncarpeted floor jabbed her and she scarcely felt it.

The walls were warm and moist from the rain that fell from a sky blistered with the long hot summer.

She crept up the winding stair to the pink bedroom, holding her breath in case the house should hear her. A dozen triumphant Lilys polka'd in the turreted room. So the blue pills worked, were more potent than any aphrodisiac, and it was worth the distressing side effects – india-rubber flesh, the bowels dragged out of her – for nights of love again. She dosed herself: one, two, three, four pills; she swallowed dutifully, eagerly now that the reward, her husband in her bed at nights, was ahead of her.

The pain was worse this time. Gutted like a fish, she thought inelegantly; perhaps her grey flesh would sprout silver scales any moment. A radical pain. A pain of expulsion – like childbirth, she imagined. She felt blood leak out of her. Then something else: a warm sac, soft as lamb's liver, moist with blood, lay between her thighs.

She lifted back her ravaged lace skirts that were soiled with a discharge from what she supposed were her menses, which were scarce and sporadic because of her illness. But this blood was too thick, too heavily clotted to be the curse of womanhood. Bad blood. Hopgate blood. Nervously, she scooped the pouch of hot flesh from her thighs and disposed of it at once in the commode beside the bed. Blue pills to purge the poison out of her. And something else besides . . . Something else, she thought.

The ceiling swooped down on her and she felt as though her soul flew up aloft in a mad dance of exultation, whizzing around the cornice of the room in a demented parody of death – in anticipation of the moment when it would achieve the order of release from clay and corruption.

But the respite was too brief and the one kind of pain was followed by another, nearly as terrible, which forced her to get up again and squat over the commode that held the nameless gory slops, forced her to emit again and again the humiliating stream of putrefaction. She tumbled back into bed and, because the pain would not desist, the pain insisted on racking her, she lifted herself half up and reached over for a little glass, a tall stoppered bottle, and the relief of laudanum.

The opiate suppressed pain and paralysed her convulsed bowels. Look at me now, the room seemed to sneer. Look at my finery. If he comes now all the fripperies will be to no purpose. He'll have to cover his face with a perfumed handkerchief, the stench is so terrible. The place reeks of your poison and the other – the nameless thing that drowns at the bottom of your commode, a pestilence, the sac of blood that should have been heir to High Withens.

13

The girl dared to suggest that he'd better fetch a doctor. She had the coarseness, the temerity to speak about what was better left unsaid: the contents of a commode. Barefaced, she'd told him obscene things, things he would not hear spoken of, ever; things that, if women knew about them, they had better leave unsaid; women's things, that must not be spoken of to a gentleman, Thank God she is not to have my child, he thought.

He dismissed the girl at once. He'd manage a year's wages and there was no need to replace the servant. He gave orders for Lily's room to be purified before he went up to her. She was small and dry on her puce satin bed. The pills were on a table beside her, and as well as another bottle of laudanum he had brought her brandy.

'Drink this!' he said. She was too weak to resist him. He felt her skin rough from loss of moisture. Her eyes were dilated and her unkempt hair leapt in wild tangles over the pillow.

'My spine gets better,' she said.

'Yes. I was right then. So keep on with the pills, won't you?'

'This cure is worse than the kill,' she said.

'Then take more laudanum, woman. It'll deaden the pain . . . if you want to live, that is.'

'But I don't want to live. Not if it means pain. The pain in my spine was never like this.' She was curled up like a small animal. 'If death isn't pain, I'll die,' she said.

He poured her more brandy and added a drop of laudanum before making her drink. 'Drink this,' he told her, holding the glass to her lips. She swallowed convulsively. 'Have you eaten anything?' he asked her.

She shook her head. 'If I eat it's as though my body wreaks vengeance on the very notion of sustenance, so I daren't consume anything,' she said.

'But your spine is nearly better; that's the thing. If you discontinue with the mercury now your recovery might be set back months. Better suffer now and recover at once than linger on, for God knows how long, a confirmed invalid with death hanging over you.'

Her mouth turned down. Her mouth was filmed with sickness. He poured another glass of brandy and laudanum for her and the opiate soothed her fears. She stretched out under the covers.

'I feel light and pure,' she said. 'I'm floating. The pain is someone else's and it's far below me.'

He poured another glass of brandy, for himself this time – a very large glass that he drank with a grim relish. Then another. He braced himself. He bent over and kissed her forehead damp, moist, slick skin with a grey pall over it.

'Bear with the suffering and love me, love me,' he urged her.

It was pathetic how her sick blood leapt to him, would no doubt leap to his touch on her deathbed even. She clasped his hand weakly in hers and with her other hand undid the ribbons over her nightgown. Then she drew his hand over her breasts. In the shuttered room her nipples looked blue and tasted full of venom. He crept into the bed beside her and though he wanted to retch he kept sliding over her, over and into her thirsting flesh.

The opiate led her into a reverie of delirium. She murmured as he loved her, 'Giovanni, Giovanni.' Over and over. 'I'm too hot,' she said. He shrugged the covers off her. Her eyes were thrown up in an unnerving parody of blindness – or death, he thought.

'My warm darling with the sun on your flesh,' she raved on incoherently, lying very still until she suddenly quickened with indelicate spasms, violent shudders that stirred him. No lady. No lady. No lady, his loins spat again and again as she fell beneath him to the brink of unconsciousness.

She thought she was dreaming as he poured the fourth glass for her. The brandy was cool. She drank it like nectar. Then she swallowed with difficulty the four pills he fed to her.

'But I've already taken four pills today,' she thought she said, but perhaps it was her dream voice that couldn't make itself heard in the real world. This isn't the real world, she thought, as she felt his body move off her. Then the soaring lightness and the soul flapped out of her.

He drew back the shutters, opened the window and breathed the fresh air. She slept sonorously, her left arm thrown above her head, resting on the dull tangle of hair. He felt nauseous; the room was too bright, the sheeny furniture too vulgar. Roses rained down the walls. No more hot-house blooms for him, he thought. Only wild flowers that have the fresh country air in them.

She woke out of the long dream in which he had loved her hard limbed and passionate, and lying on her body as the cool stream ran under them.

She awoke to sordid linen. The poisons had run out of her as she slept in the bower of poppies. He had left her. Did she only dream him? But there were the two glasses and the decanter of brandy which was nearly empty. So the pink room, that had been desecrated by her poison, was reconsecrated by his love. He had loved her. Her spine was supple but her legs were heavy under her as she stepped out of the quagmire of sheets. She washed, drenching her body with water from the ewer before she sat down awkwardly, straddling the china basin, to let the water gush inside her. She pulled on fresh clothes and heard the fibres of her muslin chatter as she dropped the gown over her head. Armies of vermin were stampeding behind the wainscot. When she tripped, kicking the basin, the water slopped out like a flood bursting sluice gates. The very ticking of the ormolu clock appalled her. Her juddering nerves! The walls of the old house were gossiping as if the long dead mistresses of High Withens had been buried alive in them. But as she strained to listen the walls went suddenly dumb on her.

She measured a thimbleful of neat laudanum to calm her nerves – a tiny drop; she didn't want to sleep again. Sleep brought her no refreshment. Her stomach made terrible noises, vulgar slurping noises, heaving and sucking as if a sludgy swamp lay within it. She walked over to the table where the laudanum was, bare feet gliding over the carpets that were softer than a velvet-lined purse. A little more poppy juice and the old house will be silenced. My stomach will be quiet, too. Just a little drop and I'll go downstairs again.

And if she dies, what then? He shrugged off the thought as though it was too gross an accusation. To dream of release meant to collaborate with the dark energies inside him. I give her ease, he thought, with the cool draughts of laudanum. And the mercury cures her. Kill or cure, kill or cure, the house mocked him. Within a year she'd have been dead anyway, he told himself. Too long about dying, my dying bride with her slow canker; she could have taken twenty years a dying.

Her dying had aged him. In a year he'd be forty. He looked at his handsome reflection. Misery suited him; the raven's wing hair had a sprinkling of grey in it. The calculating lines under his eyes merely gave him authority and his oblique smile that had the twist of mastery could wreak devastation. He only had to smile at a woman and she was at his feet like a passionate penitent. All those girls he had taught: the coy ones who had passed him scented notes, the heedless ones like Lily who had thrown themselves at him – he despised them all. He'd never loved before Agnes.

In marrying Lily he'd been restored to his inheritance. But marry Agnes and the Hopgate lineage would be revived. Good blood would flow at High Withens again.

Since the rains came and the air had cooled he felt more himself. At last the heat rash was fading, although it left shiny scars, perhaps where Lily had scratched him. But now there was no more loving, though she was still avid for it; her pulse ran too fast and she was weak from fasting. It seemed as if she was melting from inside like hot candle wax. Her flesh faded fast. But still the sick woman with the staring eyes craved him, was consumed as much by her desire as by the illness. Her desire plagued him. Lie with me, lie with me, her eyes said when her throat was too closed up to croak at him. Her breath festered. Her tongue turned black and the flesh fell away from her until it seemed desire was all that was left of Lily Hopgate.

He no longer urged the mercury on her, but he left the pills with her. The confused woman dosed herself and he neither knew nor cared to know how much she took any longer. I've done what I can, he told himself. I've cured the canker in her. It's up to her now; if her spirit has any fight in it, if she cares to combat the onslaught of mercury poisoning, that's her affair. I'm not her keeper, he thought. So he left her alone with the pills. He got rid of the lady's maid as well as the nurse, so only a couple of housemaids saw Lily when they cleaned up the daily mess or tried to feed her.

But her desire followed him much as her scent had always done. When he tried to read in the library a sudden dizziness would afflict him, a sudden falling away of concentration so that he was obliged to put away the essay, the poem, the philosophical treatise he was reading, and take up some trivia — a woman's novel, perhaps. He read most of the gothic stuff, incarcerating himself in a world of imaginary dangers where the heroines were all far more beautiful than his wife and the villains astonishingly resembled himself: darkly handsome and proud as Lucifer.

He formed an addiction to the novels which he despised for their elevation of sensation. There has to be more to life than violent emotions, he thought. There are the arts of civilised conduct, the peaceful, innocuous pastimes of the polite world, that seemed too far away now that he had permitted terror to reside at High Withens.

He thought of Agnes with her charities, her parish visits, her prescribed connections with the community. That's what I need, he told himself. To re-establish old ties, old duties, to take my part in the county society. But not with death at my side; not with a factory girl beside me.

And he fell to reading again, lurid sensational penny magazines, when he'd gone through the bound volumes in his library. But no imaginary terror was enough to release him; his addiction, like all addictions, was the more ravenous for feeding it.

He stayed up half the night trying to terrify himself with spectacular tales of vampyres, spirits, murderers, ravished heroines and maddened wanderers, and as he grew dizzier even the simply captioned woodcuts of the penny dreadfuls taxed his exhausted powers of concentration.

When there was simply no possibility of reading, because his head swam and his eyes reacted even to the dimmest of lamps as if it were a beam of corrosion; when he felt his mind stray from the connections between words in the simplest of sentences and he had to put the books and papers away, he went and simply sat in the hall, looking up at the collocation of his ancestors.

They glared at him – all the long dead, haughty Hopgates, with their faces like hawks and their piercing blue eyes. Every master of High Withens, it seemed, had had eyes the same colour as Jonathan's, the same blue-black hair, the same strong jaw with its tilt of arrogance. And they had all, without fail, married women who were both high-born and beautiful. Yet despite their rank and the eminence of blood and breeding they had lost his inheritance for him, and by his own exertions he had regained it, bought it back with the dowry of a draper's granddaughter who, after all, would die barren, whose portrait would never hang next to his amongst the family paintings. Lily's connection would be excised. When Agnes was his bride it would be as though Lily had never existed and the Hopgate blood would run pure again.

14

It was her dying wish to be taken downstairs and placed on a sofa that overlooked the garden, where she lay like a shadow on the couch that was draped with a white lace coverlet. Her hair was unbound. Her hair was the most vital thing about her as it sprang in snarls and tangles over her shoulders. She lay in the library, the warmest room on the ground floor, that looked south over the rough lawn that grew up to the tall windows. The hot breath of the south, she thought. I want the hot breath of the south to revive me.

The hot sun of the south on his skin and his breath of wine and lemon groves. His ardent speech was inflected with the passionate rhythms of revolution.

O bella liberta, O bella! His heart sang. His heart pulsed for his country's freedom in the very words he recited to her: Dante to Beatrice, Giovanni to Lily Flood, Giovanni to his motherland.

'Giovanni, Giovanni,' she murmured, 'for all your hot loving you left me – left me, while this man with his cold blue eyes, the cold eyes of the north, waits at my deathbed. The man who hates me has stayed when my true love left me for the motherland.'

Barely fifteen summers flowed in her strong veins. She could have sprung over mountain tops to follow him. She had imagined being captured by banditti, conspiring with carbonari, loving in the hot landscapes she had only seen in paintings.

Her papa, always at his lace manufactory! Governesses came and went. The spoilt, wilful daughter of the house, with her deportment lessons, her smattering of French phrases; the Italian master! Giovanni. Giovanni. The first time a man other than her papa had lain hands on her. Giovanni had placed his arms, just so, around her waist. He held her hand. His coat lapel brushed her bodice. She smelled the grape on his breath – and again she was the ripe fourteen year old, ripe as an Italian madonna with clear magnolia skin and a high bosom.

He had spoken a broken English at first, but when they danced Giovanni's words leapt into his mother tongue. And how they had danced! They danced all over the drawing room, where the carpet had been rolled up for them. They danced on out into the conservatory, out of the shadowy rectangle of the shuttered house, down into the arbour of honeysuckle at the bottom of the garden where, exhausted, they fell in an Anglo-Italian bubble of laughter, the awkward, wary words tumbling into the promiscuity of mirth.

Her blood leapt to him; if she wasn't a real lady, neither was he an English gentleman. His hand on her waist, his mouth on her lips; his greedy mouth drank her like melon juice. He unlaced her stays as if he played on a musical instrument. All his movements had the consummate ardour of a long apprenticeship in loving.

And perhaps she was more of a lady than she knew, in her ignorance, or less of one in her fervour. She remembered his almost fevered flesh in the cool spring sunshine. His heat filled her.

'O bella liberta, bella, bella liberta,' he had said when he'd removed every stitch of clothing from her.

She had thought it was for the rest of her life, the rest of her life unfurling like a flower with the hot sun of the south warming her. He loved her once, twice, thrice; she could barely remember, for the long swoon of loving turned down the lamp of daily existence. An old story. He loved and left her. Giovanni ran off to join the tortuous plot to unify Italy, left with a month's wages still owing to him, left Lily – who fell into a decline at once, then fell ever deeper into sickness – to dream about what might have been, until many years later Jonathan came for her.

Jonathan, a real English gentleman with the villainous good looks of a gothic hero. His hair was darker than any Italian's. His kisses, that at first seemed no less ardent, had all the force of authority. His courtship was artful, reciting verses from the old songs, or sensuous poetry. He had but to lift his little finger like a weary aristo and she'd come grovelling. Passionate Giovanni – whose real love was the motherland. Contemptuous Jonathan – who didn't love her at all, who loved only his pride and her money until he loved Agnes better.

Jonathan came into the library.

'Giovanni,' she said. The man looked blurred and dark to her.

'My name is Jonathan,' he said. 'Give me my English name.'

'Give me your heart,' she said.

Every organ of flesh in her squeezed dry and she was still consumed by passion, he thought distastefully. She looked oddly prettier now that the grave gaped beneath her. A luminous blue, not grey, tinged her flesh. The white lace pillows and coverlet were opalescent in the tepid morning light of the library, like an aura of ether around her. A tableau of death, he thought. He would have liked to paint her; he'd not done so much as a charcoal sketch in the past few weeks. Then he saw that she no longer had the pills or the laudanum beside her.

'You've stopped taking your medicines?'

'They don't work,' she said. 'They don't make you love me.'

'What nonsense you talk, woman. You speak as though mercury were an aphrodisiac.'

'No. It's not a love philtre. It's a poison,' she said. 'You've poisoned me.'

'I won't stay here to listen to wild accusations. If you've made yourself sick with mercury poisoning it's your fault. I only administered the tablets on one occasion. You can't accuse me,' he said.

She looked at him. Her hazel eyes with green flecks darkened, acidified to sepia. Eyes smudged by shadows that were dark as wet collodion stains.

'I risked death to purchase love,' she said.

'Then we're both gamblers.' Loathing broke out of him. 'I risked hell for High Withens.' He turned as if to leave her.

'Don't leave me to face death alone,' she said.

He sat down on a straight-backed chair at the foot of her couch, sat stiffly with an uneasy formality.

'Where's Papa? I asked for my papa to come. Surely he wants to see his dying girl again.'

'I sent for him yesterday. He'll be here soon,' Jonathan lied smoothly.

'Just yesterday? But I asked for him days ago, days ago,' she said.

'No, just yesterday. It seems long to you because you slip in and out of consciousness.'

Where's the doctor?' she asked.

'You didn't want Briggs, don't you remember?'

'But surely another physician ... any physician. There must be some ease for me. There may yet be a cure,' she said.

'The doctor came yesterday, a London man. Don't you remember anything?'

Her thoughts drifted. She had forgotten what she had been saying to him. A wisp of darkness, then his beautiful, mesmerising face.

'For a man you're too beautiful,' she said.

They were the last words he heard her say, but they were not the last words she said, not the final song her heart sang. If I were a papist I could confess, she thought. I must confess to my husband. He's not the first. I'll tell him.

'You're not the first,' she told Jonathan. He heard the croaking of her closed up throat and bent over her. Not long now, he thought, and I'll be free of her.

He didn't appear to have heard her. She tried to speak again but only heard the love song of a bull frog. 'Love

142

me. Love me,' the frog croaked under a dank stone in the clear, cold water.

His face swam into view again. Pale face, dark hair, the blue eyes colder than the grave, she thought. His arrogant chin was tinged with blue because he hadn't shaved that morning. Blue as mercury poisoning. She tried to lift her hand to look at her own blue skin but it was weighed down, as though sheets of lead had been sewn into the coverlet.

His dark hair – longer than was fashionable for a man, styled like a poet's or an artist's, too long for an English gentleman – added to his beauty; cold beauty with no heart in it. How can you be so beautiful and so heartless, she thought she asked him. Perhaps it was your beauty and not yourself that I loved after all, she realised with a sudden clarity. If you weren't beautiful I wouldn't love you. She croaked again. The noise, which had phlegm and the death rattle in it, disgusted and unnerved him.

I love only beauty. The knowledge astounded and delighted her. Only beauty. I should have been an artist, not a wife, she thought. Too late the truth! I should have painted him, not married him. She croaked desperately, 'I should have painted you, not married you!' But then her body jumped, a last bracing against eternity. 'The last dance, the last dance, Giovanni,' she said, before tumbling on the grass with him.

His wife died as he watched edgily from the stiff-backed chair. A horribly convulsive death, as if she was possessed by demons. At last he was free of her.

This was the time of guilt then? The hour, the moment when he should have been overwhelmed by the enormity of the thing, or at least filled with a terrible emptiness, when he should have been feeling either numbness or horror, all he felt was jubilation. He was free of her. His soul rejoiced that his wife had fled to eternity. No more Lily Hopgate. No more tradesman's blood. No more factory girl in his bed. His dignity was intact. He was his own man again. He felt sheer happiness, exultation. Like a pilgrim whose burden of sin has been lifted from his shoulders he was raised out of the slough of despond and he was free of her.

He rose at once and shut her eyes that were startling, wide open with a terrible recognition. Perhaps hell had gaped for her at the final moment, then, and poor Lily was even now being tossed on a pitchfork. He felt no compunction but he had to close those eyes from which death had erased the shadows. As he pressed down the eyelids an inquisitive blackbird hopped up to the tall French windows and Jonathan was momentarily entranced by the pert fragility of life in a bird: a glossy blackbird with a beak coloured bright as Seville oranges. He opened the window at once and surprisingly the bird flew in. It was as though the natural world was admitted to his house again. He didn't draw the covers over Lily. In death he had no fear of her. In death she was quite presentable, a not altogether unpleasing corpse. In death, after all, her looks could quite respectably be the lineaments of a cadaver.

She was like a wax effigy on the sofa, her spirit fled. How quickly her flesh began to stiffen. It wasn't Lily in the room with him. Whatever Lily was had gone and left her body behind like a set of discarded clothes. He felt more at ease with her body in death than he ever had in his life with her. The last few days she had worn dresses fastened loosely, because she didn't want to die in her nightgown she said, and so on this morning of her demise she was attired in virginal white muslin and for once it suited her, as if – he half smiled at the macabre thought – only death could deflower her.

When he thought about it, she'd make an interesting study for a portrait. A dead body was like a vacant house, he thought. But to record her in oils would be to grant her immortality, and he didn't want any memorial to Lily Hopgate at High Withens.

A sweetly scented breeze crept up from the valley and drifted into the library, stirring the old curtains that lifted and swathed the couch where Lily lay, covering her face from his gaze that at the very last did not find her wanting.

Jonathan felt almost at ease – almost. He walked over to the sideboard and poured a glass of port to reward his equanimity. He lit a cigar. The smoke rose and hung on the air like incense. He should think about practicalities, he supposed: the death certificate. She'd have her physician at last. A small knot in his stomach was loosened by the second glass of port. Mercury poisoning, the colour of her skin, her tongue, the very smell from her . . . but the servants knew well enough she'd been left to her own devices. No one could accuse him of anything, except perhaps neglect. He'd call in Briggs. After all, he'd prescribed the stuff for her and wasn't likely to want to advertise the dangers in his own treatment. Yes, Briggs was the man for the death certificate; he'd be in a pickle if he wrote anything but tuberculosis. Write 'mercury poisoning' and the doctor's methods would be suspect. Yes, Briggs was his man.

He finished the port and cigar, had a servant draw his bath and went upstairs to shave and cleanse the odour of death from his body.

15

His first desire was to go at once to Agnes and ask her to marry him; to press for her hand in matrimony would be a mere formality – he knew her feelings well enough and naturally her father would be overwhelmed at such an unexpected turn in his daughter's fortunes. He allowed himself to imagine the Slanes' quiet elation, to anticipate their dignified assumption of a new place in society. Agnes, the first lady of the county, the mistress of High Withens. It gave him a special pleasure to know that his love could confer position on such a bride. His first desire, when Lily died, was to be with Agnes, but he knew that such desire had to be reined in a little longer. Neither Agnes nor her father would relish a ghoulish haste to throw wedding banns over the altar fast on the interment of his wife. There was a certain decorum in these matters, and one must allow the corpse of the first wife time to cool before warming the nuptial bed with a second wife. He couldn't fool Agnes with any mock ceremony of grief, but he'd need to display a certain respect for his first wife's memory if the second was to escape public calumny.

He wrote:

My Dear Agnes,

It is all over. This morning Lily died. Her body stiffens beside me even as I write. I'll not burden you with the details of these last terrible days. It is enough that it is all over. My wife is free from her earthly sufferings at last. My wish now is to have done with the distasteful ceremonial rites that must follow such a sad event. I turn to you as my dearest friend in this. Let me petition you, dearest Agnes, to inform the Reverend Beech about my wife's death. Tell him — ask him if he would take over entirely the arangements for Lily's funeral; whatever fripperies of flowers, crapes, procession of mourners will suit. His wife is a good woman. She will know the etiquette in all this. Explain as best you can, will you? I have no inclinations in the matter other than to be left alone. My grief is a private thing and, for the present, condolences may be expressed through written missives. I could not bear a train of sympathy knocking at my door. You will understand my reluctance to receive formal calls just now. Pray give my respects to your father and rest assured that I remain, in the midst of my affliction, your affectionate friend,

Jonathan.

He penned a second letter to Briggs.

Dear Sir,

I would be much obliged if you'd pay one last call upon my wife, sadly deceased this very morning. There is the matter of the death certificate to attend to, and while I am aware that my wife was peculiarly reluctant to avail herself of your services during these last weeks I must inform you that her aversion was to any kind of medical intervention on her behalf. No other physician has been called upon to examine her.

I trust you will attend upon your earliest convenience.

Yours etc.

Now he had only to loiter in this house as in a kind of limbo until he could respectably wed. Perhaps he should forgo any opportunity to be in Agnes Slane's company for a while; to have a trip abroad, travel through Italy again. But then money was scarce, and it was doubtful that Mr Flood would be so liberal with his purse now Lily was dead. Better wait until he could take Agnes with him to Florence, to Rome, to the summit of Vesuvius. He fell into a reverie, anticipating the wedding trip.

For the moment London might be the thing. He could take in a mild bout of dissipation at the London clubs and pleasure houses – a few suppers with dollymops, perhaps. He smiled sardonically. Really dissipation wasn't his style. Perhaps he wasn't a true Hopgate after all. His only vice was an indecent haste to be with the woman he loved. To hell with decorum. He couldn't sit here in this mausoleum of a house watching over the remains of his wife like a bereaved husband. He'd deliver the letter to Agnes himself, he decided, walk over the moors in the slanting afternoon light and leave the letter at the curate's house. Hastily he put on his black silk waistcoat, a black frock coat over the dark blue trousers, and picked up his stove pipe hat. He set out for the curate's house.

His feet skimmed the springy turf of the moor. A vital, saline air was blown across the country by sinewy winds gusting up from the coastline so he was almost borne aloft by the tumultuous breezes, swept dizzily along the sharp descent to the vale of Low Withens.

The curate's house had a naked Georgian edifice. The windows were bare of lace and you could see directly on to shabbily genteel rooms fragrant with wild flowers, scoured floors and beeswaxed furniture. How he longed for clean, simple things; the light scent of wild flowers, not the heavy perfumes of hot-house blooms.

Agnes opened the door to him. No sign of a servant and no other evidence of life in the household. Her hair was unbound and fell to her waist, its sheen undeflected by the twist of curls or ringlets. The sight of her loveliness, her clean limbs in a light muslin frock, made him breathless with anticipation. Silently he handed her his letter. Wordlessly she let him in. Unpapered walls painted pale grey. His boots squeaked on the stained floorboards. Two doors led off either side of the hall which narrowed at the rear and led to the kitchens, he supposed. The door on his right was ajar. He saw shelves of books, a desk and smelled tobacco: the curate's room, then. To the left was the drawing room where she led him – an old sofa covered in blue damask, some straight-backed chairs with cushions worked with Berlin wool, prints of cathedrals, a piano forte, books and sheets of music, a tea table – that was all. They stood facing each other, not speaking; the formalities of greeting fell away. The air was thick with desire. She read his letter directly. Somewhere a clock chimed, in the hall or on the landing. A long silence. Words failed them.

She looked supple, fresh in the white muslin. He plucked a flower from a vase and threaded it through her hair. His throat almost closed up with excitement. She had never looked lovelier. The frock fell low over her bosom. He saw that her feet were bare and there was a faint scent of soap from her skin as though she had just bathed. She said nothing about Lily, breathed not a word about his wife's death as if the terrors of his presence in this empty house, his naked desire alone in the house with her, drove all other thoughts away.

'Father isn't here. He's relieving for a sick minister in another parish.' She said the words vacantly as if any implication there might be in them was lost to her.

'And the servants?' he asked roughly, desire struggling with decorum.

'No servants. There's only Cissie in any case, but the girl broke her leg last month and is up at her sister's. I'm keeping house at present.' His kiss broke off her words. She had a thin-lipped mouth, and the upper lip, puckering slightly, tasted very sweet to him.

He bent her neck back as he kissed her and her long hair trailed over the worn carpet. Did she resist him? He scarcely knew. The tacit limpness of her body impressed him with the sense of his own power. Her passivity would have to argue the case for the codes of chastity and honour for her. I'm not responsible, she would say to the silent jury. And I'm glad I'm not responsible, her limp body told her lover.

He would have taken her there, before the tall bare windows that looked on the moor, but she half fled from him. Soundlessly she ran up the uncarpeted stairs and he pursued her swiftly, caught her long hair and wound her close to him.

'If you run from me again I'll strangle you with your own lovely long hair, like Porphyria's lover,' he told her, urgently, fervently, as he pressed her on the bed beneath him. Her bed was narrow, the counterpane smoothed down without a ruck, a cast iron bedstead such as a servant might have. A painted floor and a light paper on the walls sprigged with flowers.

He pulled at her dress tapes which were fastened loosely and the frock slipped down. He tore at his own clothes and when he took off his belt the buckle snapped, and the sound of the loud twanging filled the room like a harsh laugh, Lily's laugh. When Agnes looked at him she saw the face of a stranger because she didn't recognise lust. His eyes had narrowed and his mouth was drawn back, almost grimacing at her. She marvelled at how white his skin was, almost whiter than her own. He knelt above her. She lay stiff as a board now, only half daring to resist when he coaxed up her chemise. She scarcely knew what she wanted. Fear and desire contended; desire in her longing for his touch, the need for flesh on flesh, but she was afraid because he hurt her, and even more afraid because he looked at her – a slow lascivious scrutiny of her body. To be seen naked shamed her. And the words he said were what she supposed any man said to any woman when he lay with her – perhaps even his wife, his dead wife – perhaps he'd even told Lily she was beautiful.

He pinched her slender waist. He put his face in her

fronds of hair and kissed her with desperate ferocity. He kissed her mouth as she had never been kissed. His open mouth was hard and dry. He knelt above her and then it seemed he was inside her and yet he still knelt and told her how he loved her, and so after all it seemed the most natural thing in the world, and at first she wondered what all the fuss, sermons, prayers, omens, adjurations, superstitions and damnations were about. All for nothing, she thought. Nothing at all. A fuss about nothing. He moved out of her and ran his finger along the border of lace edging her chemise. The undergarment was pristine but worn to a fine transparency, and the fragility of the frayed lawn almost stirred him more than her naked flesh. He bit at her white skin through the flimsy stuff that seemed to dissolve like a communion wafer. I must leave my mark on her, he thought. She must know she's mine after this delirium of loving. He worried at her neck, her arms, her breasts and then her thighs where she tried to shield herself. She shifted nervously away from him but she didn't grapple with him as Lily had. She was too well bred even to struggle in denying him.

All those months of stifling his true emotions, the weeks of hopeless desire, of loving Lily in a fever of revulsion, had accustomed him to a perverse loving so that now, when the woman he desired, the woman he loved above all others, lay in his arms, he was startled to feel the same violent energies course through him, a terrible anger as though loving and hating were too close, were commingled in his blood.

I'm not responsible, he thought, as livid wine stains flushed her body. He tried to be more temperate. If only she would resist, he thought. If only she didn't lie so still I wouldn't feel as though I ruin her.

He looked at her body, the slender white body beneath him on the bed. The chemise was around her shoulders like a flimsy scarf. He lifted it over her arms and it was so threadbare it seemed to drift in fragments like gossamer, like dandelion seeds, when he tossed it aside.

Her arms reached out and pulled him down towards her, so close that he wouldn't look at her. She was entranced by his long dark hair. She ran her fingers lightly over the nape of his neck. She kissed his hair, pressed her mouth lightly but fervidly over his neck, his face, his mouth. Her moist, sweet breath. He tried to look at her again but she held him close. Love me, don't look at me, she pleaded in her heart. I can love you if only you don't look at my body. Love me, don't appraise me, she thought.

I love her for being timorous and beautiful and I mustn't spoil her. I must not spoil her, he vowed again and again as though the words were an opiate that could pacify the urgent shudder of flesh.

And after, there was a brief languor, a lassitude, as though the violence that half seemed to be Lily's ghost was exorcised on the narrow bed in the arms of lovely Agnes, slender, listless, lissome Agnes, whose loving was not fraught and possessed by demons as Lily's had been. A lady in his arms at last.

He leaned over and picked up the filmy shreds of her chemise and slipped it over her arms, drew the diaphanous stuff over her breasts, her waist, so her wan body was veiled by the garment – frail as her chastity, he thought as his fingers clawed the fragile shift to ribbons, as he loved her again and again through the sheer web of cloth.

Desire was only momentarily appeased. Loving her was like the merest sip of water offered to his raging thirst. He remembered a poem by some poet he didn't recall, who imagined swallowing his mistress, drinking her down like the wine of an unholy transubstantiation.

A heady ardour clung to him. His desire for her engulfed all her possessions: the vision of her worn gowns in the half-open wardrobe, the tiny cloth boots with black silk ribbons that trailed under the bed, a gauzy reticule she had netted with her own hands, the naked wooden doll that was stiff and undressed on the mantelpiece, all her intimate, laundered garments that she had folded neatly and laid away in the press with lavender bags; he wanted to put the mark of his loving on everything.

'You ravish me,' he said, rejoicing in the old phrases of seduction. Enchantress, flower opening beneath him. She was his heart's desire, heart's ease, the only woman for him; a vision of loveliness. She had cast her allure like a net over him. He was her knight. She was the lady in the tower, the Holy Grail, the Sleeping Beauty, and his love had awakened her. The litany went on.

She thought: I'm a harlot, a wanton, a sinner, the Magdalen; the fate worse than death – a fly-blown child, an outcast, a pariah, a fallen woman. And would he marry her? He must, of course he must; he's an honourable man, she believed. But would he despise her for succumbing so easily, yielding so readily? But again he was loving her and he could not be appeased, so she stopped trembling; fear fled from her and she exulted. He must have me. He'll love me forever. And perhaps there was a measure of power for her at last in his very need; some power for her after all in this disease of loving.

She wore a new dress, a funereal frock the Beech's had discarded because a period of mourning for a deceased relative had lately passed and their daughters were desperate for bright clothes again. The gown was narrow, after the pre-Raphaelite fashion, and showed the outlines of her body.

Agnes sat facing him in the black silk dress. A necklace of jet beads glittered at her throat. She looked older in black, more stately and even more beautiful. She was barely eighteen but she held herself with a dignity, a natural grace, that poor Lily had never acquired. Her pale hair glossed to an almost silvery yellow against the sheen of her dress; the narrow gown made her look taller, sharper, curving around her hips, trailing on the floor. She wore jet earrings like the lustres of black chandeliers, heavy rings, as well as the necklace with a dozen strands that choked her long neck. On her bodice she had pinned a memorial brooch faced with a smooth empty surface of glass, behind which had been inserted pale hair curved like a swan's wing:

'What love token is this?' he teased, fingering the bauble.

'It is my mother's hair,' she said. 'My father cut a lock when she died and had swatches woven into miniature plumes and set in jet for mourning jewellery.' But his love had already banished the memory of that old grief, and she smiled at him. Her hand looked like alabaster against a jet bracelet set with a creamy cameo head that Jonathan had himself snapped over her wrist earlier when she dressed. He had kissed inside her arm just below the elbow where the black lace trimming to her sleeve frothed provocatively, diaphanously.

'My exquisite love,' he had said, and he wanted to unfasten the gloomy dress but she had spun away from him, her trailing skirts flicking out of the door behind her as she went to prepare their meal.

He pushed aside the collation of cold chicken and vegetables, almost knocking over the white wine as his hand reached for hers across the table. They dined at the small table by the bare windows in the curate's drawing room. She didn't light the lamps but had set candles on the table because she favoured the flickering, naked flames that agitated the mild air of the summer evening, spilling their molten wax on to the bruised petals she had scattered around the stems of the candelabra.

An almost holy incense filled the room: the odour of hot wax, the frail scent of crushed petals; it was as though the hunger of love dined at the table, as the simple meal, the light wine, was barely tasted, their eyes feasting on each other, as their fingertips brushed away the thin spiralling smoke of the candles and their hands clasped across the table, the hunger of love not desisting, but racking them like poison.

When he raised her hand, when he kissed the blue vein inside her wrist, she said, 'You must go. We mustn't be seen.' A small swell of panic rose in her. 'What if my father returns?'

He fed her wine. He coaxed her down, for she had half risen from her chair.

'The curate's miles away. You know he won't come back tonight. Only this one night together, Agnes. Then we have to be patient.' She stared at him and now the panic glared in her eyes, her white forehead pleating with anxiety. He still held her hand. 'Marry me,' he said, the magic words to end a virgin's story. 'Marry me,' he repeated, 'be my wife, my bride, a fit bride for me.' He covered her hand with kisses. He rose and went over to her, lifting her from the chair and kissing her white face, her neck, her bare wrist and the white arm trapped in the black band of jet.

'But your wife . . . your dead wife . . . so lately deceased . . . the funeral . . .'

'We wait a few months,' he said. 'A few months, my darling girl, a few months will appease the proprieties. By next spring you'll be with me at High Withens.'

The shadow of fear went out of her eyes which were clear again; cornflower blue eyes that matched his own. Already she had the blue eyes of the Hopgates.

'Dance with me, Agnes.'

He held her waist, drew her towards him, and they danced to an imagined music. They danced all over the curate's drawing room. Her hair spilled loose and he saw her straight, narrow back, her long scented hair, reflected in the mirrored overmantel. The skirts of the mourning gown flowed like a black river over the threadbare carpet.

'Marry me, marry me,' he urged her.

She looked at him with her serious eyes, her cornflower blue eyes, and her mouth lifted.

'Yes. I will marr —' she began her acceptance speech, but his mouth silenced her.

She recklessly drank the wine he poured for her, and a hectic flush rose on her cheeks, her eyes glittered and narrowed; her mouth was swollen because he had kissed her roughly. She didn't tell him that he had hurt her, and for the first time since her mother died she felt like a mere girl again, as though the duties of womanhood, the careful sobrieties of life as the curate's daughter, were already shed. She was a little afraid of him; the authority of his years and position, the wild reputation of the Hopgates, the history of dissipations, unnerved her. A mere girl who lay still as a doll when he loved her – as still as his dead wife, she thought blasphemously as the wine eroded her sense of decorum, made her think impious thoughts, loosened her muscles, as too much wine released a warm languor in her limbs, slackened her nerves and made her lie easy in his arms at last. The wine and his proposal caused her stomach to dip with ardour. She no longer heeded the vision of her papa stalking home to smite the defiling pitch of sin from his house. Intoxicated with the heady ardour of love and the unaccustomed wine, she went upstairs with her lover again, careless that he stayed the night in her narrow bed, reckless now that she was sure of his love for her.

'Goodbye, my clandestine love.' He smiled at her and, she wondered, did he mock her as he pressed a few sovereigns in her hand and told her to buy herself some love trinkets: the ribbons, the laces, the furbelows he would have her deck herself with when she was his bride.

She ran shamelessly down the stairs after him, embraced him at her father's door and stared hungrily after her lover as he fled, as Jonathan was swallowed up like a demon of the night by the white mist of daybreak.

'You've seen my wife?'

'I've examined the remains,' Briggs said. 'The women have done their best with the rouge pots but there's no disguising the traces of mercury poisoning.' He spoke directly. There was to be no hedging, then.

'She was desperate for a cure,' Jonathan said, 'but perhaps mercury was not the right treatment for her, doctor.'

'I outlined the dangers, stressed the need for caution well enough,' Briggs said.

'All the same, a dying woman, a woman in pain may throw caution to the wind.' Throw her life away, and for only love, Jonathan thought.

'She had a nurse to administer the medicines, or so I believed.' Briggs spoke tetchily, with a degree of professional arogance.

'Yes, a heedless girl who vexed my wife. I was forced to get rid of her.' Jonathan offered the fellow a drink but he declined to accept any hospitalities, would not even elect to sit down but stood stiffly opposite the fireplace where Jonathan slouched, drinking brandy.

'As you dismissed my services,' Briggs could hardly contain himself, 'I'm rather surprised you call me in at this juncture, Sir.'

'There was no one else,' Jonathan said directly. 'You alone knew her medical history. You alone had treated her and even in the midst of my grief I thought, perhaps foolishly, to protect your reputation. I know you did your best for my wife. I shouldn't like another physician, even one more advanced in his profession, to query the efficacy of your treatment.'

'It's a great pity your wife lacked your cautiousness,

Mr Hopgate. To possess such a degree of calculation might have been the saving of her.'

Jonathan, white-lipped and determined not to show any fear before this charlatan, put his glass on the mantelpiece. 'I don't expect your gratitude,' he said. 'My first concern is not to preserve your reputation but to let my wife rest in peace.'

'After the torments of mercury poisoning?'

'It's true she died by her own hand, however inadvertently, only I shouldn't wish to advertise it.'

'She dosed herself?'

'Yes.'

'And you weren't alerted by the symptoms?'

'I've an aversion to the sick room.'

'And the servants didn't notify you?'

Jonathan paled, whiter than leprosy. 'I won't be interrogated in my own house, damn you! If she's poisoned, however much my neglect may be culpable, your treatment is not above suspicion.' Briggs was calm, too calm, thought Jonathan.

'I won't take offence at your outburst, Sir. I'm acquainted with the many forms of ... grief, but perhaps you'd be good enough to inform me why my services were dispensed with.'

Jonathan looked at the man in the mirror. 'My wife lost faith in you,' he said

'Ah, yes. Loss of faith. Loss of faith would have killed her,' Briggs said.

Jonathan picked up a slip of folded paper from the mantelpiece. 'As I tried to explain earlier, I will not cast doubt on your treatment. I regret you were dismissed out of hand by my wife. I had to humour the dying creature, you understand ... but I wish to make amends, so . . .' He handed a bank draft to the doctor.

Briggs looked at the floridly inscribed figures. 'Thank you, Sir. I only hope I can be equal to your generosity,' he said. Jonathan looked at him bleakly. 'I'm sure you're anxious for me to do my business and get from under your feet,' the doctor continued, as he walked over to the table where Lily's portfolio still lay, and slowly, deliberately wrote out the death certificate. 'There, Hopgate. Rest assured the world will remain ignorant of your wife's . . . drug addiction. I've put her disease as the cause of her death, which, in a manner of speaking, is the truth, however indirectly.'

'Thank you,' Jonathan said.

'Good day. Goodbye, Sir.' The doctor picked up his hat and quickly and quietly left him.

Jonathan felt hot and cold all at once. Hell and heaven in a moment. Was it so easy, then? So easy to get rid of one wife and take another? The house was silent. The gallery of ancestors looked suitably humbled, he thought. Master of all he surveyed. Already he felt Agnes fill his arms, lie beside him in the great bed, their whole lives ahead of them.

He would have a quiet celebration. It was the day his real life began, after all.

'To real life, to real love,' he toasted as he drank the champagne a servant had brought him. In just a short time Agnes would join him in the toast. They would get rid of this long table and dine intimately at a console table drawn up to the hearth. She would still be in her wedding gown, her hair heavy with lace streamers. How he would relish unpinning the flowers from her hair, unfastening the floral corsage from her bodice.

He gave himself up to the pleasures of champagne and anticipation of the wedding night.

The champagne bubbled like love's sweet song: 'It will not be long, love, Till our wedding day.' The words of the ballad lifted on the wind that wailed fitfully outside the windows, a keening that rose then fell, fell away like a drowning echo into the sump of the valley below High Withens.

The glass was still in his hand when the silver moon rose on his elation. The moon lit the hall with glittering light and sparkled on the expensive chandelier that was all that was left in the great hall to remind him of his marriage to a merchant's daughter.

Not quite all that was left though; not quite all. He lit a candle and walked triumphantly to the desk where Lily's portfolio sprawled, spilling out its obsessed portraits of mythical husbands. One by one he tossed the images of himself into the fire: Jonathan as archangel, Jonathan as King Arthur, Jonathan as the redeemer of dreaming princesses; one by one the flames devoured him. 'Farewell, my dying girl,' he said as he replaced the empty portfolio on the table next to the death certificate.

'My ticket to freedom,' he laughed to himself as he picked up the sheet of paper. And perhaps he was a little drunk after all, but only a little, as he read, by the light of a solitary candle, that the cause of Lily's death was syphilis.

16

The doctor's housekeeper showed Jonathan into the drawing room which ran from the front to the back of the house, subdivided by white wooden doors. The folding doors were drawn back and from the front portion of the room came the sound of someone practising piano scales with a hesitant touch.

The rear of the drawing room was arranged as a reception area, with half a dozen papier mâché chairs lined up against the wall. The room was discreetly dim, the blinds drawn low over the stained glass doors that led out on to wooden stairs down to the garden. Only the distraught and the furtive visited at the doctor's house, he supposed, as it was customary for Briggs to pay calls at his patients' homes. His clientele was drawn from the mercantile classes who'd set up raw, opulent establishments in this clattering, jostling town.

And what was he? Discreet or furtive?

A maid came in with tea and a moment later he heard

Briggs arrive and go upstairs to his consulting room. The maid disappeared and returned with instructions for him to follow her.

The brass stair rods glinted at him. Pictures he could not later recall covered every available portion of wall space in the hall. The house, which smelt strongly of carbolic, seemed to shut out the contamination of the surrounding town.

Briggs sat behind his desk. There was a low chair for patients placed in front of the desk. At the far end of the room were more papier mâché chairs, a table and a screen. Briggs seemed larger, more imposing, or perhaps merely less diminished by the relatively cramped environs of this town house than amidst the vastness of High Withens. His sandy hair, which was balding, and his pink, soaped skin gave him a porcine air, although he wasn't a stout man. The doctor's voice was louder, almost theatrical, and more authoritative than Jonathan remembered it. A man who could touch the defiled without fear of contagion.

He knows why I'm here. He knows too well, damn him, thought Jonathan. There was a heavy, almost gelid silence.

At last Briggs spoke, a loud, bludgeoning monologue. 'You want to know why. Why you weren't informed your wife had a . . . social disease. You want to know if there was a deliberate conspiracy. Why on earth she married you. What caused her disease.'

The doctor leaned on his elbows over the tidy desk and continued in his loud impersonal voice, the voice of authority.

'I can run through your wife's medical history for you. She was first smitten with the illness – syphilis – some ten years ago, when she was still a girl, in fact. She would have contracted the disease from sexual commerce with an infected man but I'm afraid I'm unacquainted with the name or any other details regarding the gentl— the fellow concerned. The nature of her ailment was first made known to me when I was called in to treat her for a skin disease. I recognised at once the particular nature of the pustules and lesions which covered her body and I did not need to submit her to the indignities of inspection of the genitalia. In my profession, I learn to shed the moral outlook and deal with practical exigencies. It was evident, in any case, the girl was innocent for all her loss of maidenhood; she'd been cruelly taken advantage of.

'I decided in this, as in other cases I've treated, not to inform the girl or her father as to the true nature of the disease. What good would it do to bring additional misery, unthinkable social opprobrium, upon the child? The girl would have ended her days in an asylum if her father knew the truth of the matter, and I've seen too many respectable families destroyed by this kind of thing. Even where there's no family for the patient to be accountable to there's the nature of our modern treatment of syphilis – the French pox, the Italian plague, call it what you will – to consider: the indignity, some would say the barbarity of the speculum chair. I would not have a daughter of mine endure such an ordeal! So I told the girl and her father that her condition was due to a blood disorder, while following the traditional remedy for treating syphilis. And at first the mercury seemed to be efficacious, as it does appear to have been in certain other cases I've treated. Unfortunately, in your wife's case the disease reappeared some years later and again I dissembled, diagnosing a tubercular spine. It's now being claimed by so-called advanced medical opinion that the disease has three stages and what appears to be an early cure, in many instances, is but the masquerade of recovery. The disease merely sleeps and, after a slumber of maybe even as much as twenty years, reawakens. If such a recurrence is manifest the disease may then go on to its final and horrible conclusion. A sufferer may be driven insane by syphilis, Hopgate, or he may lose the use of his limbs. In some instances the victim's face might be eaten up by a canker! I once attended a woman patient whose nose and mouth were eroded by the disease; the flesh on her neck dripped away like candle wax.' The doctor went on. His calm, clear voice reads my fate like an inventory, thought Jonathan. 'There are fears that too many of our lunatic asylums are populated by the unhappy victims of syphilis in its final, most virulent manifestation than is at present accounted for.'

'I'm a condemned man,' Jonathan said. 'You've all condemned me. Why was I condemned to marriage with a syphilitic bride?'

'Ah, I assume you're asking me why I did not tell you this earlier. I had in the past cautioned her against matrimony, of course, warned her against the bearing of any children, but as time went on and it was apparent the girl was dying, I assumed, wrongly, marriage was out of the question. I took it for granted that no dying girl would find a suitor, and when I learned of the marriage I scarcely thought, hardly imagined, a bridegroom would force his attentions on an invalid, a woman at death's door.'

'There was no forcing in the case,' Jonathan interrupted. 'She was eager for . . . loving.'

'There were marital relations, then?'

'Yes.'

'And have you had any symptoms?'

'Yes.'

'You'd like me to examine you?'

'No.'

'You didn't suspect?'

'No. You told me, you all told me, my wife had
consumption.'

'I'm sorry. I didn't guess she shared your bed. Though
I recall warning you there should be no issue from the
marriage; it was mere form. I hardly suspected – a dying
woman!'

'She was my wife!'

'A dying woman', Briggs repeated, 'but who knows?
She might have lived for years if it weren't for the
mercury.'

'Lived as a lunatic?'

The thick air thinned as though it had been pared
by sabres.

'I can give you the names of certain physicians –
specialists, if you'd prefer,' Briggs said.

'Can they offer me anything more efficacious than
mercury?'

'Well, they experiment. But in any case, if your
symptoms have cleared there's a chance the recovery is
permanent. You may have nothing to worry about.'

'And if my symptoms do reappear? Is there a cure?'

'In my opinion? No. There isn't. There's no cure for
syphilis.'

*   *   *

So Lily possessed him. He would never be free of her. He was shackled to her corruption. The mark of her loving was on him forever. But none would know of it. He'd seen to that, paying Briggs yet more money to acquire another death certificate. He drank cognac as though it was water. He looked at his reflection in the mirrored overmantel. Still handsome, still vigorous, with no evidence of the disease that now slept, now slumbered – in what part of him? He unbuttoned his shirt and the silvery pigment the rash had left when it faded shone like stars in the dusky light of the evening. So Lily claimed him. Did he wait for madness, for corruption, or did he hope and live, marry and dose himself with mercury? Marry me, marry me, he had urged Agnes. And he saw Agnes with her lovely wedding dress waltz across the great hall away from him. Agnes with her fragrant hair, her bright skin, her fresh body, ruined, despoiled, contaminated. How could he face her ever again? How could he tell her that Lily was in them both, a rank poison who had got into bed with them; that his love had infected her? The curate's daughter was tainted, was soiled goods, he thought bitterly. And how, he asked himself, could he love a second bride who came to him sullied with the first's corruption?

He stared at his reflection. For a man he was too beautiful, Lily had said. Dying words spoken with her poisoned breath. Didn't she guess at the truth about herself at all? And how was it, who was it, all that time ago – who was it she'd lain with? He wasn't the first. How she had fooled him! He felt sick and suddenly powerless. His dying girl, how she'd ruined him. His ancestors leered at him. And all for his inheritance! All for High Withens! 'I've sold my flesh to the devil for you,' he said aloud as he raised his glass in a mirthless toast to the gallery.

In his dreams he gave himself up to a fantasy of revenge, digging up Lily's body from the grave and impaling it with the venom of his vengeance, driving a stake through her wanton heart, or splicing the maggots that bred between her thighs, even tearing at her putrefaction with his bare hands, flinging her carcass into cess pits. But in his dreams he was as powerless as he was in life, for Lily returned in nightmares, swaying towards him in her costly silk dress, mocking him as she opened her dead limbs to his mouth, which, parched by an insatiable, raging thirst, was compelled to drink her corruption. She came singing songs to him, tavern ditties, sauntering up to him like the harlot she was, with her mouth painted, her cheeks rouged, a smell of cheap scent – and aroused, despite himself – when he kissed her his lips met a rotting cavity of purulating matter. In his dreams, no matter how many times he buried Lily, interring her in lead-lined vaults, or throwing her mutilated body into quicklime, she returned to claim him. Lily wouldn't stay dead. She always came back for her tardy lover.

His dreams, his nightmares of Lily, were at their most violent while her body lay in the library awaiting burial. He kept away from her. He feared his own rage which urged him to violate the strumpet, break open the seal of mortality and pursue her even through the realm of death to exact his revenge. The filth to which her clay would return in the grave already mired his life. He lived her death. It was as though she had shared the rottenness of her grave with him even as she had shared her bed.

170

His revenge was puny, a posthumous rage that could not reach her. He went up to Lily's room, with its corals, its roses, its voluptuous flush of costly furnishings, and ransacked her possessions, smashing the crystal flagons of perfume, hacking with a ceremonial sword all the fastidious finery that had disguised the jade. He stabbed at the feather mattress until the white down rose and settled like an intemperate flurry of swan's wings. He lunged at her soiled nightgown, that still sprawled across the bed, with the point of his sword, and quartered the garment. The furniture was all knocked down in his frenzy and, as in a drunkard's mania, he smashed the windows so that a high, dry air vented the boudoir. And when his energies were almost consumed by destruction he caught sight of himself in a dozen mirrors. Twelve reflections parodied his rage: a regiment of mad men plundering trifles. And all at once he knew that desire, and therefore anger, had left him – so it was mechanically, deliberately, with not even a cold rage, that he hammered with the hilt of his sword at every oak-backed looking glass, lacerating his hands and his arms until the reflections were shattered, the mirrors were in smithereens and he could no longer see himself.

He drank all the time now, swift, clear measures of liquor that did not make him maudlin nor sentimental, nor lachrymose. Neither was he violent. He had spent his violence. He drank without greed but emptily; no spiritous liquid could fill the gulf of his emptiness. His handsome face was livid, his eyes narrow and red-rimmed, but all his movements were cloaked, his voice was muffled by indifference. No more temper, no more intemperance. The outward forms are all that are left of health, all that remain of life, he told himself. Only ritual to replace the blank spaces left by desire and intemperance. When desire left it took Agnes with it. When anger left, it abducted Lily. He was empty now, blank and empty as the high blue sky on the day they buried the mistress of High Withens.

He rode behind the glass carriage. Beech's wife had chosen arum lilies, and they lay like pale wands over the gleaming casket. Lily's body was drawn by milk-white steeds. She was covered with white flowers. The white of death and the black of mourning; crape bands and scarfs; dark veils. A sober procession of the bereaved. The empty forms of grief, the rituals. Carriages with the blinds pulled down. And the only one who mourned Lily was her papa, with his manful sneezing into a florid handkerchief.

Flood had placed a rough hand on Jonathan's shoulder, his rheumy eyes blistered with tears. 'She's before her maker now, Hopgate. She's free of my grief and your . . . love, was it? Did you love her?'

The master of High Withens stared ashenly at the older man who was trembling. 'I married her,' he said emptily.

'But she wrote to me.' Flood was too broken even for rage. 'Such things she wrote . . . I wish to God I'd made time to visit her. She said you never loved her.'

'The strange fancies of an invalid,' Jonathan said.

Flood looked at his son-in-law through his screen of tears. 'A year of loving was the bargain,' he said.

'Oh, there was loving,' said Jonathan.

Flood was silent for a moment, struggling with his sorrow. Then he said, 'It's true, man, I look into your eyes and see a light extinguished there. Her death has devastated you and I do you a wrong; it's my damnable grief, man. Forgive me, as surely she forgives me, beyond the grave . . . a saint in Paradise.'

The funeral procession followed Lily into the graveyard. A hot day with a too blue sky, dry and cloudless. Dry and tearless as the widowed husband.

When he heard the indecorous thud of earth fall on the coffin he looked away quickly from the chasm in the ground. He looked up and saw Agnes, heavily veiled, wearing her black dress with its trailing lace dragging promiscuously over the freshly dug soil. He stared at her. Her black veil was sucked in slightly over her mouth and he realised that beneath the web of net she was smiling at him.

17

The treacly air clung like a shroud, a broody, sulking air that she agitated with a little ivory fan. The feeble draught scarcely revived her. Her skin felt silty in the oppressive heat. She left off her stays and petticoats and her muslin frock was sappy, soaked within an hour and stuck to her flesh; a lardy, sluttish heat that greased her skin like an emollient.

She lay in unaccustomed indolence on the thinning grass beneath the willow tree, driven out of the house by the sultry air. The coolest spot in the garden was her childhood haunt behind the green tent of willow. The branches trailed in dipping fronds that curved like the dome of a bell over the secret hollow in which she lay.

Her wrist twisted and curved the reluctant breeze over her face and neck. The earth was parched and dry under her. Her thirst was terrible. She had brought out with her a large pitcher of lemonade and she refilled an already thrice emptied tumbler, sipping lazily for, despite her raging thirst, the heat was so enervating that all her actions, every movement, each breath, was sapped of energy and drawn out to a slow languorous deliberation. When she had at last drained the glass she lay supine on the earth, too listless now even to revive the dying air with her little fan. She flung her arms over her head and stared up into the weeping temple of green branches.

The funeral was the first time they had met after he had loved her. She had spoken first, after her father had condoled with him; formal tokens, not real words that revealed her heart. She had extended her sympathies and he had accepted them tersely. When they buried Lily she had felt faintly blaphemous. Her joy was too great, her elation almost burst through the rituals of mourning so that it was all she could do not to laugh aloud, seize Jonathan and lead him swiftly, ardently away from the sombre gathering.

He had given her no sign, though, not so much as a furtive glance of encouragement, but his very avoidance of her as they consumed the funeral baked meats was surely a testimony of love. They had to be circumspect. Passion, indiscreet passion, had to be tepid as courtesy.

When he was at the other end of the great hall away from her, at the gathering after the funeral, she had felt the hot pulse of his presence more palpably than she had done when he'd lain naked in her bed. It was as though the black coated figure with the white glaring face exercised seduction like an occult charm that pinned her to the chair, made her insensible of the surrounding throng who ate and drank and stood about her, seeing and hearing alone with her mind's eye only her lover.

Her throat had burned. Her stomach had swooped in agitation. The heavy cake lay uneaten, the tea disregarded on the small table next to her. She had sensed his every movement with preternatural senses. She had seen his slender, black-clad form edge through the blurred groups of the company. His face was lost to her, but she had felt his heat, was glanced by his soul as though she was a Venice glass that shivered when the poison was poured into her. She had been half faint with expectation. To pull him one moment aside, or perhaps she could steal into the library and he would see and follow her, or in the garden – a stolen moment – a kiss . . . She knew she would have succumbed right then, in his bed, while the mourners grieved below. She had thought wildly that she would risk the opprobrium of society for him.

The curate had cut in on her reveries. Without knowing what she did she had stood up and followed her father, and when he made his farewell to the bereaved husband she had said something, a phrase learned somewhere in another world, and she supposed the master of High Withens had answered her.

She was in the half swoon of sleep under the willow tree, scripting delicious scenarios of love. He would come to her, stand over her, shadowing her prostrate form as she slept. He would kneel. He would take her in his arms. She felt his kiss. They lay together under the weeping willow. She invented a stream, a beck of flowing water at their feet. He splashed her with cool water. She laughed recklessly, lifted her frock and paddled in the stream. He followed her, encircling her waist with his firm grip. When she slipped on a pebble he would not allow her to arise. He tore her clothes off. He made love to her through the coursing water.

The same heat, the same lethargy possessed High Withens. Jonathan sat in the library. His shirt sleeves were rolled up. His shirt was half unbuttoned and he wore the white trousers Lily had admired. Lily thought he looked like a poet when he dressed in white linen.

He half read, half skimmed a newspaper. A bottle of wine to slake his thirst was nearly empty although it was not yet noon.

Thwarted. He'd had a plan and that was what he had thought life was. When the plan failed, where was life? Where love? He had failed. Life deceived him. Life was a masquerade, like syphilis. You dance with the masked jade. You aim to unmask her at the end of the waltz. You are intrigued by her mystery but determined to find her out. You study the weaving of the knot, the deftly tied ribbon that fastens the blind over her features, and when you have at last deciphered the code which dictates the twists and loops of strings, figured how to surprise the doxy and swiftly, cannily untie the knot of knots and discover her, you are felled suddenly from behind. Your legs give way under you. The music stops, the dancers have all gone and your partner was only an illusion conjured by the revels. And you are too grievously injured for more dancing in any case, because when you were felled something inside you was slain. Something is dead inside you. And what do you do when desire dies, Jonathan asked the empty bottle.

The second bottle drowned questions, worries, insidious thoughts. He looked at the brimming glass.

'What will I tell her?'

'Nothing,' the wine lisped coolly. 'Tell her nothing.'

'But if she sickens?'

'She sickens! It's not your fault. You scarcely meant to infect her.'

'But I'm honour bound to explain.'

'If you tell the scandal will kill her. Let her be.'

'I should have left her alone.'

The wine tasted sweeter with every swallow.

'Lily is to blame, not you. You're innocent. You're a victim.'

'And Agnes succumbed so easily,' Jonathan explained.

'All women are strumpets,' the glass frothed.

He was surprised to see how quickly, how deliciously the contents of the second bottle had slipped down. But after all, it had gone midday and there were gentlemen of his acquaintance who'd sunk a dozen bottles by luncheon.

'Three is not so much,' the glass cooed. Cool wine, an amulet against the heat, against the heart; the best there is.

'What's done is done. Think of yourself now,' the third bottle urged him.

'But her body tasted sweet,' he slurred.

'I'm sweeter!' And indeed the third bottle tasted so rare it barely registered on the palate.

Paris winked wickedly at the bottom of his glass. Away from torpor. Away from failure. Away from fear. Of what was he afraid? Agnes? Illness? Something else – someone else? Who was it?

'Come to Paris with me,' the wine sang. 'There are doctors there with new-fangled treatments. Perhaps they may reassure you. Who says the disease sleeps in you? Look at you. You're healthy and clean. There may be years of loving. Go to Paris. These French have a know-how with the malady of love.'

How long was she to wait for him? What was a respectable, an honourable period of time? Could they not engage in at least the superficial commerce of society? Could she not see him at the wicket gate, where they had first met, outside church on a Sabbath morning? Since Lily's funeral he had not attended even one church service. He had not stirred out of doors, declining all social invitations. But this was only to be expected: a grieving husband shut away with memory and misery. No one troubled him.

She was vexed. She bit her lip. They had left the future precarious in their delirium of loving. He had proposed to her, though. She clung to that. She was affianced, but secretly. The secret lay in her like a child awaiting its hour. She remembered how hot he was for her. She smiled shamelessly. Could he not manage to send a note? Could he not have contrived something? She should have pressed him for some sort of reassurance, arranged clandestine meetings, or at least fixed when it was likely they could communicate without fear.

Like a schoolmiss she wrote 'I love you' on scraps of paper. She even drew the quill over her arm, inscribing 'Jonathan' in dark blue ink, pressing into her skin, grazing the surface so that her blood turned blue. Then she drew lacy engageantes over her arm so her papa would not see the mess, would not guess at her delirium.

She wrote powder-dry little notes: 'Sir, may I call on you?' And intemperate missives: 'I dreamed of you all

night and woke to the desolation of an empty bed' —
which she tore up, putting the fragments into her mouth
and chewing deliberately, spitting out the pap when she
was sure her secret was illegible.

In his absence she lost courage, she who had brazenly
allowed him to love her like any harlot. She was afraid
to write to him. Distance, time, made a coward of her. It
was not proper. The man should pursue. It was enough
what she had done. He knew — he must know — how
she loved him. But perhaps he did think of her and
this was his way of being chivalrous; he protected her
reputation and wanted their love to seem honourable.
She would forbear to harass him. A matter of weeks,
only a matter of months, he had said, and she would
be with him at High Withens.

She neglected her duties. Her father didn't reproach
her lassitude; this heat — nearly October and the summer
would not die — was enough to finish anyone.

She exhaled heat. Her bare feet burned on the stony
terrace at the back of the curate's house. When her
father had gone out she slipped the light gown over
her head as she went back into the empty house. She
stood naked before the bare windows of the drawing
room, on the spot where he had kissed her. She shut
her eyes. She bent back and her loose hair spread like
a fan and flicked the carpet. Again she flew upstairs as
though he pursued her. In her bright room the narrow
bed was bound and trussed with starched sheets.

She tiptoed across the floor furtively. She bent over
the drawer at the bottom of her wardrobe and pulled
it out, a tiresome process for the wood was warped
and the drawer jammed as she tugged it. From silver
tissue she lifted up a heavy garment, dragged down

with the weight of panniers, busk and whalebone. Her great grandmother's wedding dress. The satin brocade was perhaps once a delicate primrose, but the years and the dust had darkened the fabric to grainy sepia. The folds were as brittle as old parchment. She scooped up the hem of the gown, solicitous that it should not fall heavily to the floor dragging at the voluminous skirts and so distressing the cloth.

She curved and wriggled, accommodating her slender body to the unwieldy arrangements of the bodice which was like a breastplate. The panniers were so wide she would have stuck fast in any doorway in the curate's house.

The wedding dress looked hard and yellow and impossibly antique in the sliver of mirror that gaped at her from behind the wardrobe door. The bones gripped tight, suffocating her in the sultry heat. Gauds of sweat over her mouth. Her hair was slick and divided into two wings over the panniers, which tilted as though in parody of a courtesan's swaying hips when she walked or when she spun round, carefully watching her reflection.

The gown was cut low, too low over her breasts. She saw the rosy aureole peeping over the rim of the bodice, gleaming like a ruby, beaded as with sweat. She drew her white hand over her left breast. She moved closer to her reflection; not the aureoled blush of the poets' rhapsodies after all. Scarcely that. Uncomfortable in the crush of whalebone, she tugged at the bodice. In the mirror, low on her breast, she observed, like a badge of love, perhaps where his mouth in ardour had grazed her, a tiny crimson pustule.

18

He really had no choice in the matter. He had to marry her. It was his fate. When the message came – just the one word, 'Lovesickness' – he knew his fate was sealed. A blighted rose, a crimson bud pitted with black spots, fell out of the envelope. She could not have let him know more plainly that she knew the nature of her sickness.

Now at last the long heat of the summer was gone. The morning he heard from her a sulphurous fog smothered the moors, a gritty, polluted atmosphere that flung itself over the land, an asphyxiating brew that was belched out by the industrial towns encircling the Hopgate estate.

For weeks he had procrastinated, alternating between bouts of drunkenness and sobriety when the house seemed to seal itself around him like a vault. Most of the servants had gone. Now that his father-in-law's purse was closed to him, he had to maintain a more frugal household. When he had drink in him he made plans, was incisive, imaginative, blending obstacles into the distance of his canvas; but on his dry days, panic, like a palsy of the will, incapacitated him and his horrors were foregrounded, blotting out perspective. Two black ravens sat on his shoulders, twin demons that when he was sober he mockingly thought of as two wives.

He was glad of the fog. It shut out possibility that mocked him. He welcomed the erasure of everything. No more illusions of status, position; no more the delusion of true love, grand passion. I've grown up at last, he thought. I've lost the dream of happiness.

There was only one thing to be done – the wryly honourable thing: marry Agnes. Feelings no longer mattered. He would never feel again. The blood was sucked dry in him. His body was a citadel besieged by invaders who had blockaded his heart. Nothing would ever penetrate his heart again. He was isolated inside himself, a prisoner of fate.

The fog wrapped itself around him; it was madness, perhaps, to go out over the moors on such a day, but how could a lost soul miss its way? There was a little light, a yellowish haze, that left a few inches of visibility ahead of him and slowly, through an eerily muffled world as if nature was silenced by the heavy air, he made his way to the curate's house.

Lamps were lit although it was morning, because of the gloom. A maid was there this time and let him in. The curate was in his study and came out in delighted surprise but Jonathan cut short his affable welcome.

'I have some business with your daughter, Slane.' He would not, could not go through with the trite, meaningless ritual of asking for Miss Slane's hand in matrimony.

The curate would have discouraged Jonathan from seeing the sick woman, but one look at Hopgate's wild expression, that almost vicious smile, and he made do with a mere 'Well, well the poor child's not been at all fit but perhaps your visit will perk her up. Cissie, go on in and see if Agnes is well enough to see our visitor.'

And there she was, lovely as ever, perhaps lovelier for that hectic flush; that glitter of eyes gave her a certain febrile animation. She sat on the sofa propped up on cushions, an Indian shawl wrapped around her dark dress. There was the mourning brooch at her throat and her slippery hair was scraped into a tight knot. She looked clean and long-limbed as always, and he felt a sense of relief as if he had half expected some rapid degeneration of corporeality, a deliquescence, the reduction of healthy womanhood to sputum, abscess, blood and pus.

There was a lamp on the small table by her couch, a book on her lap – sermons by John Donne. There were the Berlin chairs, the piano forte, the prints of cathedrals, the ecclesiastical calm. All as it had been before. All very well. No disorder. No wildness, just this civilised domesticity and the woman very still, one hand at her white throat, the other resting on her book.

In a vase a dying bouquet of crimson roses.

It will not be long, love,

Till our wedding day.

'How are you?' he asked her, his white face suddenly dark with blood. There was a stillness in the room. A grandfather clock chimed on the landing.

'I'm beyond everything,' she said.

'You'll marry me?' he rushed in with a wild panic.

'You'll wed another corpse?' she said evenly.

'You look very well, Agnes.' He resolved to ignore her sarcasm.

'I'm not myself, that's all. I gave myself away when I lay with you,' she said.

'You must hate me.'

'I dread you.'

'Oh you musn't fear me, Agnes. I'm not an ogre.'

'That's just what you are – a fearsome man who has planted filth in me.'

'How sick are you?' He could not meet her gaze.

'How sick? Soul sick, heart sick, love sick,' she said.

'How much do you know?'

'Enough. The doctor wasn't too fastidious to go into details. He believed women in my condition were bold enough to take the unvarnished truth.'

'His prognosis?'

'He thinks I have not taken a heavy dose. I may well recover completely. I think the shock of the affair being laid before my father blunted my fears at first about the consequence of the illness on my own life.'

'He knows nothing?'

'Thank God the doctor agreed to spare him. He believes I have something called green sickness.'

'Are you in discomfort?' His voice trembled.

'A little pain; I'm often feverish and my head aches. But the worst of it . . .'

'Yes,' he said, not wanting to hear.

'It's the sensation of dirt. And I feel as if . . . down there . . .' she turned scarlet '. . . I'm infested with snakes. Like that creature in mythology who wanted to escape nether monsters, but she couldn't because they were the base part of her and everywhere she went

185

of course they went too. You look away from me. Do I shock you? How strange that my words should shock you after what your body has done to mine.'

'It wasn't my fault. It was Lily,' he said.

'Ah, the dying bride! Then it wasn't consumption?'

'She had been rotting for years,' he spat.

'And what of you?' she asked him. 'Do you have any of the symptoms of the pox?'

Again he was startled by the frankness of her speech. 'For the moment I'm free of active sickness, but it's a curious kind of liberty that may be merely a suspension of sentence.'

'Sentence,' she echoed, looking out of the window at the sepia fog. Sentenced to death. Sentenced to marriage. A life sentence. She began laughing, softly, recklessly. 'All my dreams have come true – you want to marry me.' She went on laughing.

'Do you accept?'

'Marry my sin?'

'Marry me. Live at High Withens. There is nothing for you here.'

She stopped laughing. 'No, there's nothing here for me. And we have already been made one in our sickness. We married death first, and now we're only fit to marry each other.'

'Then it's settled?'

'Yes, it's settled,' she said as if she could only echo him. She extended the hand that had been resting on the book and he raised it to his lips. A passionless, chaste kiss. 'I'll tell my father. He will think his prayers have been answered when I tell him I'm to be mistress of High Withens.'

'High Withens is all I can offer you,' Jonathan said.

'You know I'll never be a rich man,' he went on. 'The estate doesn't bring in much, and Lily spent most of her dowry on the house. But as my wife you'll occupy a certain position in society that may compensate you for — '

'The loss of health?'

'I rather hope you will recover completely. If the doctor thinks your case not to be a serious one, there is every possibility you will soon be yourself again.'

'I will never be myself again.' She spoke coldly, without even the passion of bitterness. He would have preferred it if she had railed at him, indulged in the vaporous sorrow of the hysteric, sobbed out her violence, attacked him for his violation of her health. She did not make scenes. She would be the perfect wife. She would never disgrace him. He could count on her for that. She would grace the lineage of the Hopgates even if she could not purify their bad blood.

There was a deadness between them as if the heaviness in the air had entered the house and vitiated their spirits. He thought it would be inappropriate to make amorous gestures, or even utter the endearments of love; they would seem a cruel irony. It seemed more fitting somehow to discuss practicalities.

'When would it suit you to arrange the wedding?' he asked her in a steadier voice.

'As soon as possible. I hate to live this lie in my father's house.'

'What about the proprieties?'

'Oh, you mean what will society think when we marry fast on the death of your wife?' She smiled bleakly. She leaned towards him and Donne's sermons slipped from her lap. He watched her stiffen.

Her smile slipped and she said, 'Hell gapes and you think society matters!' Then she smiled again as if the thought gave her great satisfaction.

He told her of course she wasn't bad, it was the blood of vulgar tradespeople that had brought them to this sorry pass.

'How are the mighty fallen!' she said soberly.

'Amen to that,' he agreed without irony, and if the part played by his damnable Hopgate pride in this sorry predicament occurred to him, he did not acknowledge it.

He told her to make whatever arrangements suited her, said naturally a special licence would be best and merely two witnesses would be needed. There was to be no fuss. But after the ceremony this would be like any other marriage, they would make the best of things, trust the contagion would not flourish, live happily as man and wife, live happily ever after.

'You know I love you,' he lied. 'I need you as my wife.' And he wondered his tongue didn't shrivel and blacken at such scandalous untruths, and whether her heart like his was dead and cold because syphilis had slain it.

Dispiritedly they discussed the details that should be observed and then, in an attempt to lighten the atmosphere and establish some measure of concord if not affection between them, he said, 'I thought a wedding trip would raise our spirits, and I've often dreamed of going to Italy again. You would love Florence, Agnes.' And for the first time in months his smile had nothing of dissimulation in it.

'Italy?' she said, her eyes dilating, her mouth agape. 'Oh no, I could never bear the heat. And I've heard that the stench, the . . . the foreignness of everything can be discomforting.'

He was astonished at her vehemence. 'Naturally we would not stay for the summer months. I know how they can prove a trial for an English gentlewoman. But really you need have no fear of squalid conditions. I don't have a lot of money, but when I was last in Italy I managed to live tolerably well in a succession of apartments in rather beautiful palazzos. Italy is very cheap and the poorer quarters of the towns are easily avoided.'

'I will not go abroad,' she said. 'If I am not to go under completely I need clean English air, wholesome Anglo-Saxon fare, perhaps medicinal English spa waters. A month in your beloved Italy would kill me, I know it.'

Another of his dreams to be given up, then!

'I really think you exaggerate the danger of foreign things, Agnes,' he said. 'Of course I wouldn't submit you to an unsuitable way of life, but I would have thought you would have welcomed the opportunity to travel abroad.'

Her mouth turned down like Lily's so often had, and for a moment he had a sensation that he was sitting with Lily again and her death was a dream and Agnes was still pure and virginal.

'I cannot go to Italy with you,' she repeated. 'You must understand. I don't want any hot sun festering the filth in my body. I want to be clean again and I can only become clean in England.'

There should have been calla-lilies, an ivory bridal train and a flurry of satin slippers and nuptial rice. Instead there was bleak church, on the coldest day of the year, with a sky white as leprosy, and a stony faced bride.

He remembered how, when he first saw her, he had likened her to a stone angel, the memorial on a tomb, and the wicked thought came to him that she was the marble monument raised over Lily's corpse, the petrified image of sin. Sin at his side, in a sweet blue silk dress; sin smelling clean and lovely; sin cool and passionless; sin looking grim.

She responded to the Reverend Beech's prompts like a shy virgin with a low tremulous voice. Her father, an elated witness, seemed not to be aware she was marrying a man very recently widowed. His palpable pride that his daughter had got the catch of the county, while Beech's five were still on the market and not an eligible gentleman in sight, carried them all through the ordeal of the service. The other witness was a young widow, Mrs Tow, and as they left the church Jonathan slipped a small remembrance in her palm.

After the quiet service her father pressed them to celebrate in her old home but Agnes was determined to get away quickly to High Withens.

A slow silent ride on horseback, from the valley up to a land of cumuli and engorged escarpments, sappy hollows and hopelessly entangled copses. It seemed as if they were riding forever. The earth was glutinous with fallen leaves and the pulpy detritus splashed them as they travelled, distressing their hopeful wedding clothes. Birdsong was muted here, and only the interminable shusha-shush-shusha of the beck that gushed beside their tortuous path broke in on their silence.

When they emerged from the woods on to the moors a light snow began to fall.

'It'll be a white Christmas,' Jonathan said, and the banal words fell between them and they wondered how they would ever make a life together.

Two upright coffins beyond a stagnant tarn that was swampy with waterlilies.

He looked again, and he saw High Withens with its east and west wings lowering over the valley, and the choked pond in front of the house, the only aspect Lily hadn't planned on reviving.

There was a light meal waiting for them and he poured her champagne, but all she would take was a little cake and a cup of coffee. She said she felt quite well when he asked her guardedly if she had any sickness. And he felt relief because really she did look splendid – a little thin, her face lightly flushed, and he noticed the bones on her wrists and shoulders were prominent – but wraithlike as she was, there was a certain animation to her movements. Indeed, she could barely sit still. She wasn't slothful, as Lily had been.

'More coffee?' he pressed her. 'You eat like a bird, Agnes.' He urged her to eat because a long journey lay ahead of them, and although the steam locomotive made miles seem like yards there would be delays when they came to change trains in London. They were to catch the steam locomotive to Portsmouth at Nine Elms, for Jonathan had extravagantly taken a villa in Southsea for two months, reluctantly giving up any hope of Florence.

'Southsea!' She said the name of the comparatively new resort had an exotic ring to it, and yet the coast had good salt English air with recuperative powers, and there was the opportunity to indulge in spa baths because she had heard about an establishment there where sea water was pumped into special baths that were recommended for invalids. And she looked forward to immersing herself in the saline baths, scouring herself inside and out until she was quite clean again.

She was anxious to be gone but first she must, she really must, take off her wedding dress, she said, and put on the travelling costume that had been her father's wedding gift to her.

'I'd like a bath before we leave, Jonathan,' she said.

There was a slipper bath in a box room, he told her, and he'd have one of the two female servants (apart from the cook) that had remained set the tub out in the bedroom and carry up the necessary gallons of hot water. While she went up to undress for her bath Jonathan supervised the loading of the carriage that was to take them the thirty odd miles to the railway station.

She was obliged to wait some time for the water to heat in the scullery coppers and while she waited she took some powders and herbs out of her reticule and mixed them together in a little bowl. It took ten gallons to fill the bath and the maid left her two tin jugs with lids to add more hot water when the temperature of the bath became too cool. Before she stepped into the tub she scooped up a handful of dried herbs and flowers, an old wives' concoction of medicinal powders, and stirred them vigorously into the water.

The water was green as a pre-Raphaelite version of England. The bath had a gingery purgative heat that relaxed her. Her flesh grew red. She began to sweat in the herbal steam. Greenish vapour, vapid as desire. I want to be clean, she prayed. She thought if there was time, after the herbal bathwater had grown quite cold, she would ask the girl to fetch more pails of hot water. A salt bath would be the thing to scour the viscous, clinging discharge that kept leaking out of her.

Where the herbal bath opened her pores that exuded their own humid liquor, the salt bath stung her and stripped her skin of its natural oils. She had insisted the water should be hot enough to scald her, and her skin was very tender so that after bathing, when she was dry, she had to rub a cream made from honey and beeswax into the blanched flesh.

Jonathan had checked the luggage half a dozen times, walked around the house twice to make sure nothing had been forgotten, picked at some more of the wedding breakfast, drunk too much coffee and not enough champagne, sent a maid up three times to see if her mistress had at last finished bathing, cursed roundly at the delay, resisted the temptation to go up and drag the woman out of her damn bath, and was just preparing himself to get very drunk and put off the journey until tomorrow when Agnes came down, looking pink and white and smelling like a laundry.

'About time,' he said.

'A very husbandly comment,' she teased him, feeling all lightness now that the soiled, sticky sensation was for the moment allayed. She wore a soft grey travelling costume that had a lavender sheen to it.

'You look very beautiful,' he said, trying to sound lover-like, not husbandly.

Yes, very beautiful, he thought. A real beauty – only beauty means nothing to me. Beauty is a sham.

19

They journeyed south as a heavy snow began to fall and the sky pressed close to the earth extinguishing what was left of daylight. They took a maid and the cook with them, and so the close proximity of the servants, first in the carriage then in the train compartment, stifled any possibility of intimate conversation. Though Jonathan strapped the carriage blinds down securely, and they were crushed close together in the confined space, they were soon chilled through as snow flew in scuds around the carriage.

Then the first train was bitterly cold and the black smuts from the engine mingled with the driven snow, and what seemed like a pall of grey slime rapidly coated the windows of the locomotive. And this is what she would remember of her wedding day, mused Agnes: the interminable journey through grimy air, the awkward silence of servants, and the freezing cold that gave her an ague.

But on the Portsmouth train they travelled into a limpid night. And as they reached Hampshire the milder southern air dispelled the atmosphere of ice they had brought with them. An indigo sky. The clarity of stars. A witchy brilliance.

'A beautiful, beautiful night,' she breathed, at last roused from the miseries of travelling.

They caught the last omnibus from the station to the seafront. The servants went on ahead to deal with the cold house and bride and groom spent their wedding night at The Royal Pier Hotel with its views of the sea and the Common.

'In the daylight you can see the Island,' Jonathan called out to Agnes, who was leaning over the narrow iron balcony that opened out from their room overlooking the Solent. Below her waves shrugged. Above, gulls wailed like banshees.

'I can taste salt on the air.' She licked her dry lips. Her body trembled when Jonathan came over to her. He wrapped his arm around her waist.

'Be careful, Agnes. It's a perilous ledge.' He drew her away from the rail, drew her back into the room where the lamp was turned down so there was a low, tactful light. Before he shut the glass doors she heard the siren's sigh of the waves as they dragged the land back with them to the fathomless deep.

Jonathan lifted the salty hair from the back of her neck and kissed her swiftly – a light kiss, lighter than the touch of a gull's wing.

'I'd like to wash,' she whispered. How strange it was, this virgin formality between them.

There was an edge to his voice when he said, 'I'll

go down to the billiards room and have a cigar. Will twenty minutes be enough for you?'

She nodded dully. Her head ached after the long journey. She wanted sleep. She wanted forgetfulness.

It was a comfortless bed with scratchy sheets. She was so weary, so headachy that she tried too hard to sleep before her husband's return and thus was wide awake, her head thumping, when he came in.

They both lay very still at first, still as the dead between the stiff sheets, scarcely breathing. Then he drew her to him. His breath on her neck made her shiver, his hand on her thigh made her stomach muscles clench hard as iron. He began to urge vague endearments that meant nothing to her. But if desire had gone from his dreams too, if longing drifted from his imagination, if fantasy took no part in his lovemaking, his body knew nothing of it. His body impelled him. The sudden conflagration of flesh on flesh. He had to have her.

She didn't move. She didn't stir from him. Then, as he slid on top of her, entering delirium, she said softly, moaning the words like love's own litany, words he barely registered until she repeated them, 'Jonathan! Jonathan!'

'Yes, my love?'

'Take your filth out of me. Take your filth out of me, Jonathan.'

The house they rented was close to the Common in a twisting, sinuous road that was laid out like a garden path. A white stucco house with spun sugar turrets, ice frosting crenellations, and inside, barely dry plastered walls that shivered a powdery whiteness over everything.

'It's spotless!' Agnes exclaimed, delighted because it was a new house without contamination.

When they were settled, she persuaded him to accompany her to the bathing establishment where she would take her sea-bath cure. The Clarence Rooms, hard by Clarence Pier where the ferry plied its route between the mainland and the Island, was built like a temple, with delicate columns and high, smooth walls.

'Must we really go through with this nonsense?' Jonathan tried to force a humorous tone to his voice but he felt cold and sick with humiliation, because although last night he had compelled Agnes to perform her wifely duties she had immediately afterwards got out of bed to wash away the traces of his ardour.

'I must be clean,' she said solemnly. 'I must keep myself pure,' she went on, like a zealout preparing for baptism.

He felt a bubble of rage rise in his throat. Was she trying to mangle what was left of his manhood? He must stay calm. This was a phase. She would get over it. When they got home to High Withens, in the fullness of time, she would be herself again.

They entered the Clarence Rooms together, but had to part in the long tiled hall because there were separate suites for the sexes. Within each suite a variety of special baths was offered: hot baths, cold baths, seaweed baths, vapour baths, showers and hose baths, medicinal baths, beauty treatment baths, neurasthenic baths, melancholia baths, recuperative baths, lethargy baths, gout baths, obesity baths, diuretic baths, choler baths, anaemia baths, respiratory baths, mania baths, moral madness baths, falling sickness baths, temperance baths, skin disease baths, paralytic baths, consumptive baths, cure-all baths, baths for the very young, and dotage baths for the old.

No baths were specified for the treatment of syphilis.

Jonathan decided a cure-all bath would be as good as anything. He heard the boom and rush of sea water, fifty gallons pumped in a minute, as he followed an assistant down a steamy passage. In a cool marble room he was asked to remove his clothes and provided with long calico drawers to preserve his modesty. Then an attendant hosed him down with warm seawater to loosen grime. Next he had to lie down on what looked like a marble fish slab while the man rubbed a liquor brewed from boiled seaweed into him. After the massage, a pleasant doze as a very hot bath was prepared, and the fragrant steam from the tub enveloped him in a haze of well-being.

When he was first immersed in the bath he found the water a little too hot, but the fellow indicated he was to endure this if the vitality of the seaweed and herbs was to work efficiently. Then it seemed the indulgent aspect of the process was for the moment done with, and he was asked to step out of the bath to be hosed down again with ice-cold saline water. And then – oh horror – he was again lain on the slab and huge winding sheets, which had been soaking in a pail with slabs of ice, were wound tightly around him. He was swaddled like a baby, his limbs turning blue as the circulation of his blood was restricted and he, half fainting from cold and claustrophobia, trying to be manful under the rigorous treatment, almost wept from the unendurable suffering.

When he thought he was going to die of exposure the brute of a fellow returned with shards of brittle, dried seaweed and when the sheets were removed and his body could breathe, his skin was assaulted by an exfoliating treatment. When he was rubbed raw, it seemed the top layer of epidermis flayed, a birch was produced and the heat restored to his body by a vigorous strapping with a cat o' nine tails of leathery seaweed fronds.

Then, sweet Jesus, the agony of an immersion up to his neck in a bath impregnated with sea-salt. He thought the blood would ooze at any moment.

As if, at the last, his tormentor decided to show mercy, he was placed gently in a gelid, brown bath of seaweeds. The water was larded with emollients and soothed his sore flesh, coating the thinned skin with a layer of protective grease.

And after, once more displayed on the slab, he was massaged firmly with salves and unguents so his skin glowed, his muscles drooled and he drifted into a dream of intoxicating health.

Agnes fared better. Ladies were given less rigorous treatment. She elected for the gentle baths provided for neurasthenia.

In her shift she was submerged in a stone tank filled with the chalky water of the region that drained down from the Portsdown hill. The water was tepid, not cold, and when she climbed out of the tank she was given a glass of the water to drink. It tasted smooth and a trace of white powder filmed the glass when she had finished drinking. Next, a shower of warmed sea water with its briny fizz invigorated her. The sea-plants bath which followed was a green jelly through which her limbs looked like the murky appendages of a mysterious sea creature. The glutinous flip flop of the stuff cossetted her. She squelched in it for half an hour then had another shower to wash away the slime. A hot bath and a cold bath after, then a vapour bath which she liked better; the pores of her skin were opened, exuding the grime she imagined inhabited her. Hot steam filled the room. Her lungs were saturated with heat. She breathed in thick, smoking air, like a soul languishing in Hades.

A rosewater bath was a luxury for which she paid extra. Scented water with a pot pourri of posies, that were impregnated with perfumed oils and exquisite essences, filled the bath. She did not want to get out of it. The scent was so sweet, so overwhelmingly seductive, as was the oily sheen of the water itself which was roseate and blushing. She would like such a bath every day of her life, she decided, and wondered if she could ask for the recipe to take away with her.

She was loth to leave her watery bower of flowers, and made an appointment for the next day to repeat the same treatment. Let Jonathan pay for it. Whatever he paid would not pay off the moral debt he owed her.

They strolled along the pier. In the distance they could see the steamboat head for the Isle of Wight – a low slump of land with a purplish haze over it.

'We could maybe tour the island in a charabanc,' Jonathan suggested. 'The climate is supposed to be very mild, even at this time of year.'

A salt breeze rushed in cool draughts over their wonderfully pristine complexions. They breathed in the ozone, the salty, seaweedy air.

'It's a fine day here in any case,' Agnes said, ignoring

Jonathan's suggestion. The pier was fairly crowded with promenaders although it was the winter season, and they had to push their way through groups of happy English families.

They continued walking across the Common. A military band played belligerent music. Elsewhere other soldiers enacted maneouvres on the smooth sward.

'It's hard to imagine where we tread now was once marsh and scrubland. A desolate spot, by all accounts,' Jonathan said conversationally. 'Teams of convicts were brought in to drain the land,' he continued, making futile conversation and racking his memory for the snippets of information he had gleaned from the Hollingsworth guide to Portsmouth. He must strive to sustain normal relations with his wife, he told himself. How else would they ever make a life together?

'What do you say to a jaunt over to the Isle of Wight tomorrow, then?' he reminded her.

She looked up at him distractedly. 'Oh, I've booked another course of baths at the Clarence Rooms for tomorrow. You go by yourself. You'll have more freedom without me trailing about after you.'

'This is our wedding trip,' he said evenly. 'We're supposed to be trailing about in each other's company.'

Her voice sounded cold. She removed her arm from his when she said, 'But this isn't a normal honeymoon is it, Jonathan? This isn't a wedding tour. It's a cure. This trip is about infection, not affection,' she said.

They continued walking east, following the line of newly built pastel villas that were filling the gaps between the buff Regency terraces. They walked in silence to the rhythm of military music.

There was no trip to the sylvan island. His wife spent

the next morning, and the next, and all the mornings that followed, plunging herself in curative baths.

Mornings of misery for Jonathan, who smoked and walked restlessly before collecting Agnes from the Clarence Rooms.

They headed west, climbing the iron stairs that led up to the fortified walls of Old Portsmouth. They walked briskly along the ramparts before descending more steps that wound down to narrow cobbled streets, decaying Georgian coffee houses, and the promiscuous sprawl of the dock area. Old Portsmouth was another world, a workaday world, not given over to leisure and frivolous pastime. The briny odours here were mingled with the smells of tar, refuse, open sewers and centuries old plumbing. In narrow doorways lurked strange peoples with faces and colours such as Agnes had never seen before.

'I feel a little dizzy, Jonathan.'

But he was keen to explore the tumbledown courts at the back of the High Street, to observe the exertions of the dock labourers, to stare at the broad-shouldered women who salted fish and whose sacking-cloth skirts were hitched well above naked ankles.

Agnes hung behind him, her skirts and petticoats dragging over the detritus of the squalid streets. Tardily she followed him into a smoky coffee house where it seemed she was the only woman but none appeared to object to her presence. Jonathan ordered coffee. He seemed happier than she had seen him in a long while as they sat in a small oak cubicle in the sloping wood-panelled room, where cigar smoke made the air blue and drowsy. The coffee was too strong and she was not sure if the cup was quite clean and she thought longingly of the spotless white house behind a thicket of bushes where servants were heating up water in copper boilers for the succession of baths she would have tonight.

'Have you had enough of your cures yet?' he asked her.

'Enough?' She raised an eyebrow quizzically at him and put down her coffee cup.

'Is the cure complete?' he pressed her, a little grimly.

'I feel better, but not truly cleansed,' she said, 'like a sinner who repents but awaits the absolution of baptismal waters,' she added in a high, clear voice that made him look around nervously in case anyone had overheard her.

'For God's sake, Agnes, I think you're going overboard with all these damn baths. You strike me as half crazy with this obsession about dirt.'

'Don't you want me to be completely cured?' she asked him, her eyes squinting with displeasure and cigar smoke.

'That's not the case and you know it. But it seems to me there's very little sign of any sickness in you any more. In my opinion you're as fit as you ever were.'

She leaned over the table to him, her voice very low now, and he could see the blue vein pulse in her neck. 'Don't pretend this is real health, Jonathan. Don't be fooled by appearances. There is a sickness inside us which slumbers, remember, and may awaken any time, rise up and scourge our bodies. I fight it my own way, not with your poor Lily's poisons. I'll scour the evil from me. Let me have some more bath treatments.

Indulge me. You owe me that at least,' she added, her eyes watering with the smoke.

'And you owe me a wife's dues, remember that too,' he said roughly. 'I'll pay for water cures. But you'll have to be a proper wife to me.'

Her white cambric nightgown rucked around her shoulders, she was stiff as a ramrod as he pushed into her. She lay quite still as he ground his teeth, as he ground her bones, like an ogre. Why does he have to do this, she agonised, praying for it to be over. He doesn't care for my feelings. What if I have a child? What kind of monster might it be, she wondered. The sheets were mussed; the covers slid from the bed. Her stomach muscles were taut, her fists clenching the mattress. His sucks were more like bites covering her with blemishes. He was driven in on himself, grinding himself into delirium with an aggression that dismayed her. Then she felt the slime drip within and, to his intense irritation, she was out of the bed straightaway and in the dark he heard the chink of the china jug against the ewer and the gush of water. He heard her washing, tearing at herself as if she required abrasion to remove his defiling fluids. When she returned to bed she slept on the edge of the mattress, careful not to touch him.

They went home in a freezing spring and he was glad to be back at High Withens, although his bride sighed and found the slipper bath in the bedroom unsatisfactory and thought longingly of the summer months when she secretly planned a trip back to Southsea for another sea-cure.

She was nervous as a cat, wandering all over High Withens, refusing to be still, planning, relentlessly planning to get away again. Then High Withens frustrated her attempts to organise dirt – it was too vast, too rambling, and there weren't enough servants. She scarcely made a mark on it, though she started early in the morning with buckets and pails, the dust seemed to drift through the house like an uninvited vagrant, and as soon as the lower rooms were cleansed a pall of dust descended like a cloud again from the upper regions.

She was quite worn out from all the cleaning but could not rest, and when Jonathan suggested it might be more profitable to channel her energies towards helping him with estate matters she turned a deaf ear to him.

They sat over a breakfast that was prolonged by his wife's bouts of hand-washing. She looked well, he thought, no sign of any illness, no fever or pains; she looked young, too young to be a wife to him, but beautiful as she was he was no longer troubled by fantasies of desire for her. Only at night, with the proximity of flesh, did he have to couple with her as an animal might. He wasn't responsible; he was the victim of instinct. She was flesh of his flesh now, so he could have no more illusions. And how could he truly love when he had no illusions? Love was a delusion, anyway. They were happy enough. They had made a bargain. Grand passion was for the young. He was no longer young.

A strand of hair had worked itself loose from her lace cap and he enjoyed seeing the sweet disorder. It seemed as though lust, if not love, still stirred him.

'You're looking very beautiful,' he said quietly. 'I

think the sea-cure must have worked after all; you grow more radiant.'

'Do you think so?' she said eagerly. 'I think the cure suited me so well it was a shame not to continue the treatment.'

'Yes,' he said abstractedly.

'Couldn't we try it again in the summer?'

'What?'

'Jonathan, I long to go back to the south coast. Please, let's shut up High Withens and go south for the summer.'

'But we've just spent three months in the damn place. To tell you the truth I'm glad to be back at my own fireside.'

'But my health?' she wheedled.

'Maybe next year, when I can afford it,' he conceded.

She frowned and her mouth turned down and he wondered if that was a trick all women had.

'Even if I could afford another trip I should be too busy to go off holidaying.'

'What do you have to be so busy about?' she asked petulantly.

'Well, to be blunt, if revenue from the tenant farms continues to decline, I shall be hard put to keep up this place. The old methods don't work any more, Agnes, there's been an agricultural revolution in England which seems to have by-passed the farmers on this estate. I'm determined to introduce new methods, enclose more of the common land, persuade the tenants to invest in the new machinery. I want to run a more profitable estate and I can't afford shirkers. I've dismissed the bailiff, and from now on I'll manage my own inheritance.'

When he finished speaking she got up and went over to a sideboard where a bowl of water and a cake of soap and a towel were laid out for her. As she washed her hands she called over to him carelessly, 'But it wouldn't cost much for me to go to Southsea. I could lodge very cheaply in a couple of rooms. It wouldn't cost you much for board and keep for me.'

'You couldn't posibly go alone,' he said, astonished and not a little angry.

'Oh I wouldn't be alone,' she said, reddening. 'I'd have the Belton girl with me.'

'The farmer's daughter?' he quizzed her. 'What on earth would she go with you for? I'm sure her father couldn't spare her.'

'Oh, haven't you heard?' she said lightly. 'Belton's to be married again.'

'Married? Who'd have that drunken sot?'

'But he's found sobriety. He has been saved by the Low Withens Temperance Society, and now he's not falling down drunk Miss Hemp has agreed to marry him. Not unnaturally Esther is anxious to be out of the house before her new stepmother walks in; she knows she wouldn't rule the roost any more.'

'But how do you know she'd come with you?'

'I asked her last week,' she said guiltily. 'I asked her to be my companion.'

'Your paid companion?' he said sarcastically.

'She needs little more than food and lodging, Jonathan.'

'And what of me? Isn't my wife supposed to be my companion?'

'But you've just told me how busy you're going to

be with the estate. You wouldn't have much time to spare for me, Jonathan.'

'I rather supposed you would wish to take your place alongside me. There is a part for the mistress of High Withens to play on this estate, you know,' he said angrily. 'And you of all people, with your connections with the local community, your experience of parish affairs, are most fitted to be my helpmeet.'

'I think you have idealised me, Jonathan. I always did find parish work a little tedious. I'm not the girl I was. I'm rather sick of things like duty. I want to have time for myself,' she asserted.

'You're the mistress of this estate,' he told her, 'the tenants expect you to take an interest in them.'

She fingered the loose strand of hair thoughtfully. She looked up at him and smiled slyly. 'But if the tenants knew the mistress of High Withens had syphilis, they'd bar their doors to her.'

20

The girl stared at Violetta Hemp, eyes glazed like a doll – pale blank eyes, revealing nothing.

'I'm here to take some of the responsibilities from you, my dear.' Miss Hemp's voice racketed around the dusty room. Her shawl slithered from one shoulder. She placed a heavily ringed hand on Esther's arm. 'I know you've been more than a mother to your poor sisters . . . and of course there've been other trials . . .' Her voice trailed and they both glanced instinctively in the direction of the parlour. 'But that's all in the past.'

Miss Hemp drew a chair up to the kitchen table and sat facing her future daughter. She gathered the girl's soft, seemingly boneless hands into her own, pressing them so hard the rings cut Esther's fingers.

She spoke in a loud whisper. 'Your father is filled with remorse. For everything. You understand?'

Esther said nothing. Her eyes gave no clue to her feelings.

'Everyone knows you've been an exemplary daughter and done the best for your sisters.'

'I did my duty – no more, no less,' Esther said primly. Her eyelids lowered, her hands sore from the pressure of Violetta Hemp's ardent grip, she had the faraway look of a martyr.

Miss Hemp smiled. 'Yes, that's just it. You've had a plateful of duty, and only that slip of a girl, Annie, to help you, my dear. Now perhaps, if you will let me, I'll lighten these tasks for you. You're the merest child yet – your father and I want you to have a little pleasure at last, to enjoy the affections of family life.'

'It has been my pleasure to care for my father and sisters since Mama died,' Esther said tonelessly.

'Of course.' Miss Hemp shook Esther's imprisoned hands. A demonstrative woman, she wanted to hug the girl, but was foiled by the wide wooden table. 'And your father wants you to know how, in spite of his sometimes reckless behaviour, he has always cherished his daughters.'

Esther looked at the older woman and said, 'I know well how he cherishes me.'

Miss Hemp lowered her head, her voice growing hoarse with the attempt to whisper. 'I know, my dear, everyone knows the horrors you girls have lived through. But your papa vows, on your poor dear mama's soul, the time of darkness is over. The demons that leap out of spiritous liquor have been exorcised. Your papa is no longer plagued by them.' She began stroking the girl's piteous hand, the one that was withered, shrivelled like a prune, virtually useless. Esther stiffened.

Miss Hemp rattled on. 'He's a new man, my dear. He has repented.' She smiled coyly at the sober girl. 'We must see to it that he discovers the new pleasures of a loving home life.'

A loving home – oh yes, love!

Esther's father came in and Violetta Hemp looked up, her face radiant, her shawls and scarves dipping and trailing; she looked like a gypsy reading the palm of his eldest daughter.

'I know we'll be a real family, dearest. Call in Lucy and Martha, I want to hug the dear things.'

Lucy and Martha, called in from the garden, allowed themselves to be clasped and kissed by Miss Hemp who waxed lyrical on the joys of motherhood.

Esther remained seated and picked up her sewing, stabbing the needle with her good hand through her sister's stockings, trying not to look at her father. When they had escaped from their new, soon to be mama's clutch, the two younger girls raced off to feed the chickens and Esther, alone with Miss Hemp and her father, was soon forgotten – almost invisible to these two middle-aged lovers.

Such foolish palaver!

Farmer Belton drew the buxom form of Violetta Hemp to his lap, regardless of the sensitivities of his daughter.

He was a large man, dark as his affianced love, and strong, as if hewn out of granite. Miss Hemp's ringlets were soon unravelled. His huge hands were grasping her sturdy waist, his sharp voice softened to mutter the idiocies of affection.

Her father's boots, stretched out to the fender, were caked with mud. His boots were heavy. She remembered how this usually taciturn, dour man had worn such boots to kick her mother with.

A loving family!

Had her mother loved him? Had she loved any of them? Perhaps not, for didn't she die and leave them? She had left them to fend for themselves with a father who was sodden every night with drink. When Mama died, her father was disgustingly maudlin. Weeping into his gin, lamenting his dead wife's virtues, he cried out for pity, he who had been pitiless!

She almost hated his grief more than his violence.

Grief clung. Violence rejected. Grief swamped her with his arms, his drunken tears, pinned her down with stupor. A clout about the head was preferable and quickly finished with.

Grief filled the house with lachrymose malingering, made him stay at home, lie abed, making demands on his daughters. Drink drove him abroad – to inns, stews, the houses of the disreputable – drink meant absence so the house was quiet, empty with peace. The girls were alone then; no one disturbed them.

There were demons of sobriety as well as of intemperance.

Now, with his mouth open so she could see his tongue as he laughed heartily at one of Violetta Hemp's inanities, the peace was again broken.

Her father touched that woman heavily. She, too, pawed him. Their smiles were wreathed in intimacy. He laughed loudly. His laugh was sonorous and strong as a heartbeat. Miss Hemp giggled like a spoilt girl just out of the schoolroom.

Their tears flowed too quickly, smiles lasted too

long and their voices uttering the lunacies of love were raucous.

'Make us some tea, Esther,' her father called, at last acknowledging her presence.

Miss Hemp protested that she would do it. She wasn't here to be lounging like a princess and it was time Esther had a break, wasn't it?

Miss Hemp's laughing eyes. Her father's loose smile. A certain recklessness to these ageing lovers. And something else – what was it? Esther wondered as she refused Miss Hemp's offer and herself brewed tea and cut bread and cake in meagre slices.

The very air had grown abandoned.

Not just love in these lovers' intimacies, something else. What was it? Esther stopped pouring tea and stared at her father and the woman. Miss Hemp's stout ankles dangled between Farmer Belton's legs. Her father's strong hands were carelessly stroking his Violetta. There was something else. Something different. Esther slopped the tea in a saucer at the sudden startled realisation. Why, that's what it is then, she told herself, it's not just love, not passion merely: it's freedom, freedom in their very hearts. Freedom from poverty, as the fear died in Miss Hemp's eyes. In her father's grey eyes fear had fled too, fear that was the ghost of addiction.

Agnes had noticed the difference. Esther saw that at once, the way Agnes coloured when she saw Farmer Belton kiss his fiancée on the mouth in greeting. Violetta Hemp had always been a senseless rattle but she was harmless and people had pitied her poverty and were charitable.

Belton stopped Violetta's mouth in full flow as it

gushed about the deficiencies of the farmhouse which she intended to make good with quantities of sewing and repairing and—

'Please sit down, Mrs Hopgate,' Esther cut in over the disconcerting smack of a hearty kiss.

Her father disappeared to change his clothes for supper.

The parlour seemed much smaller now that Violetta Hemp's shawls and swags of scarves and lace were already draped everywhere.

'I'll go and see how things are going on in the kitchen,' Violetta gasped, breathless with embraces.

Agnes leaned against the pile of embroidered cushions that had been scattered on the sofa. 'Well, Esther,' she smiled. 'Your trials are over at last. I won't need to look in on you so much now you'll have a new mother.'

Esther sat opposite her in a high-backed chair. 'I have only ever had one mother. She is not forgotten by me,' she said in her curious voice that lacked emphasis.

'I'm sorry. I only meant you'll have someone to care for you all again.' Agnes spoke delicately. She kept a refreshingly cool distance from the girl.

Esther spoke in a low voice, leaning forward. 'I don't want her here, in Mama's place. I'll never accept her.'

'But Miss Hemp has a heart of gold. She would never do anything to hurt you,' Agnes said, astonished. 'And think of the freedom it will mean for you, no more of the vexations of housekeeping.'

Esther's blank eyes clouded. 'I like to do the chores,' she said woodenly. 'I like things, arranging things, seeing to food, clothes, teaching my sisters.'

'Well, I hardly suppose Miss Hemp will object to you helping around the house.'

'But there won't be any space when she comes, you see. She'll fill the house with her voice, her shawls, her stoutness, and my father will be at home more too, getting in my way. When she lives here there won't be any more . . . emptiness.'

'Well, it's a small house,' Agnes agreed.

Esther sat, stiffly aware of the halo of space she always drew round herself. 'She's well named,' she said enigmatically. Esther thought of her mama, and how the brutal embraces of her father were translated to tenderness in the arms of Violetta.

Agnes was bemused. 'What do you mean?' she asked. She looked curiously at the hunched, stiff girl, her withered arm hidden by the too long sleeve of her dress.

'Violetta violates the memory of my poor dead mama. Violetta the violator, violating Violetta,' Esther said.

Looking at the girl sitting in her pentacle of isolation, sitting very still, the image of repose, a presence that did not intrude, a slight figure taking up so little space in the disordered room, Agnes felt oddly calm, comforted.

If she had a daughter she imagined it would be like this, a deep pool of shared silence.

A tremulous hand slipped into hers – unlike a man's hand that grew tentacles to trap her!

'Esther,' Agnes said softly, 'I too fear violation. I understand. Why don't you come to me? There is space for you at High Withens.'

21

Jonathan didn't like the girl, a sour-faced creature with a frizz of blood-orange hair. She had a blotchy mole at the corner of her mouth that repulsed him.

'I hope you'll be happy here,' he had said conventionally. 'You must think of it as your home.' She didn't answer, only looking at him with lowered eyelids, a curiously closed-in expression on her face. A small, oddly gelid face as if no bones lay beneath it. When she walked he noticed a marionette quality to her movements and commented on this to Agnes when they were alone.

'She was born with a withered arm,' his wife told him. 'That's why she holds herself so stiffly.'

Holding on to herself tightly, rigid as a peg-doll, that one would never give anything away – she was a canny madam, he decided.

If he wanted to avoid the girl he must avoid his wife too, it seemed, because Agnes could not stir without her companion. Not that Esther could be said to intrude in any way. She was usually silent, not speaking until spoken to, hardly daring to look up at him with her colourless eyes. She had an immobile, expressionless face, eyelids always at half mast as if she was focused on looking within herself, as if she barely registered what was happening around her; so why did he have the uncomfortable feeling she was an omniscient presence, why did he have the sensation that everything he did and said she saw and heard?

There was indefinable sharpness in the atmosphere since she had moved into High Withens; sometimes when she passed him an acrid scent, as of vinegar, lingered in the air. He really couldn't understand his wife's prediliction for Belton's daughter. She had no conversation, no musical talents, none of the feminine arts that embellish the drawing room; a dull little thing, remote as a nun. Surely Agnes would tire of that constant presence which so irritated him. Perhaps when she'd endured the girl's company, alone, in confined lodgings, for a couple of months, she'd be easily persuaded to get rid of her, he mused. In the meantime he would close his eyes to the nuisance; in a couple of weeks they'd both be gone and when they returned he would take a firmer stand with Agnes.

Esther had drawn her breath in sharply the day Agnes brought her to High Withens, it stirred such memories; it was years ago that she had first come here with her mother to wander in the grounds. They had picnicked by the murky pool and her mother collected water lilies to amuse her. Then of course the house had been shut and there was no prospect of entering. This was before her two sisters had been born, that lost Eden of time before father began drinking. She remembered her mother, laughing, smiling, the two of them throwing small stones into the still water. In her memory it was a hot day and there was welcome shade in the trees and bushes planted round the house, so High Withens seemed half drowning in rampant greenery.

After, when the weight of Papa's violence suffocated her, she fled her own house and ran wild in these grounds, peeping in through windows at the realm of silence.

Only the sound of birdsong, the scamper of wildlife.

Through the windows she saw shadowy spaces where she could hide, endless corridors to escape down. Not a soul stirred. Within the house were only forsaken possessions that could not hurt her.

When I'm grown up, she had vowed as all children do, I'll live here in the holy silence. Not a boot will shuffle. Not a voice will rise to curse me. She would live here amidst the vast, peaceful depredation. When she was grown up and an almighty rich woman.

But the house, after all, was not so silent. There were the tantrums of the master, the mistress's vexations.

'What the devil are you doing now?' Jonathan demanded.

Unblemished light filled the library. The curtains had crumbled like shrouds when Agnes took them down from the windows. Esther was arranging books in piles classified according to their state of deterioration.

'I don't know how you can relax in all this dust and filth,' Agnes grumbled.

'You'll be off again soon enough. Why should it trouble you?' Jonathan retorted. Agnes compressed her lips, not wanting to argue in front of the girl. Carefully, Esther stood up and slipped out of the room. Outside she could hear the spasm of their contorted voices, the battle of words. A long corridor stretched before her, leading into silence like a cloister. She walked away from the violent sounds. She walked quickly up flights of stairs to her own room. The luxury of retreat. Up here it was as though those two no longer existed. How unlike her father's house that had vibrated with his passions, every stir of his unquiet soul assaulting the air. Her own room in this house folded round her like a reverie. She sat in the window seat watching a flight of birds alight on the battlements of the east wing. Sitting there for blessed moments. Then a push at her door, and Agnes entered. Esther could escape the master's scenes but not it seemed the woes of her mistress. All silence broken. Peace breached. Agnes was weeping. She was distraught. The calm woman Esther was familiar with was gone. Here was a wild-eyed stranger.

'What can I do?' Agnes beseeched her.

'It's best not to confront him,' Esther advised.

'But he won't let me evade him. He stood in front of the door like a gaoler.' Agnes curled on Esther's bed. The girl sat on a window seat watching her. Agnes went on, knotting her handkerchief with anger, 'You've no idea the pressures a husband can exert, and if I stand up to him he might veto our going away.'

'Perhaps that's what is really making him so angry,' Esther said. Agnes sniffed. 'Maybe you should put off going away just now. I heard the master say he was strapped for cash, if you don't mind my referring to the matter. I've noticed men grow half mad when they're short of money.'

'I'm not one to waste money on fripperies, not like his first wife,' she said bitterly. 'I ask for little enough, and yet he's capable of denying me my one chance of good health.'

That reference to her health again. Was she with child maybe? Esther didn't understand. She knew Agnes had been ill shortly before her marriage but now she seemed quite recovered, apart from this hysteria, this obsession with cleanliness.

'I believe High Withens is set in a salubrious postion,' she ventured. 'The air seems very pure in the grounds although the house is damp,' she admitted.

''Tis nothing like so good as sea air,' Agnes said. 'And as for the house, you can see can't you, the place is too big, it needs more servants than we can afford to maintain it.'

'Perhaps you should learn to shut your eyes to imperfections,' Esther said. 'There is a serpent in every Eden.'

Agnes turned pale. 'Some imperfections I will not live with. I can't bear living with dirt,' she said. 'Oh Esther, you will love the sea. Fancy you've never visited the coast. It's divine – such bracing power, you'll never want to go anywhere else, I promise you.' In casting her thoughts like a net over the prospect of a holiday, Agnes forgot her husband. 'We will get away soon now. Then you'll see what I mean. The sea air will breathe new life into you, Esther.'

Agnes drifted away, planning, drawing up lists, marshalling arguments to put to Jonathan. For a long time Esther remained hunched in the window seat, gazing out over the grounds that stretched as far as the eye could see. Up here, high up above the frets and fevers of men, she felt safe. If only Agnes wouldn't bother her.

Agnes must not bother her.

Of Jonathan she was unafraid. He would hardly attack a paid companion. His wife's craven need was another matter.

The next morning, like a dream turned into nightmare, the scenes went on.

The same arguments batted to and fro between the assailants. Again Esther left quickly. She hastily swallowed her breakfast tea and toast and got away from them. And again Agnes followed her, still in her wrapper, upbraiding her husband's selfishness in expecting her to live in squalor as she put it. The girl, who never showed any feelings about anything, was quiet, unprotesting when Agnes said she had decided to bring forward the date of their departure. She had some of her own money put by and she would use that if necessary. Esther must make her goodbyes to her family for they would be gone God knows how long; she wasn't going to rush home to a husband who neglected her needs.

'When must we leave?' Esther asked.

'The day after tomorrow,' Agnes said shortly.

'So soon,' Esther said. To be torn so soon from this vast house where she could disappear down endless corridors.

Agnes looked mulish. 'It won't be soon enough for me. You can help me pack straight away.'

'Where shall we stay?'

'We'll put up in a hotel for a few days and then establish ourselves in rented accommodation.'

'What about your ... the master?' Esther said. 'Won't he make difficulties about such haste?'

Agnes was silent a moment, then she said, 'I've decided to take your advice and avoid confronting him. We'll leave at dawn before he awakes. After a few days, when he has cooled down, I'll write to him.'

But they would return, Esther guessed, to even wilder scenes, and she suspected when he was drunk Jonathan Hopgate's curses would be as brutal as her father's. But up here, high up where outside the birds were reeling, she was for the present beyond all of them.

In the cramped lodgings Agnes found for them it was another matter. There was pressing need for economy so they found rooms in Southsea that were clean but poorly furnished and poky, so small that Esther didn't have a room to herself. She was cooped up for hours with her mistress and, as the torpor of the steam baths and heat of drowsy tubs didn't suit her, it was only when Agnes took her baths that Esther could be alone.

The meanness of the accommodation hardly troubled Agnes and she was perfectly at ease with the solitary girl. Esther was a mouse of a child, deferring to her, serving her; she was an ideal companion. A sweet thing she would be if she ever smiled. Quiet, unobtrusive and sober as Monday morning. All the qualities Agnes had come to appreciate since her marriage to Jonathan.

It was bliss to be in her narrow white bed like a maid again; to be cleansed body and soul, to live like a nun in a shower of grace. Bliss to be waited on, attended to when the only dues she had to pay were counted in pounds, shillings and pence. No other insidious interest would accrue; Esther could make no demands on her.

At night, when the lamps were lit, the two women read. Sometimes Esther read aloud to her mistress. Sometimes, when she woke late in the morning and saw Esther already awake, fully dressed, pouring tea for her, Agnes would say, 'You're just like a daughter to me, Esther.'

Gradually she fell into the habit of not getting up till noon, and got used to Esther awakening her, helping her dress, organising her clothes, dressing her hair, shopping for her, composing letters to Jonathan for her to transcribe. Writing to her husband was such a trial for Agnes.

'What shall we say?' she complained when Jonathan wrote yet again asking for her return to High Withens.

Esther, her eyes lowered, said carefully, 'Whatever it is you want to do, ma'am.'

'You know what I want; I want to stay here always.'

'But it might be better if you went home soon.'

'Better – how better?' Agnes demanded indignantly.

Esther cast a bleak eye around their cramped quarters. 'Well, this is only a sort of temporary arrangement, isn't it?'

'Temporary? Is it too confining for you, then?' There was a hostile note in Agnes' voice that alarmed Esther.

'I was thinking of your health. I'm happy with whatever you decide. But medical opinion holds that large, airy accommodation is invaluable in promoting well being.'

'It's out of the question that I should pay more for bigger rooms. There simply isn't enough money left, Esther. It's so selfish of Jonathan to expect me to finish the treatment just when I'm beginning to feel the benefits.'

'Yes, you're looking much better,' Esther agreed. 'P'raps now would be the best time to go home, when you're so well set up. And after all, there are more physical comforts at High Withens. And much more space, which always beneficial.'

'That draughty mausoleum!' Agnes looked suspiciously at the girl. Was she going to side with her husband?

'Are you unhappy here with me, Esther? Do you want to return to High Withens?'

'Oh no, indeed,' the girl assured her. 'My place is at your side. I could never dream of leaving you.' She watched the cloud lift from her mistress' eyes. She could breathe easily again.

She brought a wrap over to her mistress.

'I can't think how I'd manage without you Esther.'

Esther placed her good hand on Agnes' forehead. 'You feel a little feverish, I think. All this fretting is bad for you. You'd better stay in bed this morning. Lie there. Just rest. Think no more about the matter. I'll devise a letter to placate the master.'

After all, High Withens could wait. Esther was in no hurry. The house had stood, and would stand yet, for centuries.

And so it began, the periods of long separation, Agnes' quest for the Holy Grail of a sea-cure, though anyone could see she was fit as a fiddle. At first she wrote Jonathan long letters giving details of the variety of cures she was attempting in Southsea; then she sent affectionate notes saying she missed him, quickly followed by brisk epistles explaining how the invigorating air, the efficacy of the baths, had convinced her she should stay indefinitely.

When he wrote demanding her return there was a long silence, and then Esther wrote to say her mistress had been crippled by debilitating headaches and a doctor she had called in had said it would be madness for her to return yet to a northern climate.

Controlling himself, he replied that of course he did not want to put her health in jeopardy, but if she didn't return immediately he himself would go down south to fetch her. And there would be no more money, did she understand? He would inform the bank not to advance her a groat if she stayed any longer.

He didn't like being alone in the house with the memories of Lily for company. Though work filled his days – he was constantly supervising the farms on the estate, reading papers on the latest developments in agriculture, harassing his tenants, devising ways to increase crop yield, remembering his duties as well as his rights in planning model cottages for the estate workers – his nights were lonely. At night a certain panic would set in. Sometimes he would give dinners for the tenants and their wives and then he drank convivially, feeling a warmth radiate throughout the house. But after his guests had gone he drank alone and the house seemed to grow cold and echo with the memory of Lily's harsh laugh. Lily was laughing from the grave at him. Sometimes he almost forgot he had another wife and when he lay down in bed he could smell the commingled scent of French perfume and mercury ointment, could hear the shuffle of soft-slippered feet, could hear footsteps walking in the room above, the rooms below him, could even fancy he heard footsteps trip across the window pane and, if he were a superstitious man, he would suspect the house was haunted by the syphilitic bride he had brought to High Withens. But he was a rational man and in the morning he would reproach himself for drinking heavily and make one of his regular vows to live soberly, to be a model of temperance.

The love of a good woman could change a man, it seemed. Mark the transformation in Belton! He embraced sobriety and Violetta Hemp with equal passion. Jonathan found himself actually envying the man. They rode back to the farmhouse together after a meeting about plans for the farm land Belton worked on the estate.

The door was open. Children spilled out whooping: Belton's daughters and neighbours' children. The windows were flung open too, and within the house a lazy disorder of drapery, books, and pictures hung askew, was curiously inviting. Of Violetta Hemp there was not a sign. She was not in the kitchen, neither was she in the parlour. Perhaps she was out visiting.

'Not at all!' Belton roared with laughter. 'Etta reckons she had enough of scattering visiting cards throughout her spinsterhood. She'll be in the dark room. We'd best not disturb her else we'll ruin the pictures.'

'Dark room. Pictures. What are you talking about?' Jonathan was mystified.

'Come in here and I'll show you, Hopgate.'

In the parlour there was a curious chemical odour, something Jonathan didn't recognise. Over the table was spread a white linen cloth, heavily stained.

'Ruined with silver nitrate!' Belton boasted. On the table was a box of glass slides and a pile of stiff paper. Belton turned the latter over to reveal a series of photographic portraits of the Beltons and their friends.

'See here my wife has captured us all. Someone gave her a camera for her repository and she has kept it for herself and intends to make a photographic record of the community.' Belton flushed with pride at his wife's talents. Then the lady herself came in, or rather flew in holding aloft wet papers that she proceeded to lay out on the dining room table.

Violetta Hemp looked like a gypsy. Her hands she laughingly held up, to show how they were blackened with collodion. Her greasy hair hung down in what looked like rats' tails rather than ringlets. Belton hugged her.

'I've been shut up in the coal hole all morning,' she giggled.

'The dark room,' Belton corrected her.

'I'm afraid there's no food cooked. Will cold mutton and pickle suffice, my dear?'

Belton assured her it would and kissed her full on the mouth in front of Jonathan. It was a chaotic repast. Violetta's chatter was ceaseless, Belton's laugh thrummed. Throughout the meal they touched hands constantly and the scent of strong chemicals that impregnated Violetta's hair and clothes and stained her skin might have been an aphrodisiac the way her husband doted.

Belton drank only water. His eyes were clear as summer rain. His hand was steady that hung about his wife's waist when after the meal they stood at the gate and waved farewell to Jonathan.

There was only one discordant moment.

'It must be a trial for you, Mr Hopgate, your wife

having to live away from you on account of her health,'
Violetta trilled. 'And I don't think our Esther relishes it
any more than you can. We had a sad letter from her,'
she went on. Her husband looked indifferent. 'Esther
says she hates the south coast. She is heartbroken at
being away from High Withens.'

22

***

Agnes returned with a high colour, looking, he thought, exquisitely beautiful; an absence that had made his heart grow fonder.

'I've missed you. I've missed you,' he said when they were in bed. It was the only place he could talk intimately with her, the only place he could be sure of not being overheard by Miss Belton's wagging ears.

'I've missed you too,' she said dutifully, stiffening as his fingers crawled up her thigh. She had felt so convinced of the truth of the maxim 'cleanliness is next to godliness' these past months, she had felt so pure after the prolonged course of medicinal baths — and now this defilement again! How could she be sure he wasn't infecting her all over again? All over again.

When he had finished she got up and washed herself.

That's it, she thought. I'll have to spend six months on a cure after a night at his side. And she began to plan her next holiday.

She seemed irritable since her return – sharp, shrewish, finding fault with everything.

'Don't nag me, woman,' was his constant lament to her. She accused him of untidiness, of slovenliness. She said he had bad breath, his feet were rank, he should bathe more often. When he sat near her, or when he sat her on his lap, she kept shrugging as if trying to shake off an importunate insect. Then came the morning she began lecturing him at breakfast before Esther came down. She said it wasn't nice for him to be always lunging at her in front of Esther. It didn't seem proper. He would shock the girl, what would the girl think of them?

'I don't give a tinker's curse what that little mealy-mouthed miss thinks,' he shouted, not caring who heard him. He shook with temper. He had a sudden urge to throw something at Agnes; his hands itched to slap her. He stormed out of the hall. He was in no mood for breakfast now, almost bumping into Esther who was coming down the stairs, and when she said 'Good morning, Sir!' he ignored her.

In the library he poured himself a glass of brandy to settle his nerves, and another to revive him. He felt that he would fly apart with anger. His anger swelled into a rage that could only be appeased by smashing, hammering, kicking, pounding, grinding, ripping, throwing, cracking, punching, dismembering, gartering, biting, murdering. He'd like to murder all women. He'd . . . he'd . . . But he had no language to express what he'd like to do.

So he wept, grossly he wept, just like a woman.

They were both very pale, both shocked, he chastened

by the mess he had made of the library, she trembling with fear.

'I really can't face such drunken rages,' she said.

'I'm sorry,' he said. 'I really don't know what came over me. It's as if I was possessed.'

'You shouldn't drink,' she said.

'If I drink, that's your fault. I need a loving wife. You're as cold as hell,' he said.

'Maybe that's because I've been through hell,' she retorted. He looked at her irritably. Was the woman still blaming him? And for what? She was strong as an Amazon.

'I've given you everything you wanted. It's your turn now. You've had your holidays, your little lap-dog companion. You've got position, a grand house. What more do you want?'

She wanted to say that it was what she *didn't* want, that was the thing, but she daren't.

'Scenes like this drain me. I need to get away.'

'But you've just come back,' he said, irritated, enraged.

'Esther thinks the climate here doesn't suit me,' she lied.

'Oh, Esther is a medical expert is she?' he sneered. 'Or does the girl merely have a fancy for another free holiday?'

'Is it beyond you to imagine some people have the ability to put the needs of others first?'

'You're saying I'm selfish, are you?'

She was at a loss. She pulled out her handkerchief and sobbed into it quietly. He relented. She looked so fragile when she cried, so broken. He went up to her, lifted her chin, kissed the salt eyes. Two moist pools of cornflowers. 'Don't cry, my love. Of course you can have another little holiday, but later in the year.' His hand cupped her breast. 'Come upstairs with me,' he whispered.

'Oh, Jonathan,' she said in a small voice, 'I've got to go out now. I promised Esther I'd take her in the carriage over to visit her sisters.'

She was still searching for another excuse to bolster the first when Jonathan pulled away from her furiously. 'Go with the little bitch. Go with her!' he screamed, letting fly a series of incomprehensible curses that buffeted the air, that assaulted her, left her bruised, inwardly battered, that strengthened her resolve to get away from him again as quickly as possible.

In the end she didn't feel up to accompanying Esther. The girl went alone, wanting to see her sisters but dreading the exclusion she would feel in that loving home.

Luckily Violetta Hemp couldn't desert her wet plates and precarious solutions, and she remained shut up in the coal hole for much of the visit. Her father was out working.

Shocked that Lucy and Martha hadn't been reading their Bible, Esther produced her own copy and intoned a dolorous passage aloud to them. Lucy and her sister squirmed. They had almost forgotten how Esther tyrannised them.

'Has that woman neglected your education?' Esther asked them sternly.

'Mama's teaching us to be models,' Lucy said.

'And Mama let us arrange the props when she took a picture of pa dressed up as Old Father Time,' Martha piped.

'She's not your mama. You must remember our

sainted mother, who will weep when you forget her, in Paradise.' Esther slapped her smallest sister with her good hand.

'I can't remember anything about our first mama,' Lucy said.

'That is because the devil has painted a black cloud over your soul. You will rot in the lake of everlasting fire if you neglect to honour the memory of Mama.'

The black cloud must have risen suddenly from Lucy's soul into her grey orbs, which darkened under the gaze of this terrifying sister. Esther's hair was like the burning bush. Her mouth was fierce with condemnation.

She bent over her little sisters. 'Only the kin of your own blood will look out for you. This new mama is not to be trusted.'

'But she loves me. She makes me look pretty in her pictures,' Martha objected.

Esther rolled her colourless eyes at the ceiling. 'You see? The devil's work. She has filled you with vanity. That woman takes your pictures to trap your souls. Listen to me,' she commanded, 'Miss Hemp married Papa because she didn't have a proper home nor enough money to put victuals on her table. When Papa dies,' she went on, her voice rising with threat, 'she will pocket all the profit he has made from the farm and cast you off without a penny. And if you have no money you will have nowhere to live and will never get husbands,' she added smugly.

Lucy looked unconvinced, but Martha was desolate and began weeping. 'I don't want to be a vagrant,' she said, her heart breaking.

'Nor will you,' Esther said. 'If you keep a holy heart

and pray to our real mama she will put it in my power to help you.'

'How?' asked Lucy sceptically, staring at her strange, half crippled sister.

A pious smile flickered on the tight mouth. 'Through my charity, my strong faith in the good Lord, I have opened the heart of my mistress to holy affection.' Esther's colourless eyes seemed filled with the scorching light of her hair. 'Last night I dreamed, my dears,' she said, although her stiff body communicated no sisterly affection, 'that our one and only true mama came down from heaven to succour me. "Have faith, Esther," she admonished, "and love your sisters, and then one day, I promise, you'll be mistress of High Withens."'

Lucy snickered. Martha was bewildered.

Esther ignored them. She seemed to be speaking to herself now as she continued. 'And I know. I feel the power of the future in my bones. Already the mistress leans on me, prefers my company to that of her husband. What a rake he is . . . he'll burn himself out like his forefathers. One of the damned. God will strike him down. Mama told me. "Esther," she said, "when you inherit High Withens take in your sisters. Even if they have no memory of me I have not forgotten them. I have interceded with the saints and all the angels. Lucy and Martha will one day be with you at High Withens."'

There were days when Jonathan's rages, even if not heard, could be felt throughout the house. Whenever he left the house to see about estate matters his resentments hung in the air, poisoning the atmosphere. Agnes was glad of Esther's company. The girl did not seem to notice, let alone mind, the master's tirades. She did not react to life as Agnes did. She was inviolate, always herself, never altered her mood to reflect anybody. When Jonathan stormed at her Agnes lost heart.

'You should take no notice. As long as he doesn't hurt you, what are you worried about?' the girl asked her. She had lived at High Withens a couple of years now and had the easy confidence of her mistress. 'You shouldn't be his barometer.'

'I can't help it,' Agnes sighed. 'He always manages to upset me. I can't detach myself from his humours.'

'You'll soon get away again,' the girl said carefully.

'And that's driving him into greater frenzy,' Agnes said. 'He already accuses me of spending all his money on cures and treatments. He hates me going away.'

Esther put down her Bible; she was always reading passages aloud to comfort Agnes, to give her the spiritual strength her mistress seemed to have lost.

'I don't think you should blame anything you do or say for the master's tempers.' She looked at Agnes from under her lowered eyelids. 'If you don't mind my saying so,' she went on in her tight little voice, 'I think the master is sometimes beyond all reason. I think the master isn't always rational. Do you know what I mean? I think, sometimes, he seems a little mad, ma'am.'

A little mad. Agnes' heart skipped a beat. Was Jonathan going insane? Or was she herself possessed by a craziness born of this doomed marriage?

Sometimes she could persuade herself it was worth the effort to humour him. When it seemed there might be no money for her little escapes or he might veto them absolutely through spite, she forced herself to look at him fondly.

* * *

After they had dressed for dinner and were awaiting their guests, Esther still in her room, Agnes said, 'Thank you for the corsage. It goes perfectly with my dress.'

Jonathan, grown increasingly negligent of his own apearance, still appreciated his wife's beauty and liked seeing her tonight, slender as a tulip in palest lavender draperies.

She was smiling at him. A weak smile, a lop-sided smile because a pucker of cunning turned down one side of her mouth. Her long neck was bare of jewellery, the small bunch of violets her only adornment.

He poured them both wine. She sat on the couch facing him, barely sipping the wine which she put down almost at once.

Jonathan drained his glass. 'Drink with me, won't you?' he asked her. Again she lifted the glass and drank quickly. Tonight she mustn't provoke him. She didn't want a scene in front of guests. She was worn down with scenes. She just wanted the time until she could get away again to pass without aggravation or violence.

When she had finished the wine he began to speak softly.

> When passion's trance is overpast,
> If tenderness and truth could last,
> Or live, whilst all wild feelings keep
> Some mortal slumber, dark and deep,
> I should not weep, I should not weep!
>
> It were enough to feel, to see,
> Thy soft eyes gazing tenderly,
> And dream the rest — and burn and be

> The secret food of fires unseen,
> Couldst thou but be as thou hast been?

'I forget the last verse,' he said. 'It's been too long since we talked of the poets, Agnes.' He rose from his high-backed chair and went and sat down beside her. 'Couldst thou but be as thou hast been?' he murmured. He put his hands around her waist, staring into her eyes that were shadowy in the candlelight. 'Is it possible for us to dream the rest, Agnes? At least at night, in the candlelight, in the almost dark, can we not dream of passion?' He kissed her mouth that turned down slightly.

His voice went on and on in her head as he kissed her; a mocking refrain: When passion's trance is overpast, overpast, overpast, overpast . . . I should not weep, should not weep, not weep as thou hast been.

As thou hast been.

But she was not as she had been.

As for dreaming the rest . . . well . . . dreaming!

His fevered mouth was crushing her mouth. And it was like no dream sitting here with this man sprawling over her lap, his greedy mouth suffocating her, his hands like a vice trapping her tiny waist, his legs pinning her down like a butterfly.

No dream existed in this high-ceilinged room, no dream in the hotly dripping candles that filled the air with acrid smoke, no dream in the slippery heat of male flesh easing her open.

She was not as she had been, sliding beneath him, exhaling short spasmodic breaths of submission, dreamlessly unfastening her stays and praying like a nightmare the girl would not come in and discover them, never dreaming to find her mistress so shamelessly abandoned; nor was it like a dream when Jonathan laboured over her, twisting her limbs askew, boring into her, beads of perspiration on his skin, the seductions of poetry stricken dumb on his mouth that could only feed on her, tasting, sucking, teeth grazing, wordlessly gnawing, all poetry silenced in the echoes that spilled from shadowy corners of the wet, sussurate sounds of lust.

Nor was it like a dream when her hairpins scattered and her hair was loose as her clothes and she fretted, as he progressed further into the delirium of entering her body, that she would be disarrayed before her guests.

And it wasn't her dream, it was a nightmare from which she must not awaken. If his dream was to go on, she must lie embalmed in the pretence that this was balmy love and she could again be as she had been – an innocent woman.

And it wasn't a dream as a voice thrummed in her head the last verse of Shelley's poem which her husband had forgotten:

> After the slumber of the year
> The woodland violets reapear;
> All things revive in field or grove,
> And sky and sea, but two, which move
> And form all others, life and love.

Life and love! As if mere dreams could ever revive them!

Agnes could not dream as her husband did, his eyes closed tight, the bittersweet delusion of wine in his mouth, swooning in a fit that was after all only the ghost of love, a phantom delirium.

She changed her dress, now spoilt by the crushed violets. She wore black so she could withdraw into shadow. The small amount of wine Jonathan had made her drink gave her a headache. When Esther joined them she could hardly look at the girl, although rarely did Esther trouble anyone by staring at them directly, her eyes were always cast down, her head to one side like a crooked goblin.

Tonight there was to be a dinner for numerous guests. A duty. Agnes' own father among the visitors, so she had to show enthusiasm. It had been necessary to humour Jonathan and if she now felt drained, despondency and fear creeping to her throat so her voice all night was tight, constricted, it hardly mattered. Not a soul sensed anything.

Jonathan was carousing. And why not? It was his family tradition and no one batted an eye at the amount of liquor he consumed.

And then, when the more censorious ladies looked at his still somehow boyish face, they would forgive him anything.

Mrs Beech preened when he offered cant compliments, such as, 'I can see where your daughters inherited their fine complexions.' Or to charming Mrs Tow: 'I hear there's a certain gentleman hereabouts is falling into a decline on your account.' He teased Violetta Hemp disgracefully. 'Your husband was saying to me only the other day how he'd trade in a gaggle of daughters for one sturdy son to take on the farm after him.'

Esther, with her blank smile, appeared not to hear him.

Jonathan staggered later when the gentlemen rejoined the female company assembled in the drawing room.

The ladies were edgy in their seats, the gentlemen, fumy with Hopgate hospitality, wanted to draw out the evening and were tardy in following the signals of suddenly shut fans and cashmere shawls drawn tightly over delicate shoulders.

When at last they were all gone, Esther slipped very quickly away to bed and Agnes half feared Jonathan, reeling, inebriate, would want to pursue his dream of love again. She needn't have worried.

Jonathan was thirsty. His tongue was parched. He had never been so thirsty and the dream he sought had become his very thirst and that insane, dementing thirst could only be slaked at the bottom of a rum bottle.

One, two bottles of finest Jamaica, downed throughout the black night, until he fell into that stupor wherein there is no hope of dreaming.

The weeks that followed were blank, day and night merging. He did not know when it was his wife left for a trip south again but he vowed that when she returned he would make her suffer for leaving.

Life went on, their life together continued, but the separations became a little longer; Jonathan's temper a little fiercer; Agnes' irritation a little deeper; only the girl did not seem to change. They settled into a pattern. When she was at High Withens, Agnes wore herself out with supervising a thorough cleaning of the tip it had become while she was away. Jonathan involved himself with the estate and heavier bouts of drinking, making love to his wife's body with less and less urgency.

And so it went on and they thought it would go on like that forever and this unhappy marriage was their interminable fate.

23

Fate. The fate of the Hopgate dynasty. There seemed no hope of a son to assume his inheritance.

And for years they had spawned so easily, prolifically, those early scions of the house. There they were in the gallery, laughing at him with their swollen codpieces, fruitful wives hung alongside them, numerous children in white lace caps, diminutive farthingales, oaken cribs laden with sturdy babes painted in miniature. Or, skulking in group portraits, the occasional bastard child.

They had spent their seed like money, profligate with both and now coffers and lineage were depleted.

The last branch withered. Fruitless.

It was their fault. Damn his ancestors for their decadence.

Or their curse. Look at that fellow in the groom's costume, attending the wife of some Jacobean Hopgate who had evidently just dismounted her horse. Didn't he have the Hopgate eyes, the hawkish nose, bitter mouth?

Did he inherit also the Hopgate pride and damn them all for condemning his bastardy by making him a servant?

A space remained on the crowded wall for his own image. The devil take it; he couldn't bear to hang a picture of himself, because already he could hear some future tenant of the house, a hideously rich coal merchant with a voice ringing like a spittoon, announce, 'And that was the last Hopgate!'

No escape in his wife's eyes from his fate, either. When he looked into her cool orbs he saw his own reflection as the grim reaper.

'Drinking already?' she complained. She walked along the gallery towards where he stood, swigging from a claret bottle.

'Nagging already? You've only been home a few days,' he countered. Her mouth tightened with disgust. He cursed her.

'Don't say such filthy things to me.' She looked white. Her voice was strangled. 'How can you expect me to stay for long in this house when you turn it into a gin palace? If episodes like last night continue even Esther will abandon me.'

'No fear of that. Esther knows where her bread's buttered even if it's a thick dollop of rum or brandy butter.' He laughed thickly. His face was blue with stubble. His eyes were crusty. There were ribs of dirt under his fingernails.

'Just look at the state of you,' she said with genuine anguish. 'You look only fit company for the scum you had here last night.'

'They're not scum. They're my friends,' he said simply.

243

'Cut-throats. Thieves. Drunkards. Even one of the stable lads,' she said hopelessly. 'How can you invite such people to the house?'

'They get me through the night. Which is more than you do,' he said darkly

She coloured then. 'Why must you always be so coarse?'

'Why must you always be so cold, dear wife?' He took another noisy swig from his bottle. He grew happier drinking. 'Come on. Come downstairs and have a drink with me.' He stroked her bare throat.

She stiffened. 'You're ruining yourself with drink, Jonathan.'

'What a fuss about a drop of claret. You should have a glass, it'd loosen you up a bit.'

'You're so loose, you're near to losing yourself,' she said bitterly. A tear moistened her eye. They were at the top of the staircase. With the skittishness of the near-drunk he suddenly lunged at her, swung her around perilously so that she nearly lost her footing, nearly tumbled down the flight of stairs.

'You could have killed me, you fool.' But he was still mauling her, pulling at her, giggling his foolish drunken laugh.

'Oh, be kind to me, Agnes. You must be kind to your husband. Your loving husband.' He tickled her.

'For God's sake, let me go.' She pushed him. He held her. She kicked him. His feet staggered and the two of them almost fell. There they were, struggling, staggering when Esther saw them.

Her voice was so low Jonathan never heard her.

'Did you hear that Jonathan?' Agnes panted. 'We've

244

got company. Esther's sisters, Lucy and Martha, have arrived for luncheon. Let me go. Did you hear? I really must go and receive them.

He let her go at last with a whim of anger turning his mood suddenly. 'Get out of my sight, then. You're a prickly armful anyway. And you can forget about coming to me to pay for any more of your fancy trips and ridiculous laundry bills. And don't think I'm going to fork out much needed money either to feed an army of your henchwomen.'

Agnes' complexion burned.

Esther pretended not to have heard the still fulminating Jonathan, but said coolly, 'My sisters thought it would be a treat for you to have a picnic, ma'am. They have made up a basket of good farm ham and eggs as well as jellies and cake, oh all sorts of comestibles. See, I've brought your wrap and some of your smelling salts; a good walk in the fresh air will be just the thing for you.'

Agnes allowed Esther to lead her away.

Jonathan drained the claret then went in search of another bottle.

At the foot of the stairs Agnes turned to Esther, trembling. 'It's no use. I feel too upset to meet Lucy and Martha. You must make my excuses. I'm sorry, but please tell them they can go ahead with their picnic in the grounds in any case,' she said.

Esther regarded her beneath her half-closed eyes. 'Don't trouble yourself about my sisters. Nothing else matters but that you should be composed. I think I know just the thing to help you Agnes.' She led the distressed woman into the drawing room and when Agnes was settled on a sofa Esther slipped out of the room and went and fetched a bottle of a brownish liquid from her own bedroom.

When she returned Agnes was sitting bolt upright again, waiting for, dreading, the eruption of the dipsomaniac storm that would inevitably break out when Jonathan exchanged his claret for a bottle of Jamaica Rum or French brandy.

'What is that?' Agnes screwed up her mouth in distaste.

'Just a tincture of laudanum,' Esther said. 'My mama always swore by it when her nerves were shredded by my father's tantrums. She called it "little mother", because of the comfort it provided.'

'Oh, I've never taken any kind of medicine. My father didn't believe in it. He was always one for natural cures in cases where the power of prayer was insufficient.'

'I'll sweeten it with honey,' Esther suggested. 'Then you may think of it more as a treat than a medicine. Sip it slowly, let it linger on the tongue. You'll maybe acquire a taste for it.'

With honey added the laudanum was more palatable. Agnes sipped it slowly as Esther instructed.

Sweet Esther. Sweet laudanum. A rushing like a river filled her heart. Her limbs soon felt deliciously light as the torpor of anguish fell away. Her very blood was still in her veins.

Esther refused to join her sisters. She would not leave Agnes alone with the threat of impending riot from the master. When Agnes had lain down, stretched languorously across the couch, Esther said; 'You can continue to dread your husband, or take this to deaden your fear of him. Just have a little sip of laudanum whenever you feel agitated; it has wonderful restorative powers.'

246

'The only thing that restores me is to get right away from him,' Agnes moaned.

'But that's not always possible, is it?' Esther said.

'Oh, don't remind me,' Agnes begged.

'I'm sorry, ma'am, but that's just the point. What you need sometimes is something that will help you forget.'

Oh to forget. What bliss! To forget a horror such as a husband ever existed!

Esther smiled as the drug took effect and Agnes dozed on the couch. The house was quiet for the moment. If she shut her eyes she could imagine she was alone, she could pretend Agnes and Jonathan no longer existed and she was mistress in their place.

Jonathan too was busy forgetting. The fury his wife dreaded, expected, failed to ignite.

This morning his mouth was dry, his throat rasped and ached – a morning for wine, cool wine, he had such a thirst on him. White wine – like a lovely woman, skittish and cool in his arms, cool, chill even as she fired him.

He wandered out of the house. Such a fine day. He had already forgotten the squabble with his wife, the brooding portraits of his forefathers.

He chose a spot close by the house at the edge of the stagnant pool against a small birch tree. He placed the bottles at the edge of the thick water nestling amongst waterlilies and lit a cigar. He breathed in deeply, rare Havana and fresh English air. Yes, a fine morning! When he leant over the pea-soup brew of algae, reeds and strangled aquatic plants he saw the water was too dark, too choked to reflect him. Neither did he see the stumbling girls until they were beside him.

It took a moment or two before he registered who they were. Ah yes, Belton's other daughters!

In her frenzy the smaller girl almost slipped into the pond. 'Oh master, master,' she was shrieking, all of a sudden squatting beside him, drumming her heels though her ashen-faced sister tried to restrain her.

It took him a while to focus on the girl's reddish-brown hair and freckled features. She was hunched beside him, clutching his arm. 'Master, didn't you see her, master?'

'See who? What is it, child?' he slurred. The girl's terror was palpable.

Lucy, trying to hush Martha, was saying, 'Quiet now, you mustn't trouble the master.' She attempted to pull her sister up to take her back inside the house with her.

'Let her stay; stay a moment.' Jonathan, registering the girl's panic with a leaden torpor, slowly stood up and leant against the trunk of the slender birch tree.

'What is it child?' He smiled a lop-sided smile at the girl. 'Has some bad animal frightened you?'

Lucy cut in over Matha's paroxysms. Her guarded expression reminded him unpleasantly of Esther.

''Tis nothing, Sir. Take no notice of her fuss. 'Tis nothing but wild fancies.'

''Tisn't. 'Tis no such thing. I saw her.' Martha broke free from her sister and threw herself at Jonathan again, a strong man who would surely save her.

Jonathan laughed. 'Why, you are a great baby!' He picked her up, swinging the child in the air.

'I saw her! I saw it!' Martha went on screaming, so Jonathan quickly put her down again.

'Saw who, what?' He bent down to the girl's level.

'Never mind your sister. Hush now. Tell me. What was it that you saw?'

She took a gulp of breath. 'As we was coming up from the hedges over there,' she pointed ahead, 'I saw a white cloud rise up from the middle of the pond and float toward you, sir. When we came closer the white cloud went all thick and like a pillar of smoke and then when we were closer still I saw it was no cloud nor smoke neither.'

'What was it, then?' he asked patiently, smiling up at her agitated sister.

'It was a ghost, Sir, the ghost of a woman, an awful ugly woman, and she was standing next to you. She was all in white but she had an ugly blue face, Sir.'

24

The ancestors of Jonathan Hopgate lamented in the seventh circle of damnation on the morning he was brought a stark corpse to be buried in the family tomb at Low Withens.

'Married to death, and at last he is one with us,' clamoured the shades of his forefathers.

'Adieu. Adieu . . . farewell,' fretted a feverish wind that urged Jonathan, widow, and the funeral procession along a track that fell from bleak moors down an arduous incline to the marshy hollows around Low Withens.

'Esther, have a care for yourself, take cover,' the widow called out to the younger woman from her carriage as a hot rain fell suddenly from a too blue heaven.

Take cover, Esther's thoughts echoed the widow. There's no sweet bower on all this wide moor that'll shelter you from the storm that's coming, she silently promised her.

The rain fell skittishly like nuptial rice. Beads of bright water hung on the long red hair and on the sparse gingery eyelashes of the paid companion. They toiled on over a sticky earth under the too blue heaven. And as they arrived at the sump of the valley a stout wind slewed the rain from the peaks of the moorland back down the valley to where the land churned and sickened.

At last, my destiny, Esther rejoiced as the coffin was lifted down from the glass carriage, and her mistress fainted . . .

On their seventh wedding anniversary, Jonathan had given his wife a gift of pearls, and in the evening as they were dressing before dinner she put on the necklace with her lovely ivory dress, and he went up to kiss her on the neck and say how well the pearls set off her beauty.

'What do you think of my gift?' he asked her, fingering the sheeny rope.

'They're perfect. I can't thank you enough.' She was in a good mood tonight. The present had softened her. He kissed her on the mouth. Her lips closed tight.

'They suit you; they look very well on you,' he said. 'They're just right for that . . . that thing you've got on.'

'My dress?'

'Yes.' He wanted to tell her that when he could afford it he'd buy her a bracelet to match. It was on the tip of his tongue to say that if she spent less of his money on travelling down south, he might be able to afford more fal-lals, but he didn't want to sour the evening.

'I'll get you a . . . thing to go with it,' he said. Now what was the word?

'A thing?' she laughed. 'You're very vague tonight, Jonathan.'

'What do you call that damn thing, like a rope, was it . . . a rope of . . .? I'll buy you a pearl manacle,' he said.

She stared at him as if somehow she had missed the joke. 'A what?'

He looked at her as if he was struggling to say something. 'A thing. A manacle?' In desperation he mimed a circle about his wrist.

'You mean a bracelet, Jonathan. What on earth is the matter with you?'

He was white as a winding sheet. When he spoke, the words sounded distorted like the words spoken by someone who was deaf. His legs felt heavy as though his boots were soled with lead. 'I've just spoken my own death sentence,' he said.

It was several years since Agnes had been up to Lily's old room at the top of the east wing; she had spared herself the worst of his illness.

At first the symptoms had been random, discrete: a mere dizziness on awakening, a certain unsteadiness on his feet, occasional aphasia. His rages increased. When he told her the disease had come back she snapped, her tears broke like a strand of pearls scattering – real tears of remorse, mourning what might have been, tears with a catch of fear within them.

He would not have a doctor in the house at first, but she supposed he must have seen some sort of apothecary or physician because he was always trying different remedies. There were the sapphire beads of mercury which he alternated with Van Swietan's liquor

– a dose of mercury in brandy. Then he had an outbreak of abscesses, and she thought that was another symptom of the disease. But he told her he had been injected with mercury salts and had to discontinue the treatment because of the acute pain this had inflicted.

Then, quite suddenly, he stopped dosing himself with anything other than the rum that stirred a fire in his brain or the fine French brandy that roused him to paralytic rages, and it was then he decided the splitting headaches were hangovers, the confusion over words the effect of drink, and that heaviness in his limbs – the stiffness and cramp in all his muscles – an ever-incipient flu caused by the dampness at High Withens.

He sat by the fire in the capacious winged chair, wrapped in a blanket like an old man. Agnes fed him dainty portions of bread and milk. She spooned the food into his mouth. She lifted a second spoonful but he clamped his lips tight before she could ladle the second helping of mush into him. The slop smeared his face.

'I don't like this . . . blub,' he said. 'Don't want it.'

'A drink, then?'

Wearily she poured a port for him. The clear hard thing on his lips – what did you call that bubble of emptiness like hard water, like ice, that spilled the red stuff into him? He spat the drink at her, a dribble of saliva and red stuff on her dress.

'Oh my God. Oh my God, how much longer?' she said.

'God? God?' The word tasted sweet. 'What kind of drink is that?' he asked her.

She picked up a napkin and wiped hurriedly at her dress. He sickened her. She couldn't feel charitable towards him. They were days now when she almost wished he was dead. She had a vision of herself unencumbered. She would sell High Withens and get a nice little villa in the South. A vista of sea-cures stretched itself before her. She wallowed in the imaginary waters of curative baths. Oh God, only to be clean again!

He was raving now, fulminating because he couldn't find the right word to curse her with. She wasn't worried, she knew he always remembered some obscenity; one was as good as another.

She rang for a maid to clear away the dishes. She tucked the mussed up blanket more securely around him. His head suddenly drooped. He began to snore noisily.

Esther followed the maid in. She walked stiffly in one of Agnes's old dresses which was too long for her. The skirts swished on the floor and occasionally tripped her but she could never be bothered to shorten them.

'For all that he falls, tumbles over chairs, can hardly walk half a dozen unsteady steps, he isn't beyond attacking me when the mood seizes him,' she told the girl bitterly. 'I'm half afraid he'll strangle me in my bed at night.' Or worse, she thought. The fate worse than death. 'It's a life sentence. Don't ever marry, Esther,' she said with a sudden vehemence. 'Don't fall into the trap that lures you with the promise of a lover. You'll awaken shackled to a husband.'

'I'd never leave you ma'am.' Esther's voice was toneless. Her eyelids were lowered. 'You shouldn't care so much for doing your duty. You shouldn't think of him as a husband. He's not your husband any more. I don't know what possesses him, but it isn't anything Christian.' She leaned over the woman with the beautiful sad eyes and whispered something.

'No,' said Agnes. 'No, I won't. I can't certify him. A Hopgate in an asylum? Never!'

'In a mansion like this? You've no need for an asylum, dear Agnes. Only find a stout fellow to watch over him; a heavy bolt on the door and you'd never even know the master was in the east wing at High Withens.'

What was this place? The light here hurt him. But the swaddles was soft. He liked swaddles. He lay in it all day. The blankets warmed him. He wasn't cold. Inside his rum-belly was hot. The fellow was rum hot too. He was a rum fellow and shared his bottle of Jamaica with him.

Sometimes the rum-fellow was a cold devil and cursed him. Wouldn't share a drop. Sometimes, he bounced him out of swaddles and made his head hit the wall. Sometimes the rum-fellow introduced his fist into Jonathan's mouth. When he watched the fellow eat meat he remembered the taste of ham-fist in his mouth and his tongue longingly poked the cavities where teeth were knocked out. A few remained. They were soft and tasted like mushrooms. He ate them when the rum-fellow refused him food.

Today was a good day. There was rum tea for breakfast. Rum soup for his lunch. The rum-fellow promised him rum possett for dinner and a rum nightcap. Rum! He musn't forget that word. The word loved him. If he forgot that word he'd be abandoned. So he kept saying it, reminding himself what a good warm word it was, warmer than swaddles.

When the light hurt him he nestled down into the

darkness of swaddles. He dived down there again when the fellow struck him or when he wanted to remember the word that loved Jonathan: 'Rum, rum, rum, rum, rum, rum, rum, di dum, dum rum,' he sobbed.

The fellow pulled him up. 'Get yerself out o' that pit, yer ruffian! Yer got a visitor.' The fellow splashed cold stuff over him. Swaddles was damp. The wooden wall gaped open. Another man came in.

'Help me stand him up,' the man told the rum fellow. They heaved, pulled at him. He stood in his nightshirt shivering with cold.

'Now close your eyes, Sir,' the man instructed him. 'And walk towards me.' He closed his eyes. He took three . . . He fell.

They put him back into swaddles again. The man spoke to him slowly. 'I'm going to give you some morphine. That'll calm you down a bit. Don't drink so much. The drink only seems to give relief. In the end it'll make things worse. Do you understand me?'

Two eyes, like swampy pools, looked up at the doctor.

Above him he could see the gold hoop that crowned swaddles. What did you call it? A halo? A martyrs crown? 'What's that?' he asked the man.

'It's a coronal, part of your bed. The bed drapes were suspended from it but they were removed when your lamp nearly set fire to them. Don't you remember?'

Remember, what kind of word was that?

The man went on. 'Do you know your name? Who you are?'

Jonathan thought: he wasn't swaddles. He wasn't rum. He wasn't rum-fellow. He looked around the bright room. The white sun glared in through twelve windows. Blank oak walls. Too much light but no reflections. Pus oozed from his dental cavities.

'Who are you?' the man patiently repeated.

Jonathan stared vacantly. He tried to think. Thinking hurt him. He pictured a flower. Tall white flowers he had seen somewhere lying on black velvet. He smiled triumphantly. 'Me, Lily. Lily. Rum Lily,' he told the doctor.

The doctor went down into the great hall where Agnes and her companion sat netting purses.

'Any improvement in him today, doctor?' Agnes asked mechanically. The doctor smiled bleakly.

'I don't think we can expect to have any improvement in your husband's condition at this stage, Mrs Hopgate. Thank you, Miss Belton,' he said to Esther, who poured him tea and passed sandwiches and cake over to him. When the girl left them to confer alone as she always did, the doctor made a request that disturbed Agnes.

'Sketch him? Illustrate his corporeal degeneration? Have my husband sit for such a morbid portrait? Are you mad?'

'I didn't expect you to say yes immediately, Mrs Hopgate. I know how shocking such a proposition can sound to one unacquainted with the exigencies of the medical profession. Believe me, I have no wish to humiliate you or your husband. Such matters are always treated in the strictest confidence, you understand. The sketches would be used to illustrate medical texts consulted by doctors and students of medicine. The sketches would be impersonal in a sense, not attempting a likeness as such of the infortunate victim, merely tracing the ravages of the disease. The more information is disseminated about this unhappy illness, the more we of the medical profession can study the symptoms, the progress of the disease – the more speedily we shall work towards finding a cure for this scourge.' He regarded the woman steadily. She shivered slightly beneath her cashmere shawl. A handsome woman. She seemed clear of the sickness, at least.

'The idea is abhorrent to me.'

'I assure you there will be no indignity. The artist will hardly be a voyeur. He will be someone professionally trained, objective, a medical artist used to such cases. He will be discreet. There is no question of any sordid revelation of the sitter's identity. And just think, Madam, examine your conscience; would you not wish to benefit mankind by playing your part to help us cleanse and purify society of this dread disease? Don't answer me now. There is plenty of time. Just remember if you do decide to let us use your husband, the process will be long term, it would be necessary to take a series of portraits to depict the various stages through which your husband's illness may pass.'

'The rake's progress,' she said sarcastically.

'Nothing so judgmental,' he replied firmly. 'As I have already told you, this would be an objective, scientific enterprise. Feelings wouldn't enter into it.'

Let them do it. Let the world in. What did she care in any case? She wouldn't be here to witness it, to be inconvenienced. She had decided. She'd break up the estate, sell off the farms, once he was declared insane. It wouldn't be long now and she'd get the doctor to agree to certify him. She'd raise enough to pay the lease on a house by the sea, to have a comfortable income. When he was dead she'd sell High Withens too. Cut off loose.

She'd forget everything. Escape the prison her marriage had become. When he was dead she'd be free again.

The young man sketched carefully, scrupulously, consulting the earlier sketches to trace the gradual decomposition of flesh.

The eyes were pulpy and wept. He looked at the last sketch he had undertaken of the patient. Then the eyelids had sat like white maggots over the eyes. Now they crumbled like cheese. The last fragments of skin were decaying where the nose had been.

A terrible absence instead of a mouth.

He went on drawing methodically with a sharp pencil. Where hair might have been in the portrait of the sick man, he left a blank. The luxuriance of the hair looked incongruous against the destroyed face. Astonishingly fine hair, still. Raven black with blue tones in it. But beauty wasn't his concern. His pencil wasn't paid to draw beauty – only truth. The rictus of diseased flesh, not the crowning glory, was his subject. The death's head stared at him. An arrogant, defiant, look-at-me grin. Long black hair was glazed to the neck by rotting matter. A last representation of the butcher's flesh, small fretting movements on the smooth paper, and the job was finished. The last portrait. He tied up his portfolio. It was over then.

Agnes came home to High Withens for the funeral. She had been immersed up to her neck, secured by a rope fastened to the bathing hut, in the briny sea, when the bathing attendant had motioned her to get out of the water. On the sloping pebbly beach Esther was talking rapidly with their landlady's maid who was red and panting having run helter-skelter over the Common with the message. Agnes' father had come down himself by train to tell his daughter she was a widow. At last she was free of Jonathan.

After the funeral, there were no baked meats on offer to the mourners. Agnes had no heart for rituals, for social niceties. She was anxious to be away again. She would sell High Withens, what remained of the estate, and there would be enough to live out the rest of her life in comfort. She'd buy a house in Southsea. She would leave High Withens to the ghosts of the Hopgates. She would never remarry. For love nor money. She was sick of men. And Esther was like a daughter, no one could have studied her comfort more. She would see that Esther was always provided for.

'Esther, fetch me my wrap,' she said. 'And call the maid to bring in the tea.' It was a relief to be alone after the ordeal of the morning. Esther brought the tea over to her, cut up the cake, Esther would have spoon-fed her if she required it. 'There's so much to be done, Esther. Legal matters, sorting out the estate. I'll probably have to put off going back to Southsea for a couple of months. Though I don't know how I'll bear it. I just hope I can soon find a buyer for this rackety place. I'll let it go cheap for a quick sale.'

Esther, small and rigid, in her too long dress, smoothed worries away as she always did. 'Do you have to find a buyer so quickly?' she asked her mistress.

Agnes looked at her in surprise. 'Of course. I want to be rid of the place. I need the money. I have to stay in Southsea for my health.'

'I've often thought,' Esther said in her expressionless voice, her gingery hair flared out like a fan, 'the change benefited you as much as anything.'

'What do you mean?'

'Well, if you lived down south all the time, you would likely take it for granted. It wouldn't be a holiday, it wouldn't be an escape, it wouldn't be a sea-cure anymore.'

Agnes looked annoyed. She put down her cup and saucer. Prettier than ever now that first youth was gone, against her black frock her light hair looked golden.

'I need the money,' she said obstinately. 'If I could get a good price for High Withens . . . You will stay with me, Esther, when I move south forever and always?'

'I should like to see my sisters, ma'am.

'Oh yes. You must still see your family.'

'Have you thought of finding a tenant for the house?' Esther asked her.

'A tenant?'

'Well, you may not find it so easy to sell and there is still an income to be had from what remains of the estate.'

'Yes, though that's little enough. You don't like the idea of my selling High Withens, Esther?'

'I've a fondness for the place, ma'am. It's part of my life. As a child I always thought it was a palace. I never dreamed that one day I might live here. It was always so small in my father's house, so cramped – all I recall is his boots creaking and kicking everywhere.'

'There's too much space,' Agnes argued. 'It's impossible to keep clean. And,' she glanced up at the gallery, 'I don't know that I'd ever feel free here.'

'A tenant might pay a reasonable sum and be responsible for the upkeep. The house would always be something to fall back on; it would always be somewhere we could return to.'

'I'll think about it,' Agnes said. She lay back on the sofa and Esther sat next to her stirring her fan over the older woman's face.

'You worry too much, Ma'am. Don't fret yourself. I'll make you a hot drink with just one drop of laudanum in. It'll help you sleep tonight. It'll make you happier about being back here. Just one little drop. It'll put new heart in you.'

The girl got up, moved stiffly with her odd, clamped gait over to the small tea table. There she worked swiftly, efficiently, mixing a hot posset. Agnes lolled on the couch. Above, in the growing dark, the gallery of Hopgates looked down on them.